Praise for

HOUSE ON ENDLESS WATERS

"Elon powerfully evokes the obscurity of the past and its hold on the present, as we stumble through revelation after revelation with Yoel. As we accompany him on his journey . . . we share in his loss, surprise, and grief, right up to the novel's shocking conclusion."

—*The New York Times Book Review*

"Emuna Elon's powerful *House on Endless Waters* is essential Jewish fiction. . . . A deeply immersive achievement that brings to life stories that must never be forgotten."

—*USA Today*

"[A] lovely novel—about history, fiction, and the importance of family ties . . . *House on Endless Waters* both posits and demonstrates the inextricability of past and present. . . . An intensely clever literary construction that never compromises readability."

—*Forward*

"A beautifully written, heartrending tale of what it means to be Jewish today—what it has always meant . . . A gorgeous, haunting literary work and highly engrossing, a page-turner at once poignant and provocative, with themes that resonate today and for all time."

—*Historical Novel Society*

"A story of love, loss, and yearning. Lyrically phrased and often powerfully visual . . . this deeply felt tale offers a rewarding meditation on survival."

—*Kirkus* (starred review)

"Readers will find Elon's lyrical prose haunting as she moves between past and present, constructing a heartbreaking, moving tale that brings understanding and acceptance."

—*Booklist*

"*House on Endless Waters* is extraordinary—a vibrant, page-turning family mystery that carries us not only deep into Amsterdam's little-explored wartime history, but also into the fascinating, complex, and often painful process by which history is crafted into story."

—Jennifer Cody Epstein, internationally bestselling author of
Wunderland and *The Painter from Shanghai*

"Intricately woven and lushly layered . . . With achingly exquisite, delicate prose, Elon explores the creative mind's power to reimagine a life and memory's power to recognize truth. An unforgettable read."

—Lynda Cohen Loigman, author of
The Two-Family House and *The Wartime Sisters*

"*House on Endless Waters* is a haunting and lyrical meditation on who we are and where we come from, on how our past shapes our present and our art. Emuna Elon's gorgeously intricate novel is beautifully written and moving."

—Jillian Cantor, bestselling author of
The Lost Letter and *In Another Time*

"An elegant, eloquent novel—a story in which time and language melt to reveal truths that could be told in no other way."

—Rachel Kadish, bestselling author of *The Weight of Ink*

"I read this book in excitement and wonder. It's not only a touching and fascinating book, but a sophisticated one as well."

—Amos Oz, award-winning author of
A Tale of Love and Darkness

ALSO BY EMUNA ELON

Beyond My Sight
Inscribe My Name
If You Awaken Love

HOUSE

ON

ENDLESS WATERS

A Novel

Emuna Elon

Translated from Hebrew
by Anthony Berris and Linda Yechiel

WASHINGTON
SQUARE PRESS

ATRIA

NEW YORK   LONDON   TORONTO   SYDNEY   NEW DELHI

WASHINGTON
SQUARE PRESS

ATRIA

An Imprint of Simon & Schuster, Inc.
1230 Avenue of the Americas
New York, NY 10020

Published by arrangement with The Institute for the Translation of Hebrew Literature
Supported by: "Am Ha-Sefer"—The Israeli Fund for Translation of Hebrew Books
The Cultural Administration, Israel Ministry of Culture and Sport

First Washington Square Press/Atria Paperback edition September 2020

For information about special discounts for bulk purchases, please contact Simon & Schuster Special Sales at 1-866-506-1949 or business@simonandschuster.com.

The Simon & Schuster Speakers Bureau can bring authors to your live event. For more information or to book an event, contact the Simon & Schuster Speakers Bureau at 1-866-248-3049 or visit our website at www.simonspeakers.com.

Interior design by Wendy Blum

Manufactured in the United States of America

3   5   7   9   10   8   6   4   2

The Library of Congress has cataloged the hardcover edition as follows:

Names: Elon, Emunah, author. | Berris, Anthony, translator. | Yechiel, Linda, translator.
Title: House on endless waters : a novel / Emuna Elon ; translated from Hebrew by Anthony Berris and Linda Yechiel.
Other titles: Bayit 'al mayim rabim. English
Description: First Atria Books hardcover edition. | New York : Atria Books, 2020.
Identifiers: LCCN 2019039570 | ISBN 9781982130220 (hardcover) | ISBN 9781982130244 (ebook)
Classification: LCC PJ5054.E49847 B3513 2020 | DDC 892.43/6—dc23
LC record available at https://lccn.loc.gov/2019039570

ISBN 978-1-9821-3022-0
ISBN 978-1-9821-3023-7 (pbk)
ISBN 978-1-9821-3024-4 (ebook)

FIRST NOTEBOOK

1

One after another the people are swallowed up into the plane to Amsterdam, one after another after another. Yoel is approaching the aircraft's door but the flow of passengers is suddenly halted by somebody, a woman in an orange windbreaker, who has planted herself in the doorway of the Boeing 737 and refuses to step inside. Yoel's thoughts are already with the new novel he has decided to write, and he thinks about this woman and asks himself which of his new characters would be capable of admitting to the primal, naked fear that besets every mortal on entering the flying trap called an airplane. Who would volunteer to disrupt with her body the "everything's alright" façade and violate the sacred alrightness to which people clutch so they won't have to admit that everything is truly chaotic.

From his place in the line, Yoel can see only the woman's back. Even through the orange plastic of her windbreaker, he can see how tense her muscles are, and over the shoulders of the people in front of him he discerns the beads of perspiration breaking out on the back of her neck and around her ears. The line starts burbling irritably; people peek anxiously at their boarding pass for flight such-and-such, clutching the rectangular pieces of paper as if they were an assurance that the plane will eventually take off. Then from out of nowhere appears a man in a resplendent uniform, with gray hair and an air of authority, who introduces himself as the purser and puts a fatherly arm around the stricken passenger's shoulders. As he gently takes her aside, the plane continues filling up, and as Yoel passes them he hears him telling her, Believe me, my dear, I have anxious passengers on every flight, and everything's alright. I promise I'll come and hold your hand during takeoff.

When he's invited overseas to promote his books, he and Bat-Ami usually fly business class, thus sparing him from physical contact with the multitudes of other passengers and from being subjected to their multitudes of looks. Since this time he's flying on his own, and mainly because he's paying for his ticket out of his own pocket, he decided to fly economy and so now all he can do is slide into his seat as discreetly as humanly possible. Just look straight ahead and downward, he reminds himself, just straight ahead and downward. Don't raise your eyes or look to the side lest your eyes meet those of somebody who might recognize you. And be very wary of people who have already recognized you and are trying to get your attention, and of the ones you can hear saying to each other, that's Yoel Blum. Or, there's that writer. Or, there's that famous guy, the one with the cap. Come on, remind me what his name is.

It has been only a week since his first trip to Amsterdam and the reception, held in his honor by his Dutch publisher, that was attended by local luminaries from the fields of literature and the media. Only a week since he and Bat-Ami had wandered through the crowds of tall people in the city of bicycles and canals, and strolled through streets, squares, palaces, and museums. In the evening, exhausted and ravenous, they went to the publisher's beautiful home on Apollo Avenue in the old southern part of Amsterdam, but had to make do with a meal of carrot and cucumber crudités: the fare on the tables was rich and varied, but here too, as at many festive events held in his honor all over the world, it was clearly evident that their hosts hadn't imagined that in these enlightened times there were still civilized people who observed the ancient Biblical dietary laws.

Before the second part of the literary event began, the Israeli guest was asked to sit on a carved chair in the center of the Dutch living room next to the stylized Dutch cabinet on whose shelves Dutch delftware of white porcelain decorated in blue was arranged, and facing the large, wide Dutch window overlooking a canal scattered with flickering reflections. His audience sat facing him, waiting for him to answer his red-cheeked host's question on the difference between Israeli writers categorized as writers of the generation of the establishment of the State of Israel and those known—like Mr. Blum, and I hope it's alright if we simply call you Yoel—as writers of the new wave.

The past cannot be hidden. Yoel pronounced the reply he always provides to this question as he crosses his legs and looks pleasantly at his audience. I believe it's impossible to write Israeli literature without referring either directly or indirectly to the archeological *tell* on which the State of Israel flourishes, the shores of which are lapped by its new and old waves alike.

Attentive faces nodded their understanding and perhaps even empathy.

Attentive faces always nod their understanding and perhaps even their empathy.

However, he emphasized in the dramatic crescendo to which his voice always rises at this point, contemporary Israeli writers are first and foremost contemporary Israeli writers. I myself hope that my writing does not wallow in the mire of the past, but carries my soul and the souls of my readers to what is the present and to what will be in the future.

The game went on. In the way that people ask him everywhere, the Dutch asked if the characters populating his books are typical Israelis. And he replied, the way he replies everywhere, that in his view, his characters are universal.

For a moment, he thought about deviating from his custom and telling

them, this particular audience, how hard he works in his writing to refine
his characters so that each of them is Everyman. In each movement to
capture all the movements which have ever been and will ever be. To for-
mulate the core of the words, their very core.

Like every writer's characters, he said as he always does, my characters,
too, live and act in a reality I am closely acquainted with. As a writer who
lives in the Israeli reality, it is only natural that my characters are connected
with that reality as well. But the stories I tell about these characters tell
about Man wherever he breathes, about Man wherever he loves, about Man
wherever he yearns.

The publisher's red cheeks flushed even more deeply as he read to his
guests from the *New York Times* book review: "It is hardly surprising that
Yoel Blum's books have been translated into more than twenty languages
and that he has been awarded some of the most prestigious literature prizes.
Yoel Blum is a magician, the wave of whose wand turns every human an-
ecdote into the nucleus of every reader's personal story."

The color of the Dutch cheeks turned a deep purple as he continued
reading: "You pick up a Yoel Blum novel and are assured of it revealing
your deepest secret: the secret whose existence you weren't even aware of."

A few more familiar, unavoidable questions, and Yoel already estimated that the evening was drawing to its expected conclusion.

But then he was asked an unexpected question by a man introduced to
him earlier as a local journalist by the name of Neumark, or maybe Neu-
berg.

If I'm not mistaken, called the questioner from his seat at the right-hand
edge of the circle of chairs. If I'm not mistaken—Mr. Blum, Yoel—you
were born here, in Amsterdam?

A stunned silence engulfed the room. Yoel too was shocked, since to the
best of his knowledge, this fact did not appear in any printed or virtual

source dealing with him and his history. He tried to recall the journalist's name. Neustadt? Neumann? Is he Jewish?

As he did so, he heard himself calmly answering: That is correct. Technically, I was indeed born in Amsterdam. But my family immigrated to Israel when I was a baby, and so I've always regarded myself as a native Israeli.

Afterward he managed to divert the talk from his personal history back to the collective Israeli one and say a few more words about Hebrew literature in these changing times. But it seemed that the matter of his Dutch origins had been placed in the center of the circle and that none of those present could ignore it. Yoel presumed that they expected him to provide further biographic details, aside from the one already provided by Neuhaus, or Neufeld, according to which the famous Israeli writer is a scion of an old Jewish-Amsterdam family uprooted in the wake of the events of World War Two.

They couldn't have imagined that the Israeli writer himself knew no further details about it either.

2

Several times a year he flies to places where his books are published in various languages, but until last week, he hadn't flown to Amsterdam, neither for the first translation of one of his books into Dutch nor for the second. In early fall, when a third Yoel Blum novel was about to be published in the capital of the Netherlands, Zvika, his literary agent, urged him to go this time and promote sales of the book. Send me anywhere you want, Yoel told him, just not Amsterdam. I can't go to Amsterdam. But Zvika continued pressing him: You can't ignore a publisher, you can't disrespect your readers. And when Yoel told Bat-Ami about it, she decided that he couldn't refuse. We're going, she said. We'll be there just for a short time.

He tried to protest. My mother, he said, demanded that I never set foot in Amsterdam.

Your mother's dead, Yoel.

The words hit him as if it had just happened.

In fact, his mother had left him long before she finally left this world. Ever so slowly she went out of her mind, then out of her soul, and finally out of her body, loosening, stage by stage, her grip on reality. Unpicking, one after the other, the stitches that bound him to her; stitch by stitch, thread by thread, until she detached herself from him completely and departed.

Like when he was a child and she'd taught him to swim, and she'd stand in the shallow end of the municipal pool holding him on the surface, her sturdy hands supporting his belly and chest while, on her instructions, his skinny arms and legs straightened and bent in swimming movements. And then, millimeter by millimeter, so gradually that he didn't even feel it, she'd withdraw her large hands from his body. Little by little, she withdrew them, little by little, until she folded her arms and only stood next to him, watching but not touching. And the first time he noticed that she wasn't holding him and that he was actually swimming on his own, he lost his balance and began thrashing around and sinking, swallowing great gulps of water until it seemed he would drown.

Afterward he got used to it.

His first trip back to the city of his birth passed mainly with pangs of remorse for having consented to go in the first place. I should have stuck to my guns, he repeatedly griped to Bat-Ami in the taxi from Jerusalem to the airport. All in all, what did my mother ask of me? She asked so little. I should have respected her wish.

What was she so afraid of? Bat-Ami asked.

What do you mean?

Why didn't she want you to go to Amsterdam? What was it she was afraid you might find there?

Nothing. What could there be after so many years? She simply didn't want me or Nettie to have any connection with the place where she lost my father, her parents and siblings, the life she might have had.

At the Ben Shemen interchange he realized he'd left his phylacteries at home and he decided to cancel the trip right then and there. Forgetting my *tefillin* is a sure sign, he explained to Bat-Ami in excited shouts, and ordered the driver to make a U-turn and drive back to Jerusalem. A Jew's *tefillin* are his self-identity, and it's a fact that I travel so much yet have never forgotten them until this forbidden and unnecessary journey.

It was only with much effort that Bat-Ami managed to soothe him. We're not in an Agnon story, she said, and at this point you haven't lost any self-identity. Following her precise instructions, the driver proceeded toward the airport while calling the taxi station and asking for another Jerusalem driver to go to the author's apartment building, get the key of their apartment from Bat-Ami's sister, who lives on the ground floor, get the phylacteries from their apartment, and bring them to Ben Gurion Airport as quickly as possible. Bat-Ami stayed on the line as she and Yoel reached the airport and as they wheeled their cases into the terminal, and even through security and check-in. She meticulously guided the phylactery courier through each stage of his complex mission, and once it was successfully accomplished and the driver informed her of his arrival at the main entrance with the embroidered velvet bag, she quickly went out to meet him and tipped him handsomely while Yoel waited for her in the departure lounge, his stomach churning.

His first structured memories begin at the kindergarten in Netanya. As he grew up and started to wonder about what had come before the kindergarten, his mother would look away, pretending she was immersed in a vital task that brooked no delay, and declare loudly and clearly: Whatever was, was. Those waters have already flowed onward.

On more than one occasion he said that he still wanted to know about the place where he was born, but his mother said: Anyone who immigrated to Israel as an infant is considered a native-born Israeli. It's like you were born here in Israel, Yoel.

His big sister, Nettie, would explain to him that that's how it is with the Dutch. They don't talk about what they absolutely don't have to talk about, and they certainly don't talk about waters that have already flowed onward. In general, she always added with the seriousness characteristic of her to this day, being Dutch is no simple matter.

In an attempt to end the meeting at the publisher's home on a pleasant note, at the end of the evening Yoel chose to relate, as a sort of encore in a different, lighter tone, one of the jokes with which he sometimes spiced his lectures abroad.

God summons the leaders of the three great faiths, he said, and announces that in forty-eight hours he is going to bring down a great and terrible flood on Earth. The three leaders hasten to gather their people— one in a church, the second in a mosque, the third in a synagogue—and prepare them for the worst. The bishop calls upon his flock to repent and utter the deathbed confession, and the imam tells the Muslim faithful more or less the same thing. The rabbi, however, mounts the rostrum in the center of the synagogue, slams the lectern with the palm of his hand, and announces: Jews, we have forty-eight hours to learn how to live underwater!

That's an anti-Semitic joke, you know, Bat-Ami murmured late that night as she curled up in their hotel bed.

She fell asleep as soon as she completed the sentence, and Yoel was tired too, exhausted as if he'd been walking the length of Amsterdam's canals for generations.

3

And now, only a week after that night, he's flying to Amsterdam again. He's going in order to start working on a new novel, after discovering, in the few days since his last trip, what he must write about. It's hard to say he isn't apprehensive about the long stay in his foreign homeland.

It's hard to say that he has no doubts about his ability to gather the necessary material, fill his notebooks with notes and interviews, and then find the strength to return home and turn those notes into a book.

But something inside tells him that if he succeeds in all this, this book will be the novel of his life; that it was for this novel that he had become a writer in the first place.

This time Yoel is flying to Amsterdam on his own, and everything he does or doesn't do there will depend on him alone. But on his first visit to this forbidden city he was terror-stricken because of his desecration of his mother's last request, and Bat-Ami took his hand as one would take the hand of a wayward child and led him to where she had chosen to lead him.

Their hosts had booked them into the Hotel de Paris, one of the many small, elegant hotels in the city's entertainment district around Leidseplein, and Bat-Ami contended that it was one of the more charming hotels they had ever stayed in. From the moment they touched down at Schiphol Air-

port, she hadn't stopped admiring and enthusing over Amsterdam's picturesque architecture, the charm of the canals, the bridges, the boulevards and
buildings, the multitude of colors and forms, and of course the well-built,
pleasant inhabitants flowing by on their bicycles in the open air.

He couldn't understand how one could get one's bearings in this strange
city that is almost entirely contained within a semicircle delineated by its
four main canals. For example, if the Keizersgracht begins at the western
end of Amsterdam and ends after a semicircle at the eastern end, then when
you see a sign saying "Keizersgracht" you know you're on the bank of that
canal, but how are you supposed to guess if you're in the center of the city
or in its west or east?

Still, right away and without any difficulty, Bat-Ami learned to find her
way through the maze of strips of dry land running between the canals.
She marched him along through that maze energetically and confidently,
as she constantly praised the universal spirit of freedom and was excited
even by blatantly touristic gimmicks like the floating flower market or by
the dangerously steep Dutch staircases.

She told him, her eyes shining, that because their staircases are so narrow and steep, the Dutch move furniture and other large items into or out
of their homes through the windows.

She was also captivated by the Dutch custom, which he found incomprehensible, of leaving their big windows exposed to full view and not
hiding their private life behind shutters or curtains. This blatant exposure
shocked him profoundly, but the happy Bat-Ami didn't stop saying to
him, Look, look at this, and Look at that, and mainly, See how nothing's
changed here in Amsterdam since Holland's Golden Age. What hasn't
happened to us Jews since then, while here, throughout all those long
years, the same buildings, the same streets, the same water, and the same
people. Just look at this guy, for example, she whispered as they went into
their hotel and the elderly, suited clerk handed them their room key over
a counter filled with Dutch clogs, miniature windmills, and pictures of

sailing ships. I'll bet he hasn't moved from that counter since the reign of Philip the Second.

It seems that it's easier for Bat-Ami on their trips abroad than it is in Israel. When she's in Israel, she shoulders all matters pertaining to the family, the home, the State of Israel, and the human race. But the moment the aircraft wheels detach from the runway at Ben Gurion Airport, Bat-Ami detaches herself from her perpetual duties and lets the world go on its way. When she's abroad, she even frees herself of the burden of her big bunch of keys. She is still always armed with her large purse and her cell phone but can finally be seen without her silvered *hamsa* ornament inset with a miniature family photograph, on which hang and jangle at all times their front door key, the key to the storeroom, the key to the garden gate, the key to the door to the roof, their mailbox key, the key to the gas cylinder cage, her car key, his car key, emergency keys to her brother's and sisters' apartments, a key to each of their three daughters' apartments, and more large and small keys to padlocks known to her alone.

4

The day after the literary evening at the Dutch publisher's home, between a visit to a museum across the River Amstel and a whirlwind tour she'd planned of the Rembrandt House Museum and the Waterlooplein flea market, Bat-Ami decided that they couldn't possibly pass through the Old Jewish Quarter without taking a look at the Jewish Historical Museum. And so Yoel found himself in a dim exhibition hall, the length of which were illuminated glass cabinets displaying mezuzahs torn from doorposts, a faded wooden sign warning in black lettering "*Voor Joden verboden*"—Jews prohibited—photographs and documents and various utensils. He thought he'd better get out of there; he thought he should respect his mother, who had wanted so much for him not to see these things. He looked around and couldn't find Bat-Ami and was gripped by panic until in the dim light he saw her sitting on one of the benches, and he made his way over to her through the knots of visitors moving around quietly, passing a group of Dutch youngsters who were following their teacher.

Bat-Ami appeared not to have noticed him and when he touched her shoulder she didn't raise her eyes to him, but with muted excitement gestured for him to sit down beside her. When Yoel sat down, he saw that she was watching old black-and-white film clips screened onto the length and breadth of the wall facing them.

Why, Yoel wondered, were his wife's eyes glued to these silent images?

When he looked at them, he saw people celebrating at a wedding festivity, the men in tuxedos, their hair gleaming with brilliantine, and the women in splendid evening gowns and elegant hairdos. He turned to Bat-Ami but she didn't turn her face to him. Her eyes were still glued to the flickering images, but she sensed his look and gestured imperatively: Look at the wall, look at the film, and he turned his head as she instructed and saw a shot of the bride and groom, and then a close-up of their parents, and a shot of the bridesmaids walking behind the bride, reverently bearing her train. Then there was a shot of a woman holding a baby girl, pointing at the camera and trying to get the indifferent infant to smile, and then one of two bow-tied young men waving at the camera, and Bat-Ami pinched his arm and tensed, and the shot of the young men was replaced by one of a young family: a man and a woman, him holding a little girl in his arms, and she a baby boy in hers. The image flickered on the wall for just a heartbeat, but even in that fleeting second, Yoel managed to discern that the woman in the picture was his mother: his mother in her early years, his mother in the days that preceded the compass of his memory, but his mother.

He stopped breathing.

Wait, Bat-Ami whispered, relaxing her grip on his arm, it's screened in a loop. It'll be on again soon. As she said the word "loop," she drew an imaginary circle in the air with her finger. Yoel swallowed saliva and nodded, but apart from the shape of the loop he didn't understand a thing.

Time after time Yoel and Bat-Ami watched the shots in the old wedding film. They sat on the bench in the center of the museum hall and saw the bride and groom, and then the couple's happy and concerned parents, and the girls carrying the train in deadly seriousness, and then the woman with the baby and her pointing finger, and the happy boys in their bow ties waving to the camera, and then—now, Yoel said to himself, pay attention now—and he stared with all his might, and on the tenth time that he saw the fragments of the film, like on the twenty-second time and the thirtieth time, he was utterly convinced that the woman flickering before him was indeed his mother. The image was grainy, but without question it was her image: the height, the massive hands, the posture. And the face, which displayed, without doubt, her broad features he loved so much, and which in the film could be seen full face and in profile as she turned her head to the right and smiled at her husband, his father. He was only a baby when his father was taken, and in time, all the photographs of his parents, together with the rest of their property, had been lost. But now he was sure that the slight, bespectacled man in the film was his father, mainly because of the warmth and admiration in his mother's eyes as she stole a glance at this man whose height was shorter than hers.

The little girl the man was holding in his arms was Nettie. He had no doubt it was her: the facial features, the expression, everything. But who is the strange infant? his heart asked. Who is that strange baby boy nestled in your mother's arms?

The baby must be you, Bat-Ami whispered as if she'd heard the question.

But it's not me, he whispered back.

How can you know?

It isn't me. Look at the shape of his head, the eyes, the hair. It isn't me.

Then perhaps, she suggested after the figures had reappeared and vanished again, perhaps, just as they were filmed, she was holding someone else's baby?

Yoel wanted to embrace this assumption. He wished he could. But the loop completed its cycle again, and again the same image appeared on the wall, and again he saw his mother holding the unknown baby the way mothers hold their own children. Not only that: he saw—for it was impossible not to—how much the unknown baby resembled her, especially in its wide cheeks and clear eyes whose corners turned slightly downward, and how there wasn't even a hint of resemblance between the face of the unknown baby and his own, dark-eyed and bony, in the photographs from his childhood taken after they immigrated to Israel and which his mother stuck, using tiny mounting squares, onto the rough black pages of the beautifully arranged album that sat on the sideboard in the living room of their apartment in Netanya.

As soon as they got back to their hotel room from the museum, Yoel took out his cell phone and brought up Nettie's number. He looked at the line of illuminated digital numbers and thought about his sister sitting at this twilight hour in her small apartment in the kibbutz located between the River Jordan and Mount Gilboa. Her face is serene, on her knees is an open book, and her old radio is playing classical music on the station to which it is permanently tuned. Her husband, Eliezer, awaits her in the kibbutz cemetery at the foot of the mountain. He is buried there next to Yisrael, their handsome, tousle-haired firstborn, who had fought in the Yom Kippur War and the First Lebanon War, but was killed not in battle but in the kibbutz date palm orchard. Yoel had never managed to picture the day the police, accompanied by kibbutz officials and the local doctor, had come to tell Nettie and Eliezer and their daughter that the power ladder they used in the orchard had hit an electric cable and that Yisrael was dead even before his strong body in its blue work clothes folded inward and hit the ground with a thump.

Nettie will soon put her book aside, sigh, and turn on the TV to watch the early edition of the evening news.

Yoel turned off his phone.

Through the window of the building opposite their hotel room he could see a kitchen in which a woman was standing washing a stainless-steel jug, and he was fascinated by her movements as she soaped and scrubbed the outside and inside with a long-handled brush and then rinsed it thoroughly in tap water. Over the past day, he had discovered that the woman lived in a two-room apartment with only a brown-and-white dog and the plants she tended in a window box. She was a good-looking woman, her straight blond hair cut short, and when she came into the kitchen, she put a floral apron over her slender figure. In the morning he'd seen her making herself a cup of coffee before leaving for work, in the middle of the day he'd seen the short-legged, floppy-eared dog waiting for her forlornly on the armchair in the living room, and at six in the evening she had come home and turned on the light, and at a distance of only a few meters from her, he'd watched her bend to put food into the dog's bowl that was evidently on the floor under the kitchen window. He wondered if she knew she was being watched and whether she cared. Afterward he was compelled for some reason to watch her beating eggs, slicing vegetables, mixing them in a deep bowl, tasting. He could hear the rattle of her dishes and kitchen tools, and almost the sound of her breathing. Almost the sound of her breathing.

Thanks to his friends at kindergarten and in the neighborhood, he had learned to make up stories at an early age.

Say, Yoel, how come you don't have a dad?

I do so have a dad! My dad's at work. My dad's in the army. My dad's on a secret mission far away from here.

Throughout his childhood, the plots his brain had woven around the figure of his absent father were filled with mystery and magic. They endowed his father with a multitude of daring roles in the military forces and in the secret services, a wide range of groundbreaking scientific studies, and vital missions across the sea.

Every time he was asked about his father and invented a new reply, he believed it with all his heart. The story his mother told him about a young man who had died in a distant and incomprehensible war was, in his eyes, only one possible answer to the question of where his father was. Only one story, which held no advantage over all the others, and Yoel saw no reason not to replace its sparse plot with more interesting ones, depending on his desires and flights of fancy.

5

He couldn't sleep that night. Bat-Ami was snoring lightly as he released himself from the confining quilt and the foreign hotel bed whose previous occupants he wondered about: had they been sad or happy, lonesome or loved? He quietly tried to find a place for himself, trying not to bump into the furniture and other objects that filled the small room, until by one of the walls he found a free area of carpeting where he was able to sit cross-legged. He needed some fresh air; he wanted to get out of the crowded room and out to the street, but he didn't go down and didn't go out because he was afraid that Bat-Ami would wake up while he was gone, and he knew that if he'd woken up in the middle of the night and seen that she wasn't there, he'd have been overcome by anxiety for fear that something bad had happened to her, that she'd left him, that he'd never see her again.

On second thought, he said to himself, would Bat-Ami indeed be worried if she woke up and didn't find him in the room? He shifted his position on the carpet and straightened his back against the wall, placing his hands on his crossed legs and looking around. How different the walls and corners of the ceiling seemed from this angle. How different the wardrobe, the bed, the woman sleeping in the bed. He heard her mumble something in her sleep and he thought: What do I know about her dreams, what do I know about her? I've always thought I know how to write people because I know how to see them, yet today I discovered that I've never really succeeded in seeing even my own mother. I thought I was close to you, my beloved mother, I thought I knew you well, and now it turns out that all the time you were carrying a missing child in your heart—and I didn't feel it and would never have guessed.

Darkness crept up to him from the four corners of the room, closing in on him, its black particles climbing over his body and penetrating his skin through its pores until he was forced to stand up, dress quickly, and flee to the street. Bat-Ami isn't me, he repeated to himself as he bent to tie his shoelaces. Bat-Ami is Bat-Ami. If she wakes up and sees I'm not there, she'll understand that I've gone out to get some fresh air and immediately close her eyes and fall back asleep.

Colored lights were flickering in a small, crowded pub across the street from the hotel entrance. A giant of a man, whose bare, heavily muscled arms were covered with tattoos, went into the pub and was swallowed up in the crowd.

Yoel moved on.

On the day that Yoel rose from the seven days of sitting shiva for his mother and went out of his house, he realized he didn't know how to walk in a world in which his mother was no longer present. Very slowly, he taught himself to walk again, and since then, it had seemed to him that he was walking properly. But at this nocturnal hour, alone in the city of his birth, where he had first learned to walk, he felt as if he had to instruct his body to execute the requisite actions again: Raise the right foot, there, excellent. Now move the right foot forward and place it on the sidewalk. Well done, Yoel, and now lift the left foot, move it forward . . .

He pulled his coat collar up round his ears, hunched his head into his shoulders, and proceeded, step by step, his eyes on his feet and the flag-stones beneath them. At the end of a row of houses, the sidewalk took an upward curve, and he looked out from inside his coat and saw he'd come to an arched bridge over a canal. He saw a bench on the canal bank and let his body collapse onto it, exhausted.

The waters of the canal flowed dark and silent along their ancient course, dark and silent and all-remembering. Yoel sat on the bench and gazed at the water as if seeking to pluck from it even a fleeting shadow or an echo left in it by his lost brother, who, by his calculations done mainly based on Nettie's estimated age in the museum film, was somewhat younger than him. His little brother.

What happened to him, to the light-skinned baby? Where had he, Yoel, been when the wedding photographer immortalized his little brother with his parents and his sister, Nettie? Did the things that happened to his little brother almost happen to Yoel too, and could that explain the early memory in which he was cast into a corner, abandoned, and his body, the body of the small child he was then, was trembling from wetness, cold, and fear? All his life he had told himself that this early memory of his was nothing but a figment of his fertile imagination; all his life he had tried to submerge this memory in the depths of his subconscious, and yet the memory had resurfaced, drawing him into the torment of a toddler that did not yet know how to put its feelings into words. Whether he experienced this anguish in reality or in his imagination, he cannot forget the hard touch of the surface he was lying on. He cannot forget how the surface seemed to rock and shake beneath him while he cried until his strength ebbed away, nor can he forget how he wanted his abandoned soul to die, to die and to exist no longer. And he is unceasingly haunted by the strange part his mother plays in this memory, his mother, who, while he lay there suffering, sat beside him helplessly.

A knot of half a dozen young people crossed the bridge near his bench, filling the night air with shards of joy and laughter, while in the canal, the dark water continued on its never-ending way, pulling with it the day that had just ended and remembering all the many sights ever reflected in it and all the many sounds.

6

As dawn began breaking, with Amsterdam still shrouded in darkness so that he could not yet put on his phylacteries and say the morning prayers, Yoel again turned on his cell phone. Bat-Ami was still asleep and appeared not to have noticed him leaving the room in the middle of the night and returning a short time ago. He stood by the window and brought up his sister's number, resolved to catch her before she left for her job in the kibbutz laundry.

In the light cast by the streetlamps, the first cyclists of the day passed by below. One, and then another, and after them two or three more. Outside the pub there was a green truck bearing the legend "Heineken," and two men in green coveralls were unloading green crates of beer bottles.

Good morning, Nettie. His voice faltered.

Yoel! she exclaimed happily. Yoel, how are you? And how's Bat-Ami?

We're in Amsterdam, he told her without further ado.

Silence. All that could be heard was the rattle of beer bottles from across the street as the men in green wheeled the crates into the pub and then began loading the empties onto the truck.

A book of mine, he explained, trying to steady his voice, a book's been translated into Dutch and . . . Bat-Ami and I flew to Amsterdam.

All Nettie managed to say after several long seconds was: You're in Amsterdam.

All that Yoel managed to ask her was: Why didn't you tell me?

She remained silent.

A large, heavy beer barrel was slowly lowered from the truck to the sidewalk.

Why didn't you tell me? he repeated. Bat-Ami and I went to the Jewish Museum here, and we saw . . . Why didn't you tell me, Nettie? Why didn't Mama tell me? How could you let me discover something like this by myself after so many years, and then only by chance?

It pained him to hurt her like this. He hurt her. It pained him.

But Yoel . . . Her voice hoarsened and her Dutch accent, which was always more pronounced when she was stressed, turned the "but" into "bot." How . . . How did you find out?

You mean it's true? he shouted despairingly, as though until that moment he'd hoped she would convince him that he was mistaken. As though until that moment he still thought she'd tell him that they'd never had another sibling and that the boy in the film, the blond baby that their mother was clasping to her heart, was another woman's child.

You've got to tell me everything. He raised his voice as if in an attempt to be heard across the sea. You've got to tell me . . .

But she remained silent.

Eventually she ended the call assertively but gently: When you come home, Yoel, when you get home, come and visit me. I'll tell you everything I know.

In a few minutes, thought Yoel, she'll put on a thin sweater against the morning chill. She'll pick up her square, orange-colored plastic basket, go out of her small apartment, and close the door behind her without locking it. She'll go down the two low steps to the aging, cracked pathway, affix the basket to the handlebars of the old bicycle standing in the shade of the fragrant honeysuckle, mount the bicycle carefully, and pedal to the laundry behind the communal dining room. She'll ride slowly, immersed in the light flowing down the hillside onto the kibbutz paths, the fields, the palm orchards.

Across the street, the green truck was now loaded with the beer barrels that had been emptied during the night.

The truck drove off.

Bat-Ami woke up.

Amsterdam was still shrouded in darkness.

7

Now he's staring out the airplane window at the fields of cloud stretching, furrow by furrow of dense white foam, from horizon to horizon.

He's going back to Amsterdam only three days after he had sat on the old brown sofa in Nettie's kibbutz apartment and had heard her tell him—hesitantly at first, but then in a continuous outpouring—what she knew about the first years of his life. As he took his leave of her at her door late that night, she was filled with remorse and sorrow and said, God help me, what have I done to you, Yoel? Why did I have to spoil what you've thought all your life? He looked into her eyes, always so light and clear, and said, Thank you, Nettie. Thank you, my sister, for agreeing to tell me the truth. Then he went down the two steps to the cracked pathway, passed the fragrant honeysuckle, and saw his dead brother-in-law Eliezer's bicycle still standing next to Nettie's in the rusted rack.

Have a safe journey, she called after him. Have a safe journey.

He took another look at her figure standing in the rectangle of light in the doorway, at her face that revealed her fear for him, and knew that her "Have a safe journey" meant "You are my brother. You are my brother and you are precious to me."

He felt like a new, different Yoel as he walked surrounded by the singing of the cicadas and frogs, beneath the canopy of poplars and rosewoods, from Nettie's apartment to where the previous, old Yoel had parked his car. Throughout the drive from the Bet She'an Valley back to Jerusalem, he told himself over and over what he had heard from Nettie and repeated aloud, How is it possible? How is it possible? He pressed down on the accelerator, speeding the car through the bends of the Jordan Valley road and following its headlight beams as they sliced through the mantle of ancient darkness as if illuminating the chapters of his life for the first time, bend after bend, fragment after fragment. How is it possible? he asked the night. How could they not have told me or hinted, how didn't I suspect or imagine?

But the night was silent, the car emerged from the hills to the open flatland, stretching from the north of the country to the south, and there was no orphanhood like Yoel Blum's orphanhood from the blackening spine of the Samaria hills on his right to the ridge of the Mountains of Gilad flickering on his left, across the River Jordan flowing parallel to the road from the Galilee to the Dead Sea. It seemed to him that the land he was driving on was a living body, his own body, and that the Syrian-African Rift was a scar running across his skin: a long, old scar that had suddenly opened and was now bleeding afresh.

As he passed the approaches to Jericho and turned onto the road that climbs toward Jerusalem, his thinking started to clear. By the time he reached the Sea Level sign, he knew he must fly back to Amsterdam as soon as possible.

And he knew he must do it alone.

Wait, Bat-Ami urged him the next morning after he'd told her everything. Wait, don't go back right away, give yourself time to calm down and digest what you've only just heard.

But Yoel didn't want to wait and he didn't want to calm down. He hurried as if somebody was waiting impatiently for him in Amsterdam. Or as if he were capable of changing the course of the events concisely related to him by Nettie, if only he could quickly get to the place where those events had occurred.

8

He hadn't left the house for the whole day before this flight, his second flight to Amsterdam. In fact, he hardly crossed the threshold of his study, where, at his desk, he had immersed himself in sorting through papers, notebooks, and documents, and arranging them in piles in drawers and in files after going through them one at a time as if he was searching for a clue. Between arranging and filing, he raised his head and looked out the window at the cars passing through the Valley of the Cross at the foot of the ancient monastery: appearing between the silvery olive trees on the slope and then disappearing behind them, and then visible again, then hidden again, and again.

Every now and then, Bat-Ami popped her head round the doorpost, peeping into the study as if she was afraid of disturbing him, and then she'd come in with a cup of herbal tea and a plate of granola cookies for him, or call him into the kitchen for one of their regular meals. She laughed, as she always laughed, at his custom of leaving his top-of-the-range laptop open in front of him, switched on and ready for action, even though he never used it. I'm sure, she said as she always does, that you must be the last writer in the world who still writes his books in notebooks, in actual handwriting.

What was he to do if with all his amazement at the innovations of the

time, and at what one could do with a shiny, compact laptop with all the bells
and whistles like the one on his desk, he is still incapable of writing on it,
neither articles nor pre–first drafts nor a first or second draft, but only uses
a ballpoint pen in school notebooks like the ones he had in his childhood,
forty pages single-line, with thin brown cardboard covers and multiplication
tables printed on the back. He's been promising himself for years that he'd
try, gradually, of course, to get used to writing on a computer like everybody
else. From time to time, he even exchanges his new laptop for a newer one in
which, so he is assured, writing is even easier and more flowing. But again
and again, he goes back to the old notebooks that he buys from the same old
wholesaler in the same little old shop in an alley near the city center.

Perhaps the day will come when he'll train himself to use a word pro-
cessor. Perhaps the day will come when he'll even train himself to live, a
day when he will walk the earth like everyone else without being overcome by the thought that in fact it's odd, even ridiculous, to be a human
being, a cluster of organs that wear out constantly as it runs here and there,
wrapped in all sorts of fabrics and making all sorts of sounds.

Toward evening, his study window seemed like a framed picture of the red-
dening expanse over the Valley of the Cross. Light illuminated from the rocks
onto the white-gray cubes of the Israel Museum, which at this time of day
seemed to him like the classic Mediterranean village described in the vision
of the museum's architects. On his last visit there, in the space inside one of
those cubes, he had come across the painting by the Dutch painter Jozef Israëls
titled *Mother and Child Walking on the Dunes*, undated, and understood, for one
brief moment, what he had been looking for all his life. The realization flashed
through his mind sharply, clear to the point of pain. But it faded immediately
and left him speechless and lost, deeply yearning and not knowing for what.

Now he could recall only the watery stains of paint gently merging into
one another: the child walking beside his mother, a child-stain merging
into a mother-stain who merges into a sea-stain and a sky-stain against a
backdrop of a fishing-village-stain.

9

He had already packed a pile of new, empty forty-page, single-line notebooks for the journey, and as he enjoyed their smell, which he loves, Bat-Ami again poked her head into his study. Galia and Zohar have come to say goodbye, she told him happily, and he put on the most paternal smile he could muster at that moment and got up and went into the living room to meet his daughters, who had probably come less to say goodbye to him and more to calm their mother, who worries about him whenever he travels without her.

Even so many years after his middle daughter, Galia, became a disciple of Rabbi Nachman of Breslov, Yoel's heart lurches every time he sees her with a sort of white turban wound around her head and her long, buttoned-up clothing. She usually comes to see them with her bearded husband and their flock of children, one of whom, a little Breslover with curled sidelocks and a fringed skullcap, had come over to him during their previous visit, fixed him with his burning black eyes, and told him: You're going to die. On this occasion, she had come with her younger sister, Zohar, and as he entered the living room he found the three women bending over Zohar's little baby and making all manner of gurgling noises. His entrance made them straighten up and strike up a banal conversation on subjects that were of no real interest to either him or them. The conversation quickly moved into the dead end known as a debate on the news of the day, and there, as expected, Galia and Zohar turned it into another political argument. This was the point when Bat-Ami, who had continued gurgling at the baby, got up as always to fetch more coffee and cookies from the kitchen, and Yoel, as always, asked them to leave politics out of it. He made this request in the same semi-authoritative tone in which he used to ask them when they were kids to return to the kitchen table the chairs they had dragged into the living room to play "train," and as always Galia replied that she wasn't talking politics at all, she was simply trying to understand why her dear sister preferred to delude herself rather than recognize reality, while Zohar laughed bitterly and said that she too wasn't talking politics, all she wanted was the possibility of living a normal life in this country at long last.

They were joined a little later by his eldest daughter, Ronit, and Zohar's baby began making small bleating noises until it fell asleep in its mother's arms. As though from outside, Yoel looked at the circle in which he was sitting in his living room with his wife and daughters, who were drinking more coffee and eating more butter cookies and talking and talking, and he inhaled a lungful of air and thought: But I'm alive. But I'm alive.

And even after everything he had just learned, it was still his mother who had taught him to be loved, taught him to be. She had protected him against the nights of his childhood when he was deathly scared of going to bed and falling asleep and wouldn't go to bed unless she was sitting on the low stool at the foot of his bed, sitting there for hours night after night until he closed his eyes and fell asleep. And if he woke up in the small hours and could see only dark and empty air over the low stool, he would give a loud and bitter shout, and only a moment passed until she came into his room, her hair in disarray and her eyes blinking at him through the web of sleep, and without a word she would sit down by his bed as if to say, I won't leave you, my child, I won't ever leave you.

10

It was going to be only a few hours until the taxi came to take him to the airport, but before he goes to sleep each night he has to rest his mind awhile. So tonight he took a sheet of paper from the package on his desk and began doodling on it.

He wrote: "Mother and Child Walking on the Dunes undated undated"

Then he scribbled the Hebrew word חתול, cat, several times, since he had recently discovered that the word actually looks like a cat, with the last letter, ל, resembling a cat's upright tail.

The word עץ, tree, looks like a tree too, he thought as he doodled, with roots planted in the ground and spreading branches.

He scribbled some more words that look like their meaning:

הר, mountain

שדה, field

בית, house (the word, he thought, has a floor and a ceiling and enclosing walls)

And also:

גג, roof

הידרדרות, deterioration

רוד, gentleness

The nocturnal silence was suddenly shattered by a burst of eerie howling. The sound of these howls had recently been besieging his windows night after night, emanating from the abyss of the darkness like the cries of grief-ridden keening mourners refusing to be comforted. Bat-Ami claimed that the howling of jackals has been heard in Jerusalem at night since time immemorial, but Yoel was sure that they have never sounded so desperate nor come so close to human dwellings. He managed to think about it less in the hours when daylight reigns in the world, but at night he was convinced that vast packs of huge wild jackals had taken over the paved paths of the Valley of the Cross and invaded the well-tended lawns of Sacher Park and that they would shortly be swarming over the neighborhood streets and maybe its buildings too.

SECOND NOTEBOOK

11

Now there is only the monotonic drone of the plane's engines, now there are only the fields of white clouds as far as the eye can see. And how hard it is to believe that life, complex relationships, a world, are stirring somewhere below that layer of foamy whiteness.

He didn't know the truth about the soul closest to him, his mother. He didn't know the truth about her even after he met her childhood friend Berta Solomon, whose existence he discovered only from a short, laconic letter of condolence she sent them when his mother died. Nettie, so he discovered, had always known about Berta, but he was nevertheless excited about the prospect of meeting someone who had known his mother before they immigrated to Israel, and so after receiving the letter, he went to meet Berta at the Dutch immigrants' retirement home not far from his native Netanya. On a wintry afternoon, he arrived at the home, which was situated in the heart of a quiet, beautifully landscaped neighborhood, which at the time was decorated entirely with local election posters. His heart was racing as he entered the building whose gate bore the name of the queen of the Netherlands, and which was fronted with Dutch-style flowerbeds around a model windmill. With the help of a lively nurse with a Yemenite accent, he found Berta, a delicate old lady with white-blond hair in a girlish haircut with a side parting, who was sitting in the lobby with a few of the other residents who had gathered there for afternoon tea. Berta was in a wheelchair, her face contorting and her limbs twitching with Parkinson's disease. Speaking was difficult for her but she somehow stammered her happiness on seeing that her friend's son had come to visit her, and she introduced him to the other elderly ladies, one of whom, an erect and pleasant-faced woman called Hennie de Levi, said: Yoel Blum? So you're Yoel Blum the writer? It's an honor to meet you, I've read all your books! And as they shook hands Yoel noticed the number tattooed on the inside of her forearm.

He joined the circle for tea, a custom his mother, too, had always insisted on at five in the afternoon. Your mother, Berta told him, didn't really want to keep in touch with me. When he asked her what she knew about what had happened to his mother in the war years, her delicate features froze while her hands continued twitching in her shrunken lap. Another elderly lady sitting on her right grumbled: They never talk about anything else in this place, every conversation is only about the war, the war, the war! In the war, she volunteered, I was hidden with some Christians. After the war my mother came to take me and nobody knew where I was, so she had to search a lot until she found me.

It was only just before six thirty, the time his new companions had warned him that they would have to say goodbye and go to the dining room for supper, that he managed to elicit from Berta some fragmented answers to his questions. When he put them all together he realized that although Berta and his mother had grown up together in Amsterdam's Old Jewish Quarter, when they reached adulthood their ways had parted. They had only met again on the "exchange train," she told him with mounting excitement, and Yoel didn't know what train or what exchange she was talking about, but he didn't dare interrupt the flow of Berta's story that she had suddenly begun to relate. I remember, she said, how all the people were already on board the train and only she, your mother, refused to get on. I hadn't seen her for a long time, but I recognized her right away: tall, stubborn . . . Her little daughter was at her side, and she stood there on the platform and said she was waiting for them to bring her son to her. The train was about to leave and everyone was shouting at her, save yourself, save your daughter, but she didn't answer and she didn't move, and some people got off the train and tried to drag her onto it, but she was stronger and continued standing there. The police were already shutting the doors, and a few people in our car held on to our door from the inside so it wouldn't close. I also shouted her name at the top of my voice. I shouted, Get on! But she didn't respond, and the train started to move. Suddenly—suddenly I saw someone running from a distance, running so fast it was unbelievable. When he got closer I saw he was carrying a little boy, and he ran straight to your mother and handed the child to her, and she finally got onto the train. And we left.

Berta was trembling violently.

I've never heard that story before, the old lady on her right whispered.

Just a minute, said Hennie de Levi in amazement. So the little boy who was brought to her, her son without whom she wasn't prepared to board the train, was you? It was you, Mr. Blum?

Yoel smiled at her. It was already six thirty and the lively nurse came into the lobby wheeling an old lady whose eyes were shut and her mouth a gaping black hole. My dear ladies, the nurse announced, you're invited for supper, and Yoel took his leave of his hostesses, who began slowly shuffling toward the lit-up dining room. He thanked Berta, who couldn't stop twitching and contorting as Hennie de Levi wheeled her away.

A picture of the suited and self-satisfied candidate for mayor flashed in front of him from a huge billboard as he went out into the garden and stood by the beautifully tended flowerbeds and the model windmill that was as tall as him. Noise came from the dining room windows and mingled with the sounds of a classical music radio program coming from one of the windows above him. From his inside jacket pocket, he took a notebook and wrote in it: "Those waters have already flowed onward."

Afterward he looked at this sentence and added a question mark to it.

12

Now there is only the monotonic drone of the plane's engines, now there are only the fields of white clouds as far as the eye can see. He hadn't known the truth about his mother, the soul closest to him. What does he know about other souls close to him?

What does he know about Bat-Ami? He'd met her when they were students at university, and he remembers that he'd liked her, but he doesn't remember if he was in love with her, and in fact he's not sure he was ever in love with anyone. He'd never had a girlfriend and he didn't expect that he'd have one, for he'd never even had a close boy friend, not in elementary school and not in high school. When he decided that it was time for him to marry, he reviewed all the girls he'd met during that period, at university and at the offices of the paper where he worked as a proofreader, and Bat-Ami Avni seemed to be the most suitable candidate. He liked the self-confidence she exuded, and he remembers, fatherless son of an immigrant that he was, that he was also charmed by the fact that she was the daughter of a big, salt-of-the-earth family that had been rooted in Jerusalem for five generations. He loved her name and he loved how everyone pronounced it in that direct, natural, sabra intonation: Ba*ta*mi. And he loved the family home in the Rehavia neighborhood that Bat-Ami's father had built of Jerusalem stone and where Bat-Ami had lived since the day she was born. If only he could marry this nice girl, he knew that he too would be able to live in the handsome house that was surrounded by evergreen pines and cypresses, and from whose windows the Valley of the Cross could be seen like the sea from a beach house.

And what does he know about his three daughters? Bat-Ami conceived them, gave birth to them, and raised them, and it seems they are still connected to her by umbilical cords through which blood pulses to this day. Toward him, on the other hand, the girls are nice, full of admiration, yet restrained and deferent. Not one of them ever talks to him about her inner world and not one of them ever tells him about what occupies her or really excites her. His sons-in-law behave toward him with the same cautious affection, and the grandchildren also pick up on the family codes, and from the day they are able to think for themselves they open their arms to hug and kiss Grandma Bat-Ami, and then move to him and stand before him and say very politely, Hello Grandpa Yoel.

It was different only with his eldest grandson, Tal. Tal, a beautiful toddler with shining eyes, would burst into Yoel's closed study, jump into his barren lap with joyous shouts, and shower him with hugs of unconditional love. Perhaps he did it, Yoel thinks, because as the first grandchild there was nobody from whom he could learn that you don't hug Grandpa Yoel. Either way, of one fact he was convinced: nobody else had touched him so deeply, neither before this child nor after him.

As Tal grew up he too discovered that his grandfather is a fortress whose walls are inviolable, and since he reached adolescence Yoel sees him only rarely and even then there is no closeness between them.

13

Daylight is starting to wane as the plane lands in the Low Country, where sea level is higher than land and the earth is webbed with veins of water and of blood. This is the earth that opened its maw and swallowed many of its lovers, and would have swallowed him as well had it not been for his mother, who rescued him from its jaws. Our life began on the day we immigrated to Israel, his mother repeatedly said throughout the years of his childhood and youth. Remember, Yoel, and never forget: You've got a mother and you've got a sister and you've got yourself. That's all; nothing else matters.

Late that evening he gets out of the taxi that has brought him from the airport, takes his suitcase and heavy hand luggage from the trunk, and walks into the elegant lobby of the Hotel de Paris. He was here with Bat-Ami only a few days ago and now he walks in flooded with the excitement of someone who has come home, but the elderly receptionist regards him with a blank stare as if he had never set eyes on him.

As the receptionist hands him a guest registration card, Yoel scans the familiar setting of the reception desk: models of windmills and brightly colored houses, porcelain delftware plates with blue decoration, wooden clogs of assorted sizes, and a large oil painting of an old sailing ship battling a stormy sea. When he completes his registration and goes to take a city map from the stand overflowing with piles of information brochures and tourist advertisements, his attention is caught by a stack of brochures about LGBT Amsterdam and next to it a bunch of leaflets advertising the Anne Frank House.

You're going to die, one of his little grandchildren had told him recently, and the boy's mother had raised her beautiful eyebrows beneath her white turban and asked reproachfully, What's the matter with you, Chesed? Why are you speaking to Grandpa like that? The boy didn't reply, and Galia smiled uncomfortably at her father. It seems to me, she suggested in a didactic tone, that Chesed simply thinks that anyone who's a grandfather must be terribly old. But our Grandpa Yoel is still young, Chesed sweetie, our Grandpa Yoel—

Not true, the child interrupted her. I didn't say he was going to die just because he's old.

Why then?

Her son hung his head with its curled sidelocks and didn't reply. A while later, after Yoel had ensconced himself in his study and was immersed in his papers, he sensed a look searing him and saw the boy standing at his desk, his eyes black flames and his nose just about level with the desktop. I'm going to die, Yoel told him quietly, and the child confirmed this fact with a nod, and they gazed at one another unblinking as Yoel reached into a drawer, took out a licorice candy, and proffered it to the small out-stretched hand, even though it was clear to both of them that no offering could lighten the sentence.

He still hadn't recovered from the humiliating welcome he'd been given earlier at Schiphol Airport. Why have you come back to Holland so soon? the huge passport control officer asked him, his voice dripping with hostility. What are you doing here?

Yoel tried to explain that Amsterdam is so lovely that on his all-too-short previous visit he hadn't managed to enjoy everything the city has to offer. Then he told the angry giant that he was a writer and that his books had already been published in Dutch and sold very well here. An armed security officer quickly appeared at the passport desk and ordered Yoel to accompany him to a side room, where he had to wait for a long time, and then be trampled to dust in a prolonged and rigorous interrogation, and wait for another eternity until his passport was eventually returned and he was allowed to go on his way.

Thinking about it now, he has to admit that logic indeed dictates a check of every foreigner entering Holland twice in the same week. But still, he was hurt as if he'd been done an injustice. Logic is on their side, but he can't free himself of the feeling that they had behaved toward him this way simply because he's an Israeli Jew.

14

In the morning he says his morning prayers by the window overlooking the pub across the street and then goes down to the breakfast room. He'd reached the hotel exhausted last night and had sunk into sleep even though he was starving, but now he looks for and finds his regular kosher menu at the buffet—plain yogurt, bread and butter, hard-boiled eggs— and he enjoys a relaxed breakfast as he scans the other diners and counts the Israelis among them. Afterward he crosses the square between the hundreds of empty tables and chairs standing outside the cafés in straight lines, awaiting the human bodies that will come in the evening and fill them with content and meaning. In the street running alongside the Keizersgracht he stops, takes the city map from his jacket pocket, opens it to study it, then refolds it and starts walking eastward along the canal bank.

Seventy-six thousand trees are planted on the banks of Amsterdam's canals to draw into their roots the water on which the city is built. So the tour guide said on the canal cruise he'd been on with Bat-Ami, and Yoel had made a note to find out the Hebrew names of these trees, but now he decides he won't do it. In Israel he calls each tree by its name and writes about the cypress and the poplar, the oak and the pine and the olive, the fig and the willow. But here he doesn't mind calling each tree a "tree," simply "tree," for what have they got to do with him?

———————

I could have been him, he thinks as a Dutchman who looks about the same age as himself passes by, riding straight-backed on an old bicycle. Or I could have been that man who somewhat resembles me in build and in his combed-back hair, sitting with a good-looking woman outside a café on the opposite bank of the canal. I could have breathed all my breaths in this air under this Dutch sky, so gray and unpretentious, from which the shafts of light shine soft and undemanding. I could have been a Dutch writer: a writer who writes his soul, that is, my soul, in the birthplace of my ancestors, and of my parents, and of myself.

Everything is beautiful here and everything is precise. Had he lived here all his life perhaps he too would be as light as those white gulls gliding over the canals, dropping to the water and immediately soaring upward again. Perhaps he too would know how to sit in one of the pubs or coffee shops opening up to the street wherever one looked, how to have a drink, to have a smoke, to stare. What would he have been had it not been for the war, who would he have been if his family had not been uprooted from this fertile soil? And had he lived here from the day he was born until this moment, and if it had not been for the secrets at the foundations of his existence, which he had only recently discovered, would he have come to be engaged in writing at all? Would he have suffered this uncontrollable compulsion to seek his words in the void of the world, would he have been compelled to tell and retell his story, would he have become a writer?

On many of the small balconies of the apartments there are crates of Heineken beer, and through the windowpanes he sees in many of the apartments, on many of the windowsills, orchids in their pots. Bat-Ami can't stand orchids. She loves the abundant plants she cultivates in plant pots, in old enamel pans and clay pots inside their apartment and on the veranda where she devotedly tends the geraniums and begonias and petunias and *Mandevillas*, fostering personal relationships with each leaf, each bud, and each petal, but she has never introduced a single orchid among them all. Orchids are coquettish to the point of kitsch, she says, their life span is too short, and there's no justification for the prestige attributed to them and the hard work that for some reason people stubbornly invest in nurturing them. Yoel, on the other hand, is usually less connected to pot plants and is more excited by the wild chrysanthemums yellowing on the Israeli roadsides at winter's end, and by the stands of hollyhocks blooming pinkly between spring and summer. But what can he do if he thinks that orchids are magnificent and full of mystery.

When Yoel thinks "Bat-Ami," he thinks first of her scent, which when they first met he identified with the scent of the garden around her house, especially the scent of Jerusalem pines like in the Naomi Shemer song that was popular at the time. Then he thinks about her voice, and then her movements, like the way she comes into the apartment and throws her bunch of keys onto the table before she sits down. And only after the scent, and after the voice and the movements, he sees her image that has remained unchanged since they were young. Unchanged? Bat-Ami grumbles when he tells her so, I don't know if you're saying it because you think it's what I want to hear, or because you don't really see me. And Yoel defends himself saying, Of course I see you, but she points at the mirror. Just look at how my cheeks have sunk, look at my eyelids, my chin and neck. My face has fallen, it's as simple as that, not to mention the ravages the accident inflicted on me. Ever since the accident I stand differently, I walk differently, my look is different. I'm different, Yoel, I've changed, and I find it hard to believe that you don't see it.

And Yoel stands his ground. In my eyes, he says, you're the same girl you were when I first met you. Even that injury hasn't left a mark on you.

The map he is holding tells him to turn left from the Keizersgracht past the Municipal Archives building and continue to Muntplein. From the top of the clock tower in the middle of the square come musical bell chimes, and Yoel thinks of his forefathers who also hear this tune as they pass by this tower.

Tourists from all over the world are walking through the square in couples and groups, talking in their different languages and voicing their wonderment at the architecture and the canals as they hurry toward the floating flower market. Yoel, too, shifts his bones along the crowded pier overflowing with tulips of every size, tulips of every possible hue, and tulips of every impossible hue. He also sees various species of lilies and he sees orchids, roses, giant sunflowers, and dahlias, but mainly tulips, open tulips and closed tulips and tulip bulbs for planting, tulips and tulips as though the Dutch aren't aware that the origins of this beautiful flower are in the Mediterranean region, that it migrated to the Netherlands from Persia through Turkey and was given the name "tulip" due to an ungraceful corruption of the Persian word "turban."

How long has it been since he saw Tal, and what was the color of Tal's hair when he last saw him? There was a time when the boy's head glistened grassy green, another time it shone deep blue, and for a very long time he had hair that was carrot red. At the last Sukkot festival, Ronit had visited them with her family, but Tal hadn't come with her. And when Yoel and Bat-Ami visited her in midsummer, Tal was just leaving the house with a few of his friends and with hair as white as snow, as white as the hair of an old man.

He must learn to find his way through the maze of Amsterdam's canals and streets, he must look and see, he must remember both what he will see and what he won't see. Flocks of tourists pass him, chattering away in their multifarious languages, standing amazed and taking photographs. They have all come here in search of attractions, whereas he has come in search of a dead child. Murder investigations usually focus on seeking the identity of the murderer, whereas he knows who the murderer is and he is seeking the identity of the victim.

15

His entire life is geared toward expectation of that one moment: the moment when he will feel he is alive. In the past he had deluded himself that it would happen only if he galloped on horseback, parachuted from a plane, or sliced through sea waves on a Jet Ski, his face to the wind. But he had never even thought about learning one of these skills, and even in his youth, when his friends clambered down rope ladders into deep caves, scaled cliffs, or raced in sailboats, he had always preferred to stay on terra firma and tell everybody it was because he had to consider his mother, who indeed was anxious even when he went on a routine school outing, but the truth is that it wasn't because of her but because of himself that he always avoided physical challenges and it wasn't because of her but because of himself that he chose military service in a home front intelligence unit. There was a period when he did think he wanted to bungee jump, his heart pounded just with the thought of his body being hurled into the void and freeing itself of the force of gravity, of earthliness, but in the end he gave up on the idea. All that trouble, of taking his cluster of organs off to the end of the world just to have it raised to some high point and be harnessed to some kind of rope and bounced into a chasm like a yo-yo, seemed too much.

In Rembrandtplein tourists are gathered round the exalted, lonely statue raised in honor of the man who revealed to humanity how light is created, a miracle that until the advent of Rembrandt van Rijn only the Creator could have worked. Yoel wends his way through the tourists and their cameras, and a bolus of sadness chokes him as he looks up at the stone image in whose stone hand is a huge stone palette and whose stone head touches the sky. Then he crosses the Amstel over the wide royal bridge whose pillars are decorated with flamboyant golden crowns, and now he is already inside the Old Jewish Quarter, and on his right is the building that once housed the four Ashkenazi synagogues that is now home to the Jewish Historical Museum. A green-blue billboard welcomes visitors and Yoel goes to the ticket office, purchases an Amsterdam City Pass for all the city's museums, and goes inside, hurrying in leaps and bounds up the spiral staircase leading to the exhibition hall.

Last week in this museum he and Bat-Ami had tried in vain to find more photographs of his family members or documentation relating to their history. The librarians in the research library and then some administrative officials had searched the documents, shelves, drawers, and computerized records for them. They had promised to continue the search after the Israeli writer and his wife returned to Israel, and most importantly, they excitedly promised to try to find the full reel of the wedding film, excerpts of which are screened on the wall, and one of them shows the writer's family.

But now, after Yoel had seen Nettie and heard what he'd heard from her, he has no further need of either documentation or photographs. All he needs is one single scene from the wedding film screened on the wall: the one and only excerpt showing a father, a mother, a little girl, and a baby. They appear for only the blink of an eye, but in that fleeting moment they are breathing and moving as if in a transparent sliver of life that has crystallized and been preserved in the dimension of time.

Remember and never forget, his mother would tell him in his childhood. You've got a mother and you've got a sister and you've got yourself. That's all; nothing else matters. They had no relatives. They had no friendly relations with other families, not even with families from Holland like themselves. Wherever he looked, Yoel the child saw families hosting and being hosted, dining in each other's houses on Sabbaths and festivals and spending leisure time and vacation time together. Only he and his mother and Nettie weren't part of the great human celebration, only the three of them regularly remained outside, that is to say inside, in the small, closed circle his mother marked out around them. We don't need anyone, she told him each time he caught her declining invitations and rebuffing attempts at closeness by likeable neighbors or people who knew her through her work at the clinic. She didn't have even one close friend, and he always thought she had chosen solitude because of her individualistic personality, because of her need for privacy and quiet, and apparently because of her critical character too, which made her judge people harshly and on more than one occasion tell them exactly what she thought of them.

He realizes only now that his mother had isolated herself for his sake. Only now, after Nettie had revealed the secret of his past, he understands that to protect that secret his mother had avoided bringing any outside entity into their small family circle. And that she had been especially careful with Jews who had emigrated from Holland, for they were liable to remember her from the past and recognize the truth she was hiding. His heart lurched when he thought about the magnitude of her effort to protect the fragile balance in which he had been raised and grown up. And to what degree of devotion, to the point of self-sacrifice, she had blocked any disturbance that might crack the delicate shell of their family cell.

He has to tell stories: back in his childhood he did not stop at the tales he invented about his father, but told his friends in the neighborhood and at school about his large and vibrant family that included grandparents and aunts and uncles and cousins in Jerusalem and in Tel Aviv, in the kibbutz and in the village. He told them about the special helicopter that nightly hovered above his house to protect him and his mother and sister against robbers and other pests. He told about the wild tiger his father had brought him from his travels, and how he raised and trained that tiger on their kitchen porch, and told about more and more exciting gifts his father brought for him from all over the world. And again about his extended family, a warm, happy family of dozens of loving relatives spread all over the country. Even Shiye Glazer, he heard himself boasting to a few children one day, even Shiye Glazer, the famous goal-scoring star of the national soccer team, is actually my cousin.

And he never understood what the kids in class and the neighborhood wanted of him. Why they mocked him and got mad at him whenever one of them checked one of the facts he related and released the results of his investigation. Where's your famous cousin? they teased. Liar, pointing at him, liar, liar, but he hadn't meant to lie, he simply didn't know, or perhaps didn't want to know, how to separate the life in his imagination from reality, which to him was imaginary as well.

16

He planned to spend only an hour or two at the museum today. Right afterward, he thought, he'd carry on to the Old South of Amsterdam and find the Jacob Obrechtstraat area: the place where he was born and where, according to what Nettie had told him, the main part of the story he plans to write takes place.

But instead he spends a long time watching the endless loop of the wedding film.

And after detaching himself from the wall on which the film is being screened, he finds himself being drawn to the various objects displayed in the museum and becomes immersed in them, entirely swallowed up by the signs, the clothes, and the utensils, by the books, the documents, and the taped interviews. Swallowed up limitlessly, swallowed up as though he has no present apart from the past of the Jews of Amsterdam.

Exhibited in one of the glass cabinets in the museum hall are Etty Hillesum's notebooks. He had read the book based on her diary a long time ago, but now there are her notebooks, her handwriting, and the figures she drew in the margins, and there is Etty, a brilliant young woman who loved life and who could have been saved through her connections in the Jewish Council, yet she chose to be taken to the place where all the Jews who didn't have such connections were taken. To console God, as she wrote in one of the notebooks, at a time when His world is causing Him so much sorrow.

There is a cabinet containing copper tableware. In others there are ration coupons and packaging from staple commodities. An identity card stamped with a "J." Issues of a daily paper. Table games. A child's dress, and below its starched collar is sewn a yellow star bearing the word "Jood." A large roll of yellow material with row after row of "Jood" stars ready for cutting out with scissors. A hard-studded suitcase bearing someone's personal details, and the word "Holland." A barrel for pickling herring. Children's toys: building blocks, a locomotive, a doll's bed, and a windmill, all made of wood. Theater playbills.

A filmed interview: A beautiful elderly lady (white hair, thick gray eyebrows, lively black eyes, a string of pearls round a graceful neck) is seated in a fine house whose window overlooks a flowering garden on the shore of a blue lake. My family was arrested, she says, because another family on the list wasn't at home and the police had to fill their quota. We didn't think, she says, that things like this could happen in Holland. Of course, if you knew about what was happening in Germany, and you knew that the Germans had occupied Holland, then you could guess what would happen here. But you still didn't believe that they might possibly arrest you, you didn't believe that you'd be taken from your home and imprisoned in a camp. No, not in Holland.

A filmed interview: An elderly man is standing in Waterlooplein in front of the two spires of the Moses and Aaron Church, which Yoel had seen across the street when he went into the museum. The man is talking about the bustling Jewish market that was right here in the square. And how, in his childhood, his father, who was a shoemaker over there (he points), would send him every day to buy him a fish from the herring seller whose barrel stood right here on this spot.

We didn't believe it. We didn't believe it. We didn't believe that such things could happen in Holland.

A scene from a short film: A train from Amsterdam arrives at a concentration camp. The sliding door of a cattle wagon opens and looking from within it are men in tailored suits, women in fox furs and high heels, children in sailor collars. They slowly start clambering down from the wagons, carrying suitcases and various other items, blinking in the sunlight and shading their eyes as they look around them.

And all this time, without stopping, the enlarged scenes from the wedding film are flickering on the hall's north wall, while on two of the other walls additional scenes of everyday life in prewar Amsterdam are being screened: Young families enjoying a picnic in the countryside. Boys in singlets playing volleyball on a lawn. Middle-aged men and women coming out of a building, taking leave of one another with handshakes, mounting their bicycles parked on the sidewalk, and pedaling off. A toddler in a swimsuit standing in a tin bath, bending to fill a small pail with water that comes up to her ankles, and then straightening up and emptying the pail over her head, smiling at the camera as the water drips from her hair onto her happy face.

Yoel glances at his watch only when the PA system announces that the museum is closing, and is reminded that time is something that passes.

As he comes out into Waterlooplein it is already almost dark, and he decides that it's enough for today and that he will postpone his visit to the south of the city until tomorrow morning. He walks to the tram stop to take a tram back to his hotel on Leidseplein but is halted as though by an invisible barrier: it's odd, but he knows, and the knowledge hits him like a hammer blow, that he must avoid traveling on public transportation. There is no reason why you shouldn't, he tries telling himself, but he is sure that as a Jew he has no choice but to return to his hotel on foot. And he's sure that great danger is hovering over him: that they, all the people passing by in the street right now, can see he's a Jew and they're determined to murder him. Maybe it's hunger, he thinks. I've hardly eaten all day. Maybe it's physical exhaustion, in the last couple of days I haven't slept for more than two consecutive hours. Nevertheless he starts shortening his steps and stays close to the walls as he looks around fearfully.

On the curb, at the edge of the busy street separating the Jewish Quarter from the golden bridge over the river, he is afraid of stepping off the sidewalk. He is sure that the drivers of the cars and buses want to run him down. The cyclists too, who at this hour are on their way home from their work or studies and are flooding the street, seem to him as though they are threatening to intentionally hit him. What's happening to me? he asks himself. He knows it's illogical but he is sure that eyes filled with hate are glaring at him from all sides. That they are all pointing at him, showing him to one another, and calling to each other in Dutch: There's a Jew, there's a Jew, kill the Jew, destroy him.

He recalls that he had read, apparently in a pseudoscientific American magazine, about Jewish paranoia syndrome. The sense of persecution is a genetic Jewish instinct, it said. An innate instinct that Jews develop based on Jewish collective memory, not in accordance with their personal reality.

But that explanation doesn't help to steady his heart rate.

You've been taken over by an imaginary fear, he tells himself. A phantom fear like the phantom pain a person feels even long after a limb has been amputated. But phantom or not, the fear paralyzes him, preventing his body from stepping off the sidewalk and crossing the busy street. He knows he can't possibly be in danger, and he tells himself three times: Everything's alright everything's alright everything's alright, but he understands that this time the alrightness won't really help him.

In the end he hurries back to the hotel in panicky flight. He refuses to believe that this frightened Yid is him, but he can't stop looking sideways and backward and only crossing streets with groups of tourists or passersby, hiding among them as if hiding behind a protective wall. When he sees policemen or any other uniformed persons, he stops his flight and hurries, his body trembling, to seek cover behind buildings, cars, or tree trunks. And by the Keizersgracht the sidewalk running alongside the canal seems too exposed, and he bypasses it through one of the more crowded streets running at right angles to it, thus lengthening his route and getting himself so lost that he doesn't know where he's coming from or going to.

He only gets back to Leidseplein in the late evening, sidling breathlessly through the busy square and slipping into an opening in a building wall to hide from a passing policeman. When he gets his breath back he sees that his hiding place is one of the entrances to the splendid, stylized commercial building with a copper cupola prominent on its roof and the name "Hirsch & Cie" in huge metal lettering that can be seen from every point in the square and the streets leading off it. Today at the Jewish Historical Museum he had learned about Leo Hirsch, the Jewish businessman who had purchased this plot of land when the entire area was desolate swampland. Hirsch and his partners drained the area, erected the building with its impressive copper cupola, and in it opened a fashion house which in those days was more modern and prestigious than any other fashion house in Western Europe. Yoel shrinks, sharpens his senses insofar as he is able, and cautions himself: Take care, syndrome or not you've got to save your skin you've got to flee you've got to run, run, run.

And he runs, runs, runs, borne like a leaf on the wind, borne, borne, borne, and he doesn't calm down even when he sees the neon sign of the Hotel de Paris from afar. Anxiety grips him lest he not be admitted into the hotel, lest he not be allowed to go back to his room, where he has left his belongings when he went out at the start of the day.

17

In the morning, after standing under the sharp needles of a hot shower for a long time, and another long time bound up in the straps of his *tefillin*, he admits that apart from Jewish paranoia syndrome, and apart from phantom fears, he had experienced something else yesterday. He doesn't believe in mysticism—he definitely leaves that entire field and its odd derivatives to Bat-Ami—but there can be no doubt that there is another explanation for what happened to him after the visit to the Jewish Museum. If Bat-Ami was here now she'd certainly say that on his way from Waterlooplein to Leidseplein last night he'd been accompanied by the tormented souls that still inhabit the streets of Amsterdam, and particularly the Old Jewish Quarter; the souls of those who had been persecuted in that place and were helpless to do anything about it, of those who were tormented and tortured and whose pleas went unheard. Those masses of Jews were here and are no longer, she would probably have said, but their grief remains in this place, all the suffering and terror remains, and on whom could those painful energies settle if not on a sensitive soul like yours?

Either way, the new novel is taking shape in his mind. He has a growing feeling that all the stories he has written throughout his life were nothing more than preparation for the writing of this one. And his confidence grows that he will indeed find the letters of his story here in Amsterdam and join them into words. Nettie can relate only the little she knows and remembers, but he will gather up the tangle of broken threads she gave him and weave them into a whole tapestry.

The sky above is clear and blue as he emerges from the hotel into the street, and he stands under that sky and studies his city map. Then he folds up the paper map, slips it into the inside pocket of his tweed jacket, and crosses Leidseplein unhurriedly. At an easy pace he passes the five stories of the handsome Hirsch building, walks southwest, and goes into the big city park, Vondelpark. Its paths are lined with trees, shrubs, and flowers and pass between lakes and sprawling lawns, and even at this late morning hour on a normal working day they are crowded with people walking their dogs, with seemingly carefree cyclists, and with people running or walking and radiating fitness, health, and efficiency.

Here is his young mother riding her bicycle along the park's main path. What is she thinking about? How did she sleep last night and what did she dream about? Does he know her—his young mother in the days before she became his mother—to the extent that will enable him to write her as a character in a novel? Does he know how she moves and talks, does he know what she thinks, does he know what she wants?

At the park's fourth exit, just as the map shows, Jacob Obrechtstraat begins, along whose wide, paved sidewalk, like the narrow streets leading off it, rows of typically Dutch-style terrace houses are arranged. Some have four narrow stories, some have five, and many have basement apartments with windows at sidewalk level. All of them are built of small red bricks and adjoin one another. At the front of each one there are two doors opening onto the street, and each story has a row of three or four high, wide windows opening onto the soft light outside and the foliage of the tall trees.

Everything is clean, everything gleams, everything is precise, and Yoel paces out Jacob Obrechtstraat step by step. A man in shorts and colorful running shoes passes him, and it seems that he's about his age and on his way home from his daily hour of jogging in Vondelpark, and that he's lived in this street ever since both of them were born here. The man turns into a house with black art nouveau ironwork framing its doorway, and Yoel thinks that perhaps it's the house where this carefree runner was born and grew up, though it's entirely possible that the house belonged to Jews, but anyway he slowly and painstakingly steps on each of the sidewalk's gray paving stones as if he is letting each house see his face, see his face and recognize in him the baby he was here so long ago.

To be a baby, he writes in his notebook, to be a Dutch baby whose mother carries him in front of her on her bicycle and the air of the world blows in his face. Leaves float down from the branches of the trees, yellow, brown, and orange, they float down onto the sidewalk and a cool breeze swirls them lightly.

Ah, and the sky slanting like a canvas. The light the Creator wears like a gown. And the depth of the splendor, the splendor that pulsed here then too . . .

He slows his pace even more as he passes the church with its great wooden doors and its two soaring spires. He reminds himself that these doors were also here back then. And then, too, the spires made the eyes looking at them gaze upward. And after the church here is the market square. The house, Nettie had told him from what she recalled from her childhood, stood in the narrow street running at a right angle to Jacob Obrechtstraat between the church and the neighborhood market square, Jacob Obrechtplein. Yoel stands in the center of the small square's paved circle, which back then had housed a permanent farmers market, and now the sign says that the market stalls are set up only on Saturdays. Yoel looks at the flat paving stones that have not been replaced since then, at the sky through the thick foliage of the oaks that covers the square, and at the four picturesque streets leading into the square, creating four corners, on each of which stands a shop: today one of them is a pizzeria, and three are house Realtor agencies.

One of the four corner shops is the one Nettie told him about. It is Martin's art shop.

18

How accurate Nettie's description was: Just before the end of Jacob Obrechtstraat, at the end of a row of stylized, well-tended homes, he comes to a big building over whose wide gate two white-blossoming trees stand guard to its left and right. He stops. He is here. This is where the Jewish hospital was. This is where he was born. Now there is another kind of medical institution here, and seen through its glazed façade is a spacious, seemingly sterile lobby in which four wheelchairs stand waiting near an elevator door, their reflections silent on the polished floor.

Right near the hospital is the synagogue that was built only a few years before the war. The synagogue too is built of small red bricks, and its façade climbing upward is reminiscent of the church up the street. Unlike the church, the synagogue is encircled by a spiked iron fence and an iron gate blocks the way to the wide steps leading to its door. As if praying, Yoel reads the words inscribed over the door in block Hebrew letters: "I have surely built thee a house to dwell in, a settled place for thee to abide in forever."

He repeats them aloud, his voice trembling: I have surely built . . . for thee to abide in forever.

On the wall facing eastward toward Jerusalem are two stained glass windows, while on the south wall there is a stone tablet inscribed with the Hebrew letters of another biblical verse. "Blessed is the man that heareth me," the letters promise, "watching daily at my gates."

Yoel sighs. You can't blame the Dutch for what happened because the
Dutch are simply naturally disciplined, they're simply used to observing
law and order and doing what they're told, and perhaps it's not only them,
perhaps most people are like that. Just as he and Bat-Ami had seen only last
week as they crossed Leidseplein, when they saw three men, apparently
Hungarian tourists, stop in the middle of the square and start performing
headstands, walking on their hands, and doing forward and backward
somersaults, and calling to all the passersby in broken English with the help
of a primitive megaphone to gather round and witness a performance the
like of which they had never seen, and within a few seconds people stopped
and gathered round them, with more and more joining them, people who
had seen the first small group and followed suit, and minute by minute the
crowd grew, even though the three performers were doing nothing more
than simple exercises and were wearing only jeans and faded T-shirts, and
they didn't sing or play instruments or put on a sketch or try to be funny,
but they just told the audience to stand in a circle that one of them marked
out with a length of rope while his friends went on jumping on the spot, and
the unbearably disciplined crowd, men, women, and their children, stood
by the rope, a huge crowd, patiently and quietly craning their necks to see
between the heads of the people closest to the rope, the three threadbare
nobodies continuing to stand on their heads and walk on their hands and
do backward and forward somersaults like third graders in a gym class.
And Bat-Ami tried to pull him away. What are you hanging around here
for, let's get on, but he couldn't tear his eyes away from what was happening there, he couldn't not see it all, including the end of the performance,
after which one of the three Hungarians took off his sweat-soaked hat and
told the audience to fill it with money and they all took out their purses and
wallets and stood in line to take out their coins and banknotes as if it were
impossible not to.

One side of the synagogue almost abuts the Jewish hospital and the other
adjoins a small park. It is an old park and the surrounding trees are now

shedding yellow leaves. In it are recently installed ladders and swings, but also a very old circular sandbox whose low concrete wall is cracked from the weight of the years, beside an old iron carousel and a no-less-old iron slide.

Yoel walks slowly into the playground, which at this early hour is empty. He goes to one of the benches, brushes off the yellow leaves that have accumulated on it, and sits down. He sits there for a long time looking at the sandbox, then raises his eyes to the ladder of the slide, holds his gaze there for a moment, and slides his gaze downward. Finally his eyes wander to the abandoned carousel, which today is painted red and blue and who remembers what color it was decades ago.

He allows his heart another spin on the carousel and listens to the voices that have been waiting for him here since way back when.

19

Three Realtors' offices surround the small market square, their windows covered with photographs of apartments for sale or rent in the nearby neighborhood. He looks at the photographs showing the interior of the apartments and knows that most of the kitchens are renovated and modern, and most of the furniture is modern too, but the walls have been the same for many years. And the apartments are the same apartments.

This is where the story unfolds, he tells himself, in an apartment like this, in a building like this, in one of these streets.

His eyes wander, and on a narrow building adjoining the Realtor's office that was Martin's shop he sees a small, faded sign he had missed. Hotel, the sign says. Mokum Hotel.

How excited Bat-Ami had been last week when she discovered that the Dutch refer to Amsterdam as "Mokum," that is, the Hebrew word "*makom*" (place). That a "*haver*," friend, in Dutch vernacular is "*haber*" and a lunatic is a "meshugge."

Yoel goes through the door beneath the sign, along a narrow passageway, and down three steep Dutch steps, and comes to a glass sliding door opening onto a small, shabby lobby. The place seems deserted, there is nobody behind the old wooden counter that is gouged with scratches, and it is only after several long minutes that a side door opens and a dark-skinned young man appears yawning hugely, stretching his wrinkled shirt over his chest, puts a paperback with an illustrated cover on the counter, and with a surprisingly pleasant smile and in excellent English introduces himself as the Mokum Hotel receptionist. They quickly fall into conversation. Yoel hears himself telling the young man that he's a writer doing research for a novel set in Amsterdam and that he's thinking about renting a room in this hotel on a monthly basis. A writer! his interlocutor exclaims in earnest excitement. A real writer! Their talk continues and it emerges that the receptionist's name is Achilles and that he too writes and loves writing. Still, the truth is, he confesses, pointing at the book on the counter, that he mainly loves reading and he and his girlfriend are continually reading the biographies of leaders from all periods and analyzing the biographies they read, because they think that the most enthralling thing is deciphering the latent motives of the figures they read about, getting behind the scenes of the historical events and understanding what really happened. She's been his girlfriend for a long time, he says with a happy smile, and they've already read and deciphered the stories of Abraham Lincoln, Helen Keller, Mahatma Gandhi, Moshe Dayan, Marilyn Monroe, and many more. In fact, they've been in love since their childhood, but before he marries her he wants to save a lot of money. My father's British and my mother's Indian, he says with a sort of British-Indian smile. I give all my wages to my mother because if I keep the money the chances are I'll spend it without noticing.

Yoel glances at the upside-down cover of the book on the counter. He can't identify the portrait on it and wants to ask if it's a biography too, and if so, whose. But a deafening metallic pealing suddenly fills the air followed by more and more peals and Achilles stops talking, shuts his eyes, and counts the peals one after the other on his fingers. When silence falls again, he says: It's eleven o'clock! And his expression is one of wonderment and surprise as if until he heard the ringing of the bell he wasn't sure that eleven o'clock would arrive today too.

That's the bell of the church across the street, he explains reverently. The church of Our Lady of the Most Holy Rosary.

Achilles goes on talking about his relationship with his parents, about his wonderful beloved and the books in which she and he love to search for hidden layers and riddles, until Yoel takes advantage of a brief pause between sentences to inquire if there's a room he can rent by the month, and Achilles slaps his forehead and apologizes for chattering, stifles another yawn with the same hand while the other smooths his shirt, and invites his guest to choose a room from the hotel's offerings himself.

The rooms here are quite small, he apologizes with another yawn in the faltering elevator, whose stops and starts are accompanied by groans and grunts, but I hope we'll be able to find us one that will be suitable for our literary writing. Yoel nods his thanks and wonders if there is any such a place in the world that is suitable for literary writing. He also wonders if Achilles's use of the first person plural means that he intends to share with Yoel the responsibility for the said writing, and perhaps even to labor with him, shoulder to shoulder, on quarrying the words out of the rock. The first room he shows Yoel has four ascetic beds, one for each of the four whitewashed walls. Like two stony-faced sentinels looking into the room through its only window are the twin spires of the church across the street. Yoel looks at the table under the window, imagines himself writing under the constant supervision of these two, and thinks that perhaps he'll be able to draw from them a supreme literary inspiration of a kind he hadn't experienced so far.

Standing in the next room in a straight row are eight identical beds. You can choose whichever bed you want, Achilles says, and chuckles. But Yoel thinks that if he takes this room he won't choose one of the beds but all eight. He'll sleep in a different bed every night, he thinks, and dream a whole different dream every night. Perhaps he'll even move from one bed to another during the same night, and have a completely new dream every hour in each one.

From time to time his eyes light on wallpaper whose edges are curling or on a layer of wooly dust, but he decides to keep quiet, and eventually Achilles takes him up to the fourth floor in the groaning, grunting elevator. I wanted to show you one more room, Achilles says as they walk down the corridor, it's a smaller room and is at the back of the hotel with a less beautiful view, but maybe you should take a look at it anyway. And at the end of the corridor he yawns and opens the door of a corner room the size of the bathroom in Yoel and Bat-Ami's apartment in Jerusalem.

Almost all its floor space is taken up by a sagging bed, a narrow double bed or perhaps a wide single one, that crouches in the middle of the room as if the room belongs to it, and by one of the walls is a sad, thin chair pushed up against a Formica-topped table with an old TV set on it. Yoel takes all this in skeptically, but then he notices that instead of a window the room has a sliding glass door leading onto a small balcony. He goes out on the balcony, whose width he can span with his legs apart, and whose railing is rusted and perhaps even slightly unsafe, and he looks over the railing and is amazed to find that down below, like in a living picture, he can see the backyards of the two rows of houses running at right angles to the market square.

I'll take this balcony, he announces quickly. I mean this room.

20

Yoel is standing in the pristine lobby of the Hotel de Paris, on the other side of the display of clogs, the model windmill, and the rest, and saying goodbye to the elderly receptionist who seems as indifferent to his departure as he had been to his arrival. After a short taxi ride from Leidseplein to Jacob Obrechtstraat, he walks, his bag heavy on his shoulder as he pulls his suitcase behind him, to the narrow entrance of the Mokum Hotel, carefully descends the three steep steps, and enters the lobby.

Achilles joyfully emerges from the side door, places before him a registration form, and ceremoniously proffers him a pen, and Yoel takes it and tries to fill out the form, but immediately replaces the pen on the scratched counter and from his shirt pocket takes a pen that writes. It's a great honor for us at the Mokum Hotel to have a real writer staying with us, Achilles tells him, and it turns out that the book he is so immersed in is a biography of Napoleon, the third one he's reading about this enigmatic conqueror, this time in French. It's a great honor for us, he repeats with a white-toothed smile, and Yoel again wonders about his use of the plural and on whose behalf he is speaking, for it seems that apart from the two of them there's nobody else in the hotel.

I thank you, he says.

At your service at all times, says the young receptionist, but immediately qualifies this statement: That is, at your service from seven in the morning till seven in the evening.

So at seven in the evening someone comes to relieve you?

Not exactly. From seven in the evening till seven in the morning there's nobody at the reception.

And what happens if a new guest arrives during that time?

Nobody does, because during that time the front door's locked. And by the way, from seven in the evening till seven in the morning the elevator doesn't work either.

You mean that from seven in the evening till seven in the morning one can't come into the hotel or leave it?

Achilles bursts out laughing. Of course you can come and go! What put that into your head?

But you said that the front door's locked, and the elevator . . .

Yes, but there's a back door. And of course you can use the stairs.

When Yoel tries to get into his new room there's something inside that's stopping the door from opening. When he pushes against it he discovers that what's blocking it is the door of the wardrobe standing close to the doorway. Both doors are scratched and dinged, apparently from previous collisions, and once he's inside he shuts them. He locks the door, but when he tries to put on the safety chain to ensure his privacy all he finds are a few links of what was once a whole chain. He drags his suitcase inside and puts his shoulder bag on the bed, which is either a wide single or narrow double, he still can't decide, but which actually looks comfortable, and he opens the bag, takes out his brand-new laptop, and places it on the Formica-topped table. He pushes the clunky old TV set to the edge of the table, disconnects its cable from the wall socket, and replaces it with his laptop plug, lifts the computer's lid, runs two fingers over the shiny black keyboard, and presses the power key.

And he goes out onto the balcony.

The two rows of houses stand beneath the railing, tangible and teeming with life. Each row has its back to the other one, and between the two rows, beneath the apartments' back windows, are the backyards. Parts of the yards at the far end are hidden by trees and bushes, but he can see the ones closer to the hotel in their entirety and he starts scanning yard after yard. He makes a note of every plant he sees and of each piece of garden furniture, a child's tricycle, a swing strung from a branch, a rubber ball that has rolled under a bench, and a doll forgotten on a square of lawn.

Through one of the second-floor windows of the third building in the row to the right he sees the profile of a curly-haired woman sitting in front of a computer screen. All around her, covering the entire area of the wide table, are mountains of papers in bundles and loose, and the woman is shifting restlessly on her chair, her hands moving over the keyboard and halting every now and then in a gesture of despair or surrender.

As he passed in the street Yoel had seen a psychoanalyst's clinic shingle on the building's façade, and so he now decides that the restless woman at the computer is a psychoanalyst. She's writing her reports on today's sessions in the clinic and is restless because she's not sure about her diagnoses and her reports are liable to affect her clients' lives and even seal their fate.

Through one of the windows closer to his balcony, in the first building in the row on the left, he sees a wall covered with framed pictures. The dim light doesn't allow him to see any details, but beneath the pictures he sees a sort of wide chest of drawers on which there are various objects, apparently small sculptures and other pieces of artwork. Between the sculptures and objets d'art is an animal with light, spiky fur, apparently a pet, apparently a dog.

In another window that is lit up he sees one side of a kitchen: a work surface, a sink, a stove. Everything is white, meticulously arranged, squeaky clean. To the right of the stove there is a white salad bowl.

When he is assailed by hunger pangs, Yoel goes into his new room and nibbles rice crackers from the food package that Bat-Ami provided for him. On the corner of the table he places the electric kettle she had packed for him, the jar of instant coffee, and the ceramic mug, but he's got no milk and he'll have to go to the nearest supermarket that's located—so Achilles had told him—beneath the square between the Stedelijk Museum of modern art and the Van Gogh Museum, right opposite the concert hall with the gold harp on its roof.

21

Like airports, hospitals, hotels, and banks, supermarkets look the same everywhere in the world and are laid out in accordance with the same universal systems as if they've been distributed all over the globe using the same diligent copy-paste. This one, too, is operated in exactly the same way as its duplicates wherever they may be, but of all the people in the world, only Yoel doesn't know how to insert a coin to release a shopping cart from the line of carts chained to one another since it is Bat-Ami who usually takes care of his material needs at home and abroad, and it is she who releases a cart for him in every supermarket they go to.

In the past year he had decided to try to learn to share the household chores like today's young couples do, and as part of that decision he had even accompanied his wife to the neighborhood supermarket once or twice, but even on that once or twice it had been her who had taken care of the technical details. All the more so when they were abroad, for then he was usually occupied with meetings with readers, literary lectures, and preparations for meetings with readers and for the literary lectures, whereas Bat-Ami's time was hers to enjoy the beautiful places they visited, rummage in flea markets, and take care of their meals.

So with Bat-Ami not there he is standing inside the entrance to the supermarket and looking around ashamed and helpless because of his lack of this basic universal skill, until eventually a nice Dutch lady comes along and helps him to insert the right coin into the right slot and release a shopping cart just like everyone else. And he is on his way, wandering between the shelves and scanning the rows of foreign products, and he has no idea what they are since printed on each package is what it contains but it's all in Dutch. Much later he is standing in line at the checkout, and in his cart are four huge cucumbers, a packet of cherry tomatoes, three apples, and a carton of milk that is perhaps not a carton of milk but a carton of something else that the Dutch pack in cartons that look like milk cartons.

On his way back to the hotel, the blue plastic supermarket bag in his hand, at the top of the street running from the concert hall to the small market square he passes a small café whose shutters are being raised at that very moment to welcome the new evening. According to what he'd read yesterday in the Amsterdam guidebook for the Israeli tourist that Bat-Ami had bought before their trip and without which she didn't leave the hotel, this café is one of Amsterdam's old "brown cafés," so called because of the color of their interior walls, floors, and furniture, which are all made of natural brown wood. The brown café next to the Concertgebouw, says the guidebook, is famous for its well-known Dutch intellectuals, which include professors, writers, musicians, and theater people.

Yoel slowly walks by the lovely frontages of the houses whose backyards he had earlier looked at from his balcony in the Mokum Hotel. There are but few pedestrians in the narrow street, and most of the people passing are on bicycles or in cars. But in front of him on the sidewalk, her back to him, is a young woman and her two children. She is tall and sturdy in a tailored woolen coat, her flaxen hair is gathered above a strong nape, and her gait is erect and confident. He trails behind her and behind her little girl, whose blond hair is plaited into two thin braids, and she is walking beside her mother's tall figure, holding on to the side of the baby stroller her mother is pushing, and from this rear angle and the distance between them he can't see the face of the child in his checkered coat sitting in the stroller.

The woman's legs are solid and strong, the little girl's matchstick legs take two or three steps to each one of her mother's, and the wheels of the stroller turn and turn. Yoel hears the pleasing sounds of the conversation between mother and daughter, he hears the wheels turning and the baby's burbling as they pass the building housing the psychoanalyst's clinic, and they walk as far as the midpoint between the brown café and the market square and stop there. From her purse the woman takes a key and inserts it into the front door lock. Yoel slows as she opens the door wide, tells the little girl to go inside before her, and then wheels the stroller inside and goes in too. And the door closes.

Yoel approaches the house and sees that the threshold is covered by fallen red leaves. Red ivy climbs beside the front door and the leaves that fall from it pile in the entrance like a puddle of blood.

Opening sentence of the story:

Sonia goes into the house without treading on the red autumn leaves piled in the doorway.

THIRD NOTEBOOK

22

Sonia goes into the house without treading on the red autumn leaves piled in the doorway. Eddy had smiled when he noticed it this morning and suggested that he get a broom from their apartment and clear the way for her. But Sonia, also smiling, asked him to leave the leaves, and her, alone. This autumnal message makes me happy, she told him. And fallen leaves aren't dirt, Edika. You have to admit that the threshold looks much lovelier with this colorful garb than without it.

She steers Nettie into the hallway, comes inside with the stroller, closes the door, and descends the steep staircase with both hands gripping the metal handle of the heavy stroller as it bounces in front of her, step after step. Nettie follows her down, counting the steps in English as her father had taught her only yesterday. Eddy is always teaching the child new skills, and Sonia thinks that it's perhaps a good thing that he's away from home so much. If he spent more hours with them, the little girl wouldn't have time to be little.

Apart from this point she doesn't find anything positive in the fact that Eddy works sixteen hours a day at the hospital and sometimes even more. They'd moved here a short time after she'd become pregnant with Leo, and she thought that the proximity to the Jewish hospital would give them more time together. The high rents in this area meant they could only rent this small basement apartment in Anouk's parents' house, and Eddy's increased presence in the life of their small family was supposed to make up for the decline in the quality of their housing. But it quickly became clear to her that the proximity to Eddy's place of work didn't increase the amount of time he spent with her and the children, but ate away at it even more. It seemed that the news that the brilliant young doctor lived so close to the hospital, right round the corner in fact, led his employers to think that he should spend all day and all night in the internal medicine ward. Every new patient, or a change in the condition of a not new patient, was grounds for them to call him back to the ward, even when only a short time had elapsed since he had completed a long, fatiguing shift and had finally gone home. When she plucked up her courage and went to see the hospital director, Professor Sherman, to complain about it, he had looked at her pityingly. I most definitely understand you, he said. Though I'm sure that you of all people, dear Sonia, a former staff member here and who will apparently be one in the future too, are prepared for a degree of personal sacrifice for the success of our important hospital and for its good name. Especially in these times that are difficult for all of us.

Maybe we were mistaken, she thinks now as she takes off Nettie's and her own coat. Maybe we shouldn't have moved here.

She takes Leo's coat off last, and only then the baby breaks his silence and lets out a weak wail.

You're a good boy, too good, you know? she says as she takes him out of the stroller, clasps him to her bosom, and lays him down on the bed to change his diaper. You're allowed to cry, she whispers into his blue eyes, which are gazing at her with complete trust, you're allowed to, my treasure, especially when you're as hungry as you are right now.

Nettie, who had hurried to her wooden dollhouse in the corner of the room as soon as they got into the apartment, comes over to stand next to her as she sits down to nurse Leo. I'm going to give my babies only breast milk too, she announces.

You'll be a good mother. Sonia smiles at her. You'll be a wonderful mother.

23

Yoel makes himself a cup of coffee and goes out onto the balcony again, back to the two rows of houses below, to them and their backyards. Daylight is slowly fading; in the windows electric lights come on and figures flit in the lighted windows.

In the big window to the right the restless psychoanalyst is still bent over her keyboard, over her mountains of papers and files and over the minds of her clients.

She types something quickly and leans back, stretching her tired arms sideways, reads what she has written on the screen and her shoulders reveal dissatisfaction.

There is now light in the closer window to the left, and he can see some of the framed paintings hanging on the wall there. He can also see that the low, wide piece of furniture under the pictures is indeed a stylized chest of drawers, and that exhibited on it are various statuettes and objets d'art, in the center of which, most surprisingly, still lies the same thin, light-colored dog, a dog that looks amazingly similar to a fox or jackal, its long tail folded beside its haunch and its look directed at the writer standing on the balcony of his hotel room and looking right back at it.

A young man dressed in black comes trippingly into the gleaming white kitchen on the lower floor. His slim body moves as if in a graceful dance as he fills a white kettle and, with the same dance movements, picks up the white bowl that was upside down on the white drainer, places it on the white work surface, and piles some vegetables next to it. From a white drawer he takes a white knife and starts chopping a perfect red tomato on a white cutting board.

The church bell chimes six times. In the right-hand row of houses, Yoel tries to locate the house whose door had swallowed the woman who had earlier been walking in front of him with her little girl and her baby. He thinks she went into the house in the middle of the row, so he stands on his balcony and looks as hard as he can at the middle house and says to himself quietly: That's the house. That's the house. Slowly and painstakingly, his eyes glide over the small red bricks that the five stories of that house are built of and pass over its white window frames. They reach the chimney rising from the corner of the roof, its plume of smoke curling into the endless sky.

Bathed and sated, Leo had fallen asleep a short time after the bell of Our Lady chimed six times. Sonia wants to read Nettie a bedtime story and get her to sleep too before the nightly argument between the enemy's anti-aircraft batteries and the British bombers begins.

It looks like Eddy won't be coming home tonight either. It was good that she'd managed to pop into the hospital while Nettie was in school, leave Leo with one of her friends in the surgical unit, and drag Eddy away from his work for a short while. They didn't waste this precious meeting on talk but simply sat together at the far end of Eddy's department, smoking their cigarettes quietly and stealing a few minutes of intimacy as if they didn't have a common roof under which they could meet, as if they didn't have two beautiful children he'd given her in love, and as if they were still the same youngsters struck by mutual attraction that they'd been when they first met.

Now she and Nettie are sitting in the kitchenette of the basement apartment, chatting amiably about the day that was and the day that will be and eating their supper of thin lentil soup and potatoes. In the long, low window that meets the ceiling above the dining table and their two heads, every now and then they see the feet of passersby on the sidewalk.

A door slams on the top floor of the building and right away mother and daughter exchange the amused smile of people sharing a secret. After the sound of the slam comes, as expected, the delicate pitter-patter of feet hurriedly descending the stairs, down and down until they come to a stop on their floor. A knuckled knock on the door and Sonia gets up, opens it, and pretends surprise as she calls out: Anouk!

Anouk bursts in. Her face is pale and in her arms she is carrying a rolled woolen blanket from which a tiny pair of feet is dangling.

Och, dear Sonke, she pants. I'm so sorry to disturb you again in the middle of your family meal. . . .

Why is she saying "family meal"? Sonia thinks. Can't she see it's just me and Nettie?

It's alright, she replies, you're not disturbing us, and right away, as if an automatic mechanism has been activated in her, Anouk bursts into sobs. I'm so frightened, she explains, and all at once a cascade of tears covers her lovely porcelain cheeks. I think that this time Sebastian's dangerously ill. . . . Martin tells me to calm down, he doesn't consider my feelings at all . . . but I'm so worried. I don't know what I'd do without you. . . .

Sonia unrolls the blanket and takes her neighbor's son in her arms. She feels, as she does each time she holds him, how bony and stiff his body is compared with the soft and pliant body of her beloved Leo. And a familiar feeling of compassion for little Sebastian rises in her because of the anxiety with which his mother constantly surrounds him and also because of how he looks: Sebastian Rosso, she thinks, seems to be the least cute child in the world, and without doubt the least cute child she has ever seen. Babies, like the helpless young of other animals, usually have sweet, rounded faces that arouse an instinctive feeling of sympathy and a desire to protect them and care for them. Only Sebastian Rosso has a long, pinched face, a large nose, and small, grave eyes. His face actually looks to her like that of an old man and remarkably similar to the face of Anouk's father, the banker de Lange.

At this moment his pinched face grows paler, the little eyes darken as they look at her, the narrow lower lip curls, and Sebastian—even though he ostensibly knows her well from his frequent visits with his hypochondriac mother—fixes her with his little eyes and bursts into horrific screams that make Nettie jump up from her chair and from her plate of food, and wake Leo from his sleep.

Eddy and Martin had met at medical school and remained friends even after Martin quit medicine in the middle of his third year and transferred to philosophy studies.

Martin would visit Eddy and Sonia after they got married and Sonia loved listening to his original thoughts on the meaning of Man's existence in the midst of the great chaos. She tried her hand at matchmaking between him and the smartest and most profound of her friends, but Martin found no interest in the girl. And how surprised Sonia and Eddy were when he knocked on their door one evening and with him was the beautiful, cheerful daughter of wealthy parents: Anouk de Lange.

Martin and Anouk married and lived on the top floor of her parents' house. When Sonia and Eddy told them they were financially unable to rent an apartment near the Jewish hospital, Anouk suggested that they take the newly vacant basement apartment at particularly low rent.

By the time Sonia manages to quiet Anouk and her son and reassure Anouk that her son isn't dying but just has a slight chill, Leo is wide awake. The soup on the table is already cold. And after Anouk finally wraps her screaming bundle in its blanket and goes back up to her own apartment, the nightly air raid starts to fill the city with explosions and flashes of flame. Sonia snuggles under the bedclothes with her two children and hugs them to her with all her might, clasping their little bodies to her as if trying to fuse them into herself and turn the three of them into one.

24

Yoel goes out into the night, walks to the nearest tram stop, and gets on the first tram that comes along. After six or seven stops, in a flash decision, he gets off at Dam Square and finds himself standing outside the Royal Palace, on whose roof stands a sculpture of Atlas bearing the weight of his eternal burden. He wants to be swallowed up in the crowds of people in the square, most of whom are youngsters walking or standing in couples or small groups, laughing and talking, and as they pass him he hears fragments of their conversations, many of them in Hebrew. That was really something, someone says to someone else in Hebrew. We've already been to Van Gogh, says someone to someone else in Hebrew. And one voice in a group of youngsters crossing the square in the opposite direction asks in Hebrew: How can you know? And the question goes off with that group but continues resonating in Yoel's ear, for truly, how can you know. How.

He approaches the somber National Monument in the middle of the square and he doesn't feel good, he doesn't feel good. He can't remember if he ever felt good, and in the dark he can't find the numerals that, according to the Israeli tourist guidebook, should be engraved on the back of the monument in commemoration of the years that Amsterdam was under foreign occupation. He looks at the stone lions crouched heavily on both sides of the monument, and it seems to him that they are opening their huge stone mouths not in a terrifying roar but in a wide, tired, dreary yawn.

He wants to be swallowed up so he flows along with the crowd from the square into one of the alleys leading off it and drifts onward until he is stopped in panic by a display window encircled with red light bulbs and his face flushes as if he is an adolescent boy. Of course he had read and heard about Amsterdam's red light district, but he is totally shocked in that fleeting moment when he sees—just out of the corner of his eye, but sees—that it really is the figure of a woman standing in the window surrounded by red lights, standing like a product for sale, and this window is only one of a series of more red windows like it, and in that same blink of an eye Yoel hurries away and flees and now he's at the door of a small, dimly lit bar, and a waiter hands him a flyer with a menu, and Yoel glances at it and realizes that the small, dimly lit bar is a local coffee shop, a place for smoking drugs, and he lays the flyer on a table, stammers an apology, and flees.

The air raids continue. Sonia is lying in bed between her two children, staring at the ceiling and praying to the God of her forefathers in whose existence she has long stopped believing. She tries not to fall asleep because as soon as she closes her eyes, even for a moment, she dreams that Nettie and Leo are falling, drowning . . .

You're scared of living, Bat-Ami teases him affectionately, though not without disappointment, every time he opts to remain in the confines of the known and familiar rather than taste new experiences. When she was here with him she'd tried in vain to persuade him to go into one of the many inviting coffee shops from which a sweetish aroma floats into the public domain. It's completely legal, she reminded him, what can possibly go wrong if we sit inside awhile? For my part, just have a cup of coffee or even a glass of water, and don't consume anything, God forbid, that your mother didn't acclimate you to in your childhood. But he refused her and in the end they didn't go into a coffee shop even once. There may be Israelis there who might recognize me, he tried to explain, but she dismissed his excuse with a laugh: You're scared of living, my dear, you're simply scared of living.

What does he want, and what is he afraid of? What could possibly happen if he sat in a coffee shop? And what could possibly happen if he went behind the display window illuminated with red lights and the woman standing there—the same woman he'd seen only out of the corner of his eye, and only in a flash, but the sight of her figure won't leave him—draws the red curtain behind them both. There were times when going to a hooker had featured on his list of extreme adventures, like bungee jumping or hang gliding from a cliff top, experiences which could shake a man out of his chronic nothingness and inject a feeling of living flowing inside him. At the time the thought of a red-lit window such as this could arouse in him, together with the feeling of disgust, a sort of body-soul tumult. Whereas now he thinks about the unfortunate woman standing inside the square of dusty lights and waiting, one hand on her hip and her private parts on display, and he can feel only revulsion, repulsiveness, wretchedness, and he continues drifting and flowing with the crowd filling Dam Square and the alleys leading from it, until on one of the corners he is drawn to a sign saying "Irish Pub" and into a large space filled with flashing blue, yellow, red, purple lights and bursting at the seams with beat music and three levels crowded with people partying. He takes off his coat, finds himself a small vacant table next to the wooden balustrade that fences off the upper level, orders a beer, and relaxes in his chair beneath a bunch of black and yellow balloons hanging from the ceiling, relaxes in the midst of all the human bodies sitting or standing or going up and down the stairs from one level to another. A young waitress brings him a small green bottle, and he empties its bitter contents down his throat and immediately raises his hand to order another.

Not far from him there is a happy racket, a group of young people are apparently having a sort of drinking contest because there's a boy standing in the middle, tilting his head back and opening his mouth while the whole crowd is chanting encouragement and another young man holds a big bottle of vodka and pours it into the open mouth as if into a decanter.

Yoel drinks another beer and gazes at the green bottle in his hand.

In the last autumn of her life his mother told him she had decided to knit him a bottle-green sweater.

On each of his visits to her she'd tell him happily about the wonderful bottle-green wool she'd buy and the unique sweater she'd knit him out of it, and on every visit she'd measure him for this new sweater. The color will suit you, Yoel, she'd promise each time she got up heavily from her chair, and every time she'd take her yellow tape measure from the sideboard and place before her the adult man who was once her little boy.

Lift your arms to the sides, she'd order him, and now I'll take your measurements, Yoel, so don't move. . . .

How many times had he stood like that in her room at the old-age home, between the sliding door of the bathroom that was wide enough for her walker and the old armchair that had wandered here from the apartment where his mother had lived for so many years? How many times had he stood, his back straight, chest out, and arms outstretched sideways, and felt the tape measure stroking his nape, stretching across his shoulders and the length of his arms, encircling his biceps, and sliding down his back? How many times—and not once had he attempted to remind her that she'd already taken his measurements yesterday, and the day before yesterday, and every day last week and the week before. He just did what she told him, submitting completely, not moving a millimeter, looking at the framed family photographs on the wall beside the institutional metal fan and hearing his mother moving around him, groaning and panting but satisfied and perhaps even happy. He never got tired standing like that, his raised arms motionless like the wings of a grounded bird, as she remeasured lengths from his armpit to his waist, from his right shoulder to the left one, from his neck to his wrist, over and over again.

A giant screen on the pub wall is showing sporting events that Yoel doesn't understand. On the bottom level, which he can glimpse through the balustrade next to his seat, wooden balls are being shot into the pockets of a colorful pool table. How I enjoyed those repeated measurements my mother took for the sweater that would never be knit, he thinks. I wish I could go back and stand in front of her, go back and feel the touch of her precious fingers gliding over my body and lovingly counting each centimeter. Now the members of the vodka gang behind him burst into applause as the winner of their drinking contest is announced. In the meantime the music from the sound system changes; now it is drumbeats, and Yoel's heartbeat adjusts itself to the rhythm.

Anouk is the only daughter of Jozef de Lange, his delight, the apple of his eye, and his ally. De Lange frequently fires insulting remarks at his wife, or simply ignores her, but his admiration of his only daughter is boundless. And perhaps it is such admiration that Anouk also expects from her husband, Martin, because Sonia often hears her complaining that Martin doesn't devote enough attention to her. Mar-tin! She raises her spoiled-child's voice. Mar-tin, bring that here already, and, Mar-tin, take that away, and, Mar-tin, where have you been, and, Mar-tin, why don't you answer me, and, Mar-tin, how many times do I have to ask something from you, and, Mar-tin-Mar-tin-Mar-tin.

From the day Sebastian was born the flow of her complaints swelled and turned into a real torrent. Added to her routine complaints were more and more displays of envy. The foolish girl wept frequently that she was no longer beautiful in Martin's eyes, that Martin was no longer interested in her, and that her heart told her that he's got a lover, and maybe not only one. And Sonia whispered to Eddy: Poor dear Martin, why does he have to suffer all this? But wise Eddy smiled. Don't worry, my Sonia. Everyone gets exactly what he chooses, and chooses exactly what he needs.

I dam my soul, Yoel writes in his notebook, with a resolute finger I stop up each hole that opens in my dike. He's finishing off a third bottle of beer when, as if out of nowhere, a man and woman smiling from ear to ear appear at his table and in excited Hebrew introduce themselves as Danny and Ofra from Tel Aviv, who are presently on vacation in Amsterdam and simply must tell him how much they love his books. And he, who always responds to compliments like this with a big shy Thank you, is astounded to hear himself reply to Danny and Ofra: I'm glad you like my books, because I, for instance, don't like them at all. And as the two stand facing him slack-jawed, their excitement replaced by wondering if the highly respected author is being serious and how they should react, he points at the stairs beneath the balustrade and informs them that he's sorry but he simply must, after all the beer he's drunk, cut short their exhilarating conversation and immediately go downstairs to the toilets on the middle level.

In the meantime the air raids continue shaking the house and the world. Nettie and Leo are fast asleep in the way of children who trust in their mother's power to protect them simply because she is their mother. Sonia gently detaches them from her body, lays her daughter down on one side of her and her son on the other, and lies on her back between their calm breaths. Since she can't rely on the God of her Fathers after deciding that He does not exist, she reminds herself that it is not Amsterdam and its inhabitants that the bombers are trying to hit, but the occupying army's bases near the city. She thinks about her Eddy, who is almost certainly busy treating the wounded and sick. And about how she clung to him when they said goodbye this morning, burying her face in his chest through his doctor's white coat that filled her nostrils with the pungent smell of antiseptic. When she looked at him closely she saw his eyes red with exhaustion. And even behind the thick lenses of his glasses she could see the sorrow seeping into the light gray circles around his pupils.

What, my heart, what's the matter?

Eddy shook his head without replying and she understood that he had received more news about what was happening in the countries to the east of Holland. Aside from his many other talents, Martin knows how to tune in to distant wireless stations and it is he who gives Eddy these disturbing updates. At first Eddy would tell her about what he had heard but had recently stopped, and she had stopped asking. Since the occupation their life is complicated enough without being overburdened with what is going on in other places. And she raised her hand to Eddy's sad face and stroked his cheek that was covered with two-day-old stubble.

Now, in their bed in the basement apartment, she is lying between their two sleeping children and staring at the ceiling. Above that ceiling in their apartment, spread over the three middle and main floors of the building, live Anouk's parents: the Jewish banker Jozef de Lange, a short, fat man whose square shape is usually encased in a well-cut gray suit in whose waistcoat pocket is a gold watch and chain, and his wife, who looks like a bitter, aging version of her daughter, Anouk. The banker frequently takes out his gold pocket watch and looks at it importantly, but it stays in his pocket as he climbs the steep stairs to his apartment, as he has to hold on to the banisters with both hands in order to pull his heavy body from step to step.

And in the top-floor apartment, above the de Langes' ceiling, live Anouk and Martin and little Sebastian. Even though some danger might be hovering over the heads of the Dutch Jews, Sonia says to herself, she and Eddy and their children are safe and protected by virtue of their being the subtenants of one of Amsterdam's wealthiest and most respected Jews, who is well connected with the municipal and political corridors of power and influence. She has no doubt that if the need arises, Jozef de Lange would offer them his protection both by virtue of the fact that they live under his roof and, perhaps most importantly, by virtue of the fact that they are the good friends of his only daughter, Anouk, and his beloved son-in-law, Martin.

Either way, she soothes herself, letting her eyes close, there's no cause for worry. It's common knowledge that harsh and frightening things, like those that are reportedly happening in certain other countries, can never happen in Holland.

25

In the morning Yoel has difficulty deciphering how the hot water system of the shower in his room at the Mokum Hotel works. The shower is operated by three taps regulating the heat of the water and the force of its flow, and each tap is opened by turning it in a different direction, and whichever way he turns them—all three together, or two, or each one separately—all he gets is either a few drips of ice-cold water or a full blast of scalding water. However hard he tries he can't convince the taps to produce shower water of a sane temperature. And the shower head is cracked in several places as well, so that the water doesn't flow downward but spritzes in every direction. When he finally manages to turn off all the taps and exit the shower stall, he discovers that the bathroom floor is flooded up to his ankles.

Seven thirty in the morning, it is still dark outside, and behind the windows he can see from his balcony, light bulbs are being turned on. In the sky to the east pale sunbeams are spreading, painting a pinkish strip, as if with the stroke of a thin brush, above the outlines of the trees and houses and the smoke rising in two thin plumes from two smokestacks distant from one another. He stands in his big glass doorway until the world becomes clearer; new light rises into a soft blue sky with scattered clouds.

In the ground-floor lobby he catches Achilles in the middle of a wide yawn which, when the young man sees him, becomes a wide good-morning smile. Yoel asks him how he is, and Achilles smoothes his rumpled shirt and tells him that last night he and his beloved finished reading the Napoleon biography and again realized that the point is always the story behind the scenes, the untold story that holds the key to what really happened.

Yoel goes into the breakfast room and sees that he's not the Mokum Hotel's only guest: in the middle of the room are four corpulent ladies seated at a table loaded with food and speaking loudly in Italian. All four are actually talking at the same time, not one of them is listening to anyone else, and to the sound of this raucous chorus he approaches the modest buffet laid out along the wall, passes a tray with slices of salami of various colors, a tray of slices of hard cheese, a tray of croissants, and a basket of white rolls, and finally puts on his plate a wrinkled apple and a dry tangerine that he takes from the fruit bowl that had probably been sitting on the buffet table for quite a few days. After some slight hesitation he fills himself a bowl of cornflakes and milk, makes his way to the far side of the room, and sits down by a glass door overlooking the hotel's backyard that adjoins, so he notices, the end of the row of backyards overseen from the balcony of his room.

The quartet of Italian ladies is eventually joined by one of their husbands. The group is then joined by a young woman and a little boy, and later on the young woman's husband, and another young couple, and two youths, and a thin girl who refuses to sit down, and finally an older rotund gentleman who looks like the husband of another one of the members of the founding group. All of them—except for the girl who refuses to sit—chew slices of salami and cheese and croissants, shout loudly at one another, and only stop chattering in their melodic language to burst out now and then, and in unison, into loud, happy laughter.

Sniffing among the garden furniture in the backyard are a white cat and a striped one, both huge and furry and bearing colorful collars. When one of the young Italians goes outside for a cigarette, the two cats leap toward him, mewing demandingly, as if it is clear that he has come outside with the sole purpose of feeding them delicacies. The white one lays its forepaws on the young man's thigh as if trying to climb up his jeans, and the striped one jumps up onto the garden table, almost dislodging the lighter from his hand, while the young Italian expels a jet of smoke without even bestowing a glance on the two furry beggars.

Yoel gets up, passes carefully behind the vibrant Italian enclave, and goes to the buffet to pour himself a cup of coffee. Unlike the Hotel de Paris breakfast room, which has a cutting-edge machine that knows how to make five different kinds of coffee, here there is only a simple thermos jug—and right now the jug is empty. He can make himself a cup of coffee in his room, but he doesn't feel like dragging himself up to the fourth floor in the elevator, and he looks around, and in the kitchen adjoining the breakfast room he finds the aproned hotel worker, a thickset woman with gleaming coal-black skin and hair braided into long dreadlocks. When she hands him the filled jug he sees that her eyes are deep set and warm, and that in the depression below her lower lip shines a tiny silver drop.

The happy, loud Italian keeps ringing out, and Yoel makes his way back to his corner table, where he finds Achilles standing by the glass door, his face ashen.

They've come inside, he says to Yoel in a voice replete with tension.

Who has?

The cats! Somebody left the yard door open and the ca . . . the damn cats ca . . . came inside!

And you . . . ?

Yes, sir, I hate them.

Hate them?

They nauseate me. I . . . well, the truth is I'm scared of them.

So why do you keep them here?

Keep them? No, they . . . they just come here from the other yards, they belong to people in the neighboring houses, and I just can't bring myself to . . .

The black worker comes out of the kitchen laughing and in her arms is the white cat, its back clasped to her bosom and its paws flailing in an attempt to free itself from her grip. Achilles backs off in trepidation as she passes him, and she throws the disgruntled animal into the yard, closes the glass door, and turns, still laughing, to drag out the striped cat that is still sniffing around under one of the tables.

Och, Josephine! Achilles calls out with tremendous relief now that his territory has been cleansed of the two invaders. What would I do without you, dear Josephine?

Josephine smiles, her round face shining like a black moon.

In the coming days Yoel would learn that Curaçao, the region from where Josephine had emigrated, is located on an island rich in cacti and flamingoes in the southern Caribbean Sea. He will learn that Curaçao was a Dutch colony which to this day belongs to the Kingdom of the Netherlands, the Kingdom of the Low Countries, that is, to Holland. And he will try to understand the matter of the Dutch colonies, the Dutch perception of themselves as the chosen people, and how the great economic success of Amsterdam in its golden era, coupled with the Protestant philosophies of the time, had strengthened in the Dutch the belief that they had been destined to fulfill a divine mission in the world.

26

The child Yoel didn't eat a thing, nothing, unless his mother spoon-fed him.

One day she declared: There's no such thing as a child who doesn't want to eat. There's only a child who is spoiled.

And she announced: That's it, I'm not feeding you anymore.

When mealtime came she sat him down at the table in their apartment in Netanya and put in front of him a plate with pieces of boiled chicken, slices of sweet carrot, and mashed potatoes. She and Nettie also sat down and started eating, and when she looked up from her plate and saw that the child was not moving, she said: You don't want it? So don't eat! And the two of them went on enjoying their meal while he sat on his chair, on his booster cushion, and looked at them sorrowfully.

Thus one meal went by, and more after it. Whole days passed and little Yoel didn't eat or taste even a morsel. His mother saw how his skin was graying, his eyes sinking into their sockets, and his tongue whitening. He grew so weak he could hardly stand.

Until that lunchtime when the three of them again sat down at their modest table and Yoel was again sitting there in complete silence, blackening capillaries under his sunken eyes and his lips cracked. His mother looked at him, and looked, and suddenly slid her chair toward him in a sharp movement and with that same resolute sharpness picked up his spoon, loaded it with potato puree from his plate, and brought it toward him, and Yoel opened his dry mouth to the spoon. One after another his mother brought him spoonfuls of ground meat and mashed potato, one after another like heartbeats of love, and the boy opened his mouth to the spoon, raking in the food with his lips and tongue and chewing and swallowing with gusto, his eyes fixed on his mother's and on the tear that glistened in one of them and slid down her cheek.

From that day forth to the end of second grade, or maybe even the middle of third, his mother fed him all his meals. Spoonful after spoonful. Beat after beat. All his meals.

Anouk. Her thin, doll-like figure.

Her beautiful face that remained beautiful even when it frequently displayed bitterness and insult.

Her honey-blond hair cut in a straight line at the level of her cheeks.

The way she tucks one leg under her body when she's sitting.

And the graceful movement of her finger that is constantly brushing a lock of hair from her face to behind her ear.

Anouk's Martin continues to spend his days in his shop in the little market square. Like all the Jewish-owned businesses the shop had been expropriated long ago. But the banker de Lange, who had given the shop to Martin in the first place, managed to transfer its ownership to one of his non-Jewish friends and register Martin as the friend's employee, just until the storm passed and this absurd occupation finally ended and life in Amsterdam returned to normal. The banker has great affection for his talented son-in-law, and even the hardships of the war do not prevent him from continuing to give Martin money to develop the exceptional collection of art for which the shop is famous. Enthusiastic art lovers come from far and wide knowing that a serious lover of art should not purchase a work of art in Nieuwe Spiegelstraat, the street of art shops that runs down from Centrum to the Rijksmuseum, before making a detour of a few hundred meters to the south, to this enchanting shop in Jacob Obrechtstraat.

Martin loves discussing works of art, especially those of Dutch artists and particularly the ones who touch upon the infiniteness within reality. He loves enamoring his customers with the works he loves, though it seems that as far as he is concerned managing his successful shop is just a way to provide for his family while he immerses himself in what he loves more than anything else: studying. Since he dropped out of medical school he had managed to start studying architecture and philosophy, excelling in both fields, and then terminate his academic studies because he wanted to continue studying on his own, according to his personal taste. In the end Eddy decided that his dear friend is an incorrigible autodidact. De Lange, who would have given his daughter the moon had she asked for it, gave him the shop in the square and suggested that he trade in whatever he chose. And Martin, of course, chose to trade in the object of his great passion, art. Between customers he delves into his books and his studies, and of late he is reading everything he can find on the study of infinity, which enthralls him from the mathematical aspect as well as philosophical thinking and artistic expression. It is no secret that he longs to engage in art practically too, and that in his youth he studied painting and planned to become a painter. But many years have passed since he last held a brush in his hand, and in the recesses of his shop a splendid easel that Anouk bought him stands waiting in vain. I'm not good enough, he tells anyone who asks him why he doesn't paint, the world doesn't need another mediocre painter.

A perpetual flame burns in Martin, burning him from the inside and igniting in him an aspiration for beauty, for truth, for connection with all things all the time. He is a scion of one of the distinguished families of the Spanish-Portuguese community that is steeped in both wisdom and material assets, and which has lived in Amsterdam for centuries. His father wanted him to be a doctor, but the soul interests Martin more than the body, the spiritual more than the material, and whenever a battle rages between his wife, Anouk, and his son, Sebastian, over the food she cooks and cooks and the little one refuses and refuses to put into his mouth, until sooner or later they both burst into tears, Anouk because Sebastian doesn't eat, and Sebastian because his mother tries to force him to eat, then along comes Martin and lifts the exhausted toddler from his chair at the table strewn with dishes of pureed food in a variety of colors and textures. He sends his wife to rest in her bed, and stands, his son in his arms, facing one of the works of art hanging on the walls of their apartment, and he talks about it and the artist that painted it until the sobbing stops and Sebastian, his nose dripping and his breathing still uneven, points at the painting on the wall and smiles contentedly.

At night, after spending the evening with Anouk and Sebastian, and sometimes with Anouk's parents or his neighbor and good friend Eddy Blum, Martin goes back to the shop. Until recently he and Eddy would go out with their wives, who would dress up and put on makeup for the occasion, to the theater or a concert or just some nice place where they could sit and enjoy a drink. Then came a long period when they didn't dare go far, and they only went to the brown café on the corner of their street. He and Eddy deep in theoretical conversation at the bar, or the four of them—he, Eddy, Sonia, and Anouk—at their favorite corner table, where they were sometimes joined by their friend Vij, who owned the café, and other friends too, and they drank beer, chewed roasted nuts and hard-boiled eggs, and talked about the local and world situation until they cried from laughing as if this life were one huge joke. Now they spend the evening hours in a heavier atmosphere and stay within the five floors of the house. Martin rarely sees Eddy, whose free evenings are few and far between because of his workload at the hospital, and even when he's at home he doesn't have much patience for their friendly chats. And late at night, after Anouk has gotten Sebastian to sleep and fallen asleep herself, Martin walks down the dark, empty street and steals into his shop without turning on a light. He passes carefully between all the pictures and objects standing in the dark, ignores the easel staring at him sadly, and goes into the storeroom at the rear whose door is covered with a heavy curtain. There, his thin body disappearing among his secret wirelesses, Martin sets sail into the vastness of infinity in his search for remote radio frequencies.

27

A pathway as straight as a ruler, paved with light-colored marble, crosses the perfect lawn of Museumplein as far as the façade of the stylized building of the Rijksmuseum, which looks like a fairy-tale royal palace. The lawn gleams, a light breeze ruffles the row of trees lining the grounds, wooly clouds graze in the blue sky, and Yoel is one of the many tourists visiting the famous site on this pleasant day.

As he stood outside the Concertgebouw waiting for the traffic light to change and following the traffic flowing in perfect order along the wide avenue, with the soaring Concertgebouw on one side and Museumplein spread out on the other, through the street noise he heard the monotonic thrumming of a Scottish bagpipe.

He looked at the orderly flow of trams, buses, cars, and crowds of cyclists of all ages, and didn't understand what Scottish bagpipes were doing here, but now, on the verge of the marble pathway, there's the piper: a large, broad, elderly Scot wearing traditional Scottish dress—a pleated kilt of red-and-black tartan, a matching cloak, a tall fur hat with a white feather, shiny white boots, and checkered knee socks decorated with red tassels. The man is walking in small circles, blowing into the chanter of his cumbersome traditional instrument the traditional Scottish notes, which, at this moment, are filling the grassy square to which—as Nettie had told him in her apartment in the kibbutz at the foot of Mount Gilboa—Sonia and Eddy would flee every time Martin warned them of a police raid and they had to get out of the house, leave the children with him and Anouk, and find refuge within the Rijksmuseum's walls, walking through the exhibits as if they were just two ordinary art lovers and hoping no one would ask for their papers.

He would have to weave the story of his life with the few torn threads Nettie handed him. I'm sorry, Yoel, she told him, I can only tell you what I remember, and it's not a lot.

When he asked if she could describe Martin and Anouk's apartment for him, she replied that she doesn't remember. I was only a little girl, she said, her eyes moving around her modest room, lingering on the framed photograph of her firstborn son, who had been electrocuted in the date plantation at the foot of the mountain, and moving on to the window that opens onto the same mountain and the same plantation. And after we left Amsterdam I went through so much, she added apologetically, the newer memories suppressed the old ones.

But when he'd called her from Ben Gurion Airport to tell her he was going back to Amsterdam, she told him that the day after his visit with her she was sitting in her usual place in the kibbutz laundry mending hems on the members' work clothes, and suddenly the picture of Martin and Anouk's apartment had appeared in her mind in all its tangibility.

I remembered, she told him excitedly, how we'd go up to them, up more and more steep stairs that seemed to be unending, and when we got to the top and their door opened, on the wall facing the door I'd see a big painting of the sea. Their walls were covered with oil paintings. How could I have forgotten?

On the first evening of their first trip to Amsterdam, only a few hours after they'd landed, Bat-Ami had seated them in a low, enclosed canal cruise boat and they had sailed along canals, passed under bridges and through narrow canals where the sides of the vessel had almost touched the walls of the buildings, until they emerged into the river and thence to the sea, bathed in the lights of the port and drinking beer and chewing peanuts as the boat returned to the city, and their guide, a tiny, not young woman in a tiger-striped jacket, talked incessantly into her microphone and explained in English that "canal" in Dutch is "*gracht*," that at Anne Frank House there is a long queue day and night, that at the bottom of the canals there are tens of thousands of stolen bicycles, and that anyone staying in the Ice Museum for more than ten minutes freezes and turns into an exhibit.

Now he's striving to remember what else that tiger-woman had said, but he mainly recalls the whisper of the water as the boat sliced through it and the pain that the city's beauty roused in him through the boat's glass walls. At the time he did not yet know that there had ever been a couple called Martin and Anouk Rosso and he did not yet know about their son, Sebastian. But Amsterdam's beauty had wounded him even then, as only the beauty of a treacherous city is capable of wounding.

He presents his museum ticket at the entrance and goes inside, between the historical walls of the Rijksmuseum and beneath its high ceilings. He walks slowly, like the seemingly excited tourists from all over the world, between medieval Dutch four-poster beds and carved Dutch sideboards and portraits of chubby, self-important Dutch nobles choking in their high, starched lace collars that don't allow their heads to move. He wants to get to the classical paintings, which, according to the museum map, are waiting for him on the second floor, but he finds himself lingering on the ground floor, drawn to a comprehensive exhibit of Christian icons, and another step or two and he is surrounded by paintings and sculptures of mother and infant, mother and infant, mother and infant. All these painted and sculpted mothers and infants of course depict Jesus and his mother, Mary, but before they depict Jesus and Mary they are first and foremost real infants in the real arms of real mothers, and it is not difficult to see how each of the real mothers loves her real infant with real love and keeps him close to her real heart, even though some of the painted infants look less like infants and more like miniaturized old men.

Walking slowly Yoel moves from mother to mother, infant to infant, love to love, lingering for a long time at each pair until he is finally rooted to the spot in front of a black marble stand on which there is a glass cabinet

containing a wood statuette about forty or fifty centimeters tall of a delicate young mother smiling lovingly at an innocent babe radiating chubby
sweetness who is playing with the bunch of grapes in her hand and nestling
against her body in total devotion, in the total faith of one who is assured
that he is loved and protected, loved and protected. It is hard for Yoel to
leave this statuette and the sign on the black marble stand which says that
it was fashioned by the Dutch artist Van Veggel. And he stands there for
an eternity and another eternity, his eyes on the infant's devoted repose,
the mother's embrace, her feet peeping from beneath the folds of her long
skirts, their tread so delicate and so confident.

When he eventually moves on, deciding it is time to look for the stairs
to the second floor, he is stopped by an oil on canvas in which dozens of
frightened women are trying to save their babies from the drawn swords
of brutal soldiers. They stand no chance: most of the babies have already
been slaughtered. Some are still clinging, bleeding, to their helpless mothers' arms, and the small plump bodies of others are strewn on the ground.
One of the soldiers is grasping the leg of a baby whose mother is trying
to shield him; another mother is trying to ward off a spear raised over her
child. The explanatory sign says that the etching depicts the *Massacre of
the Innocents*, inspired by the New Testament story of King Herod, who, in
an attempt to kill the infant Jesus, sent his soldiers to Bethlehem to kill all
the infants under the age of two. Yoel presumes that this is fiction, but still
his heart goes out to the slaughtered baby whose mother is bent over him
in the bottom left-hand corner of the painting, bringing her face to his as if
still believing she can breathe life into him.

And he can take no more—he hurries outside to escape the gloom of
the museum and all the infants and their mothers come out with him, clinging to him with all their might and refusing to let go. Outside he is blinded
by the light, the wailing of the Scot's bagpipes pierces his ears, the vast
lawn of the square is unbearably green, and he realizes that he had spent
a long time in the museum, for beyond the long marble pathway cutting

through the lawn in a line as straight as a ruler, the sun has moved to the west, dropping behind the buildings across the avenue, its rays shattering against the golden harp on the roof of the Concertgebouw as if kindling it with flames. People, all of whom were once their mothers' babies, walk on the grass alone or in pairs or with their children or their dogs, some sit down to rest on the molded metal benches spread out along the pathway, while others carry paper bags from the museum shop holding a poster with a print of Vermeer's *The Milkmaid* or a mug with a reproduction of Rembrandt's *The Jewish Bride* or a silk scarf on which Van Gogh's *Almond Blossom* is printed. Yoel quickens his pace. He reaches the end of the pathway and makes a sharp turn into the winding street to the left, and walking quickly alongside the tram tracks, he walks and walks until the grasp of his mother's lost baby on his coattail weakens and it stops pursuing him, and there is the row of beautiful houses which, like all the buildings in this city, have not changed for hundreds of years, and there are Dutch people of his age who have lived in them since they were born and to this day, and he walks and walks until he comes to a little bridge over a canal, beyond which start the stalls and shops of the municipal market, and only then he stops walking.

Only then he stops walking, and he stands on the bridge, leans against the iron railing between some parked bicycles, and feels the raindrops falling on him and falling. He stands, leaning on the rail under the water of the rain and above the water of the canal, and looks, looks for a long time, at what isn't there. Like in the Zen garden in Kyoto that he and Bat-Ami had visited years ago: a garden in whose center are fifteen stones, but from every angle at which you observe these stones, you can see only fourteen of them, and the idea, as their tour guide explained, is not to look at the fourteen visible stones but at the fifteenth hidden one.

He stands above the water of the canal, above his own upside-down reflection between upside-down buildings and upside-down trams and upside-down clouds, he stands in time between water and water and between infinity and infinity and strives with all his might to look at what is hidden, at what isn't there.

28

A Van Gogh painting: the garden of the asylum where the artist was an inmate in the last year of his life. Trees encircle the asylum building but their tops are not visible in the painting. Neither is the sky. And a bent man in dark clothing is walking alone in the garden, one foot stepping off the paved path.

Anouk was in the final months of her pregnancy when the basement apartment in her parents' home was vacated by the subtenants who had lived there for many years. Martin suggested that it be rented to his friends Eddy and Sonia Blum, who were looking for a place to live in the vicinity of the Jewish hospital, but the banker's wife was afraid of taking in a couple with a young child, and the banker preferred that his wife give up this meager supplementary income and not rent out the apartment at all. It was only after Anouk explained to her parents how much she needed—in her condition—a doctor and nurse close by that Eddy and Sonia moved into the house with their daughter, Nettie, and their embryonic son.

On Saturday morning Yoel goes to the synagogue in Jacob Obrechtstraat. In Jerusalem he prays alone at home on weekdays and the Sabbath. On Saturday mornings Bat-Ami enjoys wearing a long skirt and a fine hat,

and tip-tapping along in festive shoes to one of the big synagogues on King
George Street or to one of the small old synagogues in the Shaarei Chesed
neighborhood. Yoel prefers to stand wrapped in his prayer shawl by one of
their apartment's windows, usually the one overlooking the Valley of the
Cross, but here he is, in Amsterdam, in front of a synagogue built before
the war by Jews whose financial status enabled them to move from the
Jewish Quarter to the Old South. A synagogue whose exterior red-brick
wall is inscribed with the words of King Solomon: Blessed is the man that
heareth me, watching daily at my gates. The entrance to the synagogue is
blocked by two young men wearing white silk yarmulkes who introduce
themselves to Yoel as community security personnel. Since they do not
recognize Yoel as one of the regular worshippers, they ask him to identify
himself by means of the Jewish password, in other words to give them the
name of the Torah portion of the week.

   Now he is inside and only three and a half quorums, some thirty-five
people, occupy the two floors of the big synagogue, under the magnificent
crystal chandeliers and the stained glass windows bearing the symbols
of the twelve tribes of Israel. His mother left the tradition of her parents'
home and returned to it due to the war, and none of his daughters share the
same level of observance as him and Bat-Ami: Ronit is less religious than
them, Galia is more religious than them, and Zohar isn't religious at all.
She had recently brought that child of hers into the world, a child without
a father, and Yoel can't understand how she will raise her over the years,
and what she needed this burden for. He looks around and thinks it entirely
possible that the synagogue's dark oak benches are also the benches of
the Jewish worshippers of prewar times, facing the carved holy ark that is
apparently the same one. He knows that both Eddy and Sonia and Anouk
and Martin are not regular worshippers but thinks that perhaps they might
attend the synagogue infrequently. And as he tries to locate them in the
rows of benches, the cantor begins the prayer for the State of Israel and the
congregation rises to beseech Our Father in Heaven to bless the State of
Israel and the Israel Defense Forces and also King Willem-Alexander; his
mother, Queen Beatrix; and the Netherlands.

On Saturday afternoon the banker de Lange and his wife entertain their Jewish friends, the wealthy industrialist Van Leeuwen and Justice Visser and their wives.

A pleasant atmosphere prevails between the three couples as they sit in the grand drawing room on the ground floor of the building, right above Eddy and Sonia's basement apartment. A pleasant atmosphere, though today as well, and in front of their guests, the banker frequently reminds his wife that she doesn't understand a thing and suggests she shut up while he and his friends discuss the worrying events taking place at this time in their occupied city. Recently, all the Jews had been required to register in a special census, and in the Jewish Quarter there was a roundup in which scores of them were arrested. The labor unions in the city declared a strike in protest and identification with the arrested Jews, but it was quelled after only three days and since then the occupation laws in Amsterdam have been enforced, mainly by the Dutch Green Police.

They all agree, and Mrs. de Lange joins the consensus with a cautious sidelong glance at her husband, that the Jewish elite, of which they, of course, are part, must do everything possible to calm the atmosphere and preserve, and even strengthen, the equal status enjoyed by the Jews of Amsterdam from time immemorial.

From the balcony of his room in the nearby hotel Yoel looks at the de Lange house and knows that the respected group sitting in the drawing room at this Sabbath afternoon hour does not yet know that the day will soon come when there will be a need for Jewish children to be taken from their parents and hidden. The banker and his friends are also unaware that more and more Jewish businesses in Amsterdam will shortly be expropriated. Severe restrictions will be imposed on Jewish-owned property. The authorities will confiscate from Jews money, furniture, works of art, and so forth. The day is not far off when Jews will be forbidden to mix with members of non-Jewish society in public places, schools and labor unions will be closed to them, and Jewish students will be unable to study at the universities. The occupation authorities will order the establishment of a Jewish Council in Amsterdam. The banker Jozef de Lange will be appointed a member of the council. His friend Van Leeuwen will be among the council's leaders and his friend Justice Visser will employ all the means at his disposal to preserve the honor of Holland and minimize the damage caused by the German occupation. Autumn will come, followed as always by winter, and one morning Justice Visser will come, as he does every morning, to the Supreme Court, and awaiting him there will be a notice informing him that he has been dismissed from his post because he is a Jew.

On this pleasant Saturday afternoon the three respected friends and their wives decide to come to the aid of the Dutch homeland in these difficult times, to harness the best of their powers for its sake and hope for the best.

And on his balcony in the hotel Yoel sees how the warmth of the autumnal sun cradles the backyards and fills their gardens with the chirping of birds and the flight of butterflies. In one of the yards in the right-hand row two blond children are kicking a ball around. In a yard to the left a woman is weeding her garden while the big striped cat dozes on the ground beside her, its paws spread. A young man is sitting at the top of the stairs descending to another yard on the left, his finger flicking the screen of the smartphone he is holding while a longhaired young woman, apparently his wife, is playing with their little child at the foot of the stairs. This yard and the next are separated by a hedge that prevents Yoel from discerning the figure emerging from the house into the yard at this moment, the figure of a man or a woman. Before he makes up his mind which of them it is, the figure walks to the edge of the yard and then back to the house, disappearing through the door that closes behind it with a soft click.

29

Earlier, at the kiddush that followed the morning service in the synagogue, Yoel was standing at the edge of the foyer where tables had been set up for drinks and the cloyingly sweet sponge cakes, when one of the worshippers who was also on his own started a conversation with him. He introduced himself with his surname, Raphaels, and was happy to hear that Yoel was from Israel and was interested in the history of Dutch Jewry during the war. I don't know if I can help you, he said, since the war years were the years of my early childhood and I can only remember that I was hidden with a Christian family, and that I was happy there. I've only started going to synagogue in recent years, he confessed, and it's important for me to attend this particular one because my father used to pray here before the war, that is before he was taken and didn't return. I come by tram from the New West part of the city every Saturday morning, he added with an apologetic smile, and at first I didn't know that Jews are forbidden to travel on Shabbat, but I still do even after it became known to me because it's important to me to be here.

They carried on talking, and in reply to Yoel's questions Raphaels told him that he had been born in Amsterdam and hidden in one of the southern villages. I don't remember the day I arrived at my parents' who hid me, he said. But I remember well the dreadful day when I was taken from them and returned to my biological mother.

The two no-longer-young Jews stood facing each other amid the commotion of the kiddush, each with a disposable plastic cup in one hand and a slice of cake in a paper napkin in the other. Until that day I was a happy child, Raphaels sighed. I didn't imagine that I wasn't really the son of the father and mother who raised me with so much love, nor that I wasn't really the brother of their four happy children.

He fell silent and so did Yoel. What could he say?

I was angry, Raphaels went on, gazing into his plastic cup. I was angry with my biological mother for taking me away from my family, and I was no less angry with the parents who raised me and then allowed that strange woman to take me away from them.

Raphaels bit into his cake, ate it all, and with a finger brushed the crumbs into a little pile on the napkin and ate them too. Perhaps he and I had met in the streets of this neighborhood when we were babies, Yoel thought. Perhaps our parents had known each other before the war. And if they hadn't, perhaps Raphaels's biological father had met Eddy Blum on one of atheist Eddy's rare visits to this synagogue.

It's strange, eh? Raphaels smiled as he wiped his lips with his now empty napkin, rolled it into a little ball, and stuffed it into his empty cup, which he put on the table. Strange that I'm telling you all this after meeting you such a short time ago.

I find it very interesting, Yoel replied encouragingly.

You have to understand, Raphaels went on, that for years and years I didn't tell a soul about it. In fact, I haven't even told this story to myself!

Yoel put his cup and the slice of cloyingly sweet cake on the table on which mainly empty bottles and crumpled napkins remained. Going by Raphaels's brown suit, his shiny brown shoes, and the furrows around his eyes whose color matched his suit and shoes, Yoel tried to guess if he was single or married, loved or lonely.

The congregation started to disperse and the two of them turned to leave.

I've started talking about my past only lately, Raphaels confessed, thanks to a Jewish organization that began bringing hidden Jewish children together, I mean Jewish adults who were hidden in their childhood.

At the meetings I saw that there are more people like me, you understand? And I began . . . they help me to open everything that was closed, you see? They help me to understand that anyone who experienced things like that, especially the ones who were passed from hand to hand, it has a complicated effect on them.

And Yoel thought about the three of them, him, his mother, and Nettie, sitting at the table by themselves, always by themselves, on weekdays and Sabbaths and festivals. And how once, when his mother had relented in the face of his urging and pleading, she had agreed to accept an invitation to a Rosh Hashanah Eve meal from neighbors whose son was his classmate, so they brought their hosts a splendid box of chocolates and excitedly entered an apartment filled with light and gaiety, and his classmate's talkative mother seated them at the festive table with lots of jovial, shining relatives and bowls of apples and honey for the New Year to be good and sweet, and pomegranate seeds so our merits might multiply like the pomegranate, and moist dates, *tamar*, so those who hate us be *tam*, extinguished, but the fish, that is the fish head, placed on a platter in the middle of the table so we should be heads, not tails, fixed its dead eye on Yoel, on Yoel of all of them, it glared and glared until Yoel couldn't stand it any longer, and when they all rose for kiddush he fled the table, the family, the gaiety, and went to the stairwell, where his mother found him sitting on the top step waiting for her.

I started to understand my life, Raphaels said as he and Yoel stood on the Jacob Obrechtstraat sidewalk. Now I'm trying to become reconciled with all my dead parents, biological and nonbiological alike.

It's good that his city pass gives him free access to the museums, and Yoel can find refuge in these protected havens on the Sabbath too. In the last week, the Jewish Historical Museum, and especially its library, had become his principal place of work, and the three museums of art in Museumplein that are so close to the Mokum Hotel are where he thinks and breathes. This time he decides to go to the Van Gogh Museum first, where on the floor he will perhaps find a fragment or two of his heart that broke when he was there yesterday, but on the west side of the square he sees a quiet line of weekend tourists waiting by the entrance, a line that stretches for hundreds of meters along the sidewalk. Fat raindrops start falling and from one end of the line to the other umbrellas, scarves, coats, and anything that comes to hand are opened over heads.

So he goes back to the Rijksmuseum, and as he has done since the incident of the dead babies, he skips the first floor and quickly goes up to the second. There, on the main wall next to the stairway, are paintings by the Dutch-Jewish painter Jozef Israëls, and Yoel doesn't find the undated one of the mother and child walking on the dunes, a painting which when he saw it at the Israel Museum in Jerusalem, a closed door in his soul was opened for a moment, just for a moment, and it was a closed door of whose existence he was unaware until then. But he enjoys seeing here several of Israëls's other seascapes in which figures of simple fishermen and their families are done in clear, almost transparent waves of watercolor that blend with the sea and sky as if they are all truly one.

His eye is drawn to a painting of a stormy sea on the right-hand wall close to the exit. Thick layers of oil paint tumble onto one another in strong brushstrokes and it seems that the painter worked with broad body movements and at breakneck speed and shaped the waves with a sharp knife. Yoel looks closer at the title and sees it is *The Sea at Katwijk* by Jan Toorop and is surprised that the painter's name is foreign to him even though the painting itself seems familiar.

30

How to write the first time that Sonia encounters one of those wooden signs imprinted with the words "*Voor Joden verboden*" in black letters. How to describe what she thinks and how she reacts. And where does it happen? At the entrance to the municipal market? A tram stop? The entrance to a museum? The public library?

The second time she encounters such a sign.

The third.

My mother, Raphaels told him on Saturday, always said that from the day she handed me over to be hidden, she lost all emotion. In order to hand me over she had to detach herself from herself, and afterward she never managed to get back inside herself and continued, long after the war ended, living outside herself and observing her life without any emotion. Without any emotion? Yoel asked. And Raphaels nodded. She looked after me and the two additional children she had after the war, but she was never happy and never sad. . . . When my younger sister yelled at her that she's a block of ice she didn't get upset, she just nodded and said, Yes, you've got an ice-block mother.

Yoel goes into the Albert Cuyp Market, where among the shops and stalls he is glad to find a small branch of the Maoz Vegetarian chain with which he is familiar from his trips to New York and other places. He orders a falafel with tahini and salad and then, sated and calmer, he takes an afternoon stroll through the market's streets. Gently, gently, as if repressing his pain, he walks between the stalls and the people, many of whom are probably tourists like himself; he passes great piles of gleaming fruit and garishly colored vegetables; he passes the cadavers of unidentified fish and various types of seafood; he passes stalls laden with bags and dishes and clothes of all sizes and colors.

They come here, he thinks, here they walk, here they buy. The market hasn't changed since then, the stalls haven't moved from where they were, the sky hasn't been replaced by another sky. Am I a block of ice too? he asks himself, for according to studies quoted by Raphaels, in many cases the emotional neutering of the parents had also adhered to their children, passed down to them like a genetic defect even though during the war they were babies and didn't remember anything about what had happened to them. I, for example, don't know how to get excited, Raphaels had told him, it seems to me that I live more or less on one uniform level.

Let's buy some almonds and nuts, Yoel tells them silently, stopping at the nut stall, and they stand with him, Martin and Anouk on one side and Eddy and Sonia on the other, but suddenly a woman who's not in the story pushes between them and says to him in Hebrew, What an honor, what a great honor it is to meet you here, Mr. Blum, and Yoel nods courteously and flees, trying to become swallowed up in the crowds of people but almost colliding with a big, well-built man he recognizes as a former member of the Knesset or maybe a retired IDF general, who is striding toward him with his wife, a well-known socialite or perhaps a TV news presenter, that is, Yoel is sure he'd met them both somewhere in the past, perhaps he'd even been quite close to them, but right now he has no idea who they are and under what circumstances this close acquaintanceship had been formed.

Yoel Blum! the man roars in the voice of a TV game show presenter, and Yoel wonders if in fact the man is the TV presenter and his wife the former member of the Knesset, but he has no idea, and meanwhile both of them,

first the man and then his wife, are embracing him warmly and strongly
in the middle of Amsterdam's crowded market and planting wet kisses
onto his cheeks. What are you doing here? they ask him in tremendous
surprise, as if it is a well-known fact that only they, whoever they are, are
allowed to wander pleasurably through the markets of the world, whereas
he is not supposed to leave Israel's borders, perhaps not even the borders
of his study, unless it's for a worthy official objective. Public relations, eh?
the man roars, slapping Yoel on the back. That's what you're doing here,
you winner, you! You think we don't know? Yoel politely declines their
invitation to spend some time with them either today or tomorrow at the
charming coffee shop they'd found right beneath their hotel, but he doesn't
manage to take his leave of them, or rather doesn't manage to get them to
leave him alone until after he'd heard about all their Dutch experiences,
the coffee shops, the windmills, and the wonderful cheese market in Alk-
maar, oh, the cheese market, and until he'd been asked to help them make
a decision: the man, who Yoel is almost certain is a former member of the
Knesset or a retired general, or a former member of the Knesset who is also
a retired general, feels that before they return home he and his wife should
visit the Jewish Historical Museum; his wife, on the other hand, says there
are enough historical Jewish sites in the world, and one goes to Amsterdam
not for Jewish history but for the fun. We're interested in what you think,
they tell him with pleading looks, and when Yoel replies that it's hard for
him to decide, the man capitulates and admits that the Jewish Historical
Museum is apparently not one of this city's main attractions. Quite so, his
wife concurs, especially since the Dutch were always good to us and the
Jews here didn't really suffer.

The couple eventually releases him and they hurry on their way, but not
before hugging him again and wetting his cheeks once more with loving
kisses. Yoel follows them with his eyes until they disappear round a bend,
he looks here and there to verify that he is not being watched, and then
he approaches one of the stalls selling cheap flashlights, key rings from
which dangle a pair of tiny Dutch clogs, mechanical monkey drummers,
and other cheap toys and gadgets made in China or thereabouts. Among

all these treasures he looks for and finds a pile of black stocking caps, and he takes one, simple and black, pays two euros for it, and on the spot, he removes the casquette cap that has become author Yoel Blum's trademark. He replaces it with the knitted stocking cap, pulling it down over his skull until the edges come down to his ears.

Yoel doesn't wear a yarmulke. In his view, wearing a yarmulke—cloth or knitted, black or colorful, large or small—is to declare one's belonging to one of the religious or social streams, and he doesn't belong to any of them. He is a liberal and would actually prefer not to cover his head at all, but he began wearing a cap for his mother's sake and continued to do so only because he didn't want to cause her sorrow. After everything she'd been through and after she'd immigrated to Israel with him and Nettie, his mother had made a commitment to observe the precepts of the Torah, and heaven forbid that he cause her sorrow, heaven forbid that he let her see him with his head uncovered. Not even after her death.

Among all the people flowing hither and yon in the crowded street of the Albert Cuyp Market he stuffs his casquette into his pants pocket. Then he starts looking in the row of clothing stalls. He feverishly moves hangers back and forth until he finds a sort of biker's leather jacket, and much to the stallholder's surprise, he buys it for twenty-three euros. The jacket isn't real leather but a sort of shiny metallic faux-leather plastic. But a jacket like this, he notes to himself with satisfaction, author Yoel Blum wouldn't wear even if you paid him, even if you begged him. He removes his tailored jacket, folds it meticulously, and puts it into the plastic bag the stallholder had given him. Instead of his old jacket he puts on the faux-leather, faux-biker one, and now he is relaxed. So long as he's dressed like this no one will recognize him.

Not far from the market, at this late autumn afternoon hour, Anouk is strolling along the Herengracht at Martin's side as he carries little Sebastian on his shoulders.

Anouk, yes, Anouk, knows how to enjoy the beauty of each fleeting moment. This particular moment for instance, this moment of this late autumn afternoon, a special, onetime moment when she is strolling along the canal bank beside her Martin, who is carrying their little Sebastian on his shoulders, she sees how the touch of the light on the water on this particular stretch of this particular canal creates a onetime spectacle the likes of which have never been nor will be again. Look, she whispers to Martin, see how magical it is! And Martin sees her glowing face and feels how her happiness is overflowing and washing over and cleansing him too.

And he knows that without her, what is he. What.

31

Although life is hard for them, they're still sure that this bizarre, inconceivable war will remain in Holland for six months at the most.

This morning the sky finally cleared after three consecutive days of rain. It's Nettie's birthday and Sonia is about to take her to school when Eddy arrives from the hospital for a short surprise visit. When the war is over I'll buy you a proper birthday present, he says in that shy way of his, but in the meantime, dear Nettie, I'm giving you this gift with my love. He proffers a small parcel wrapped in used gift wrapping, and the child beams and takes the package, and her tiny fingers excitedly tug at the string because she loves presents, loves birthdays, loves her father, loves opening birthday presents from her father. She opens the wrapping and there is the present: a pear! Her father has bought her a real pear for her birthday! She puts the beautiful yellow fruit on the table and looks at him, beaming, for pears are unobtainable in occupied Amsterdam. It's been a long time since anyone in Amsterdam has seen a pear. And how she loves pears! At this moment there is no present in the world that could make her happier.

This morning the sky finally cleared after three consecutive days of rain, and again Yoel finds himself fleeing and immersing himself in the three museums that stand facing each other so close to his hotel.

Vincent paints the vase of purple irises in the year of his suicide, against a yellow background and with a few stems already drooping. He also paints the landscape of the area where he is living, but instead of completing the sky he practices sketching faces, leaving behind entire canvases of started faces, and over the entire surface of an old painting in which he had once painted another vase with different flowers, he daubs a green-gray layer on which he creates a face whose shapes and bulges he marks by emphasizing the shadows. He paints a lot of potatoes: potato picking, potato meals, and, close to his death, a painting he calls *Evening*—a potato-picker couple resting in their house at the end of the day, the woman sitting mending an item of clothing, the baby asleep in its crib, a cat curled up by the blazing hearth.

Sonia comes outside with the two children, takes Nettie to the teacher's house, and pedals back home with Leo. She parks her bicycle in the usual place at the curbside, takes the baby from the front carrier, and sees Anouk standing by the house, leaning on Sebastian's stroller and sobbing loudly. Her doll-like body is trembling in her pink dress and her smooth honey-blond hair, cut in a straight line to the height of her tiny pearl earrings, falls onto her manicured hands with their red nails that are covering her face under her white hat.

Sonia hurries to her. What's the matter, is the child alright?

Sebastian is sitting in his stroller and seems composed, but Anouk's tears have smeared her eye makeup and she can hardly speak for sobbing and choking. It seems that earlier this morning, after she had dressed herself and Sebastian, she had gone, as she usually did, to the public playground adjoining the synagogue. But the other mothers playing with their children, women she meets on the playground benches almost every day, and Sonia sometimes meets them there too, had driven them away shamefully. They are usually glad to see Anouk and are friendly, and she usually sits and chats with them about babies and husbands and life, but today they gave her malevolent looks. You can read, can't you? they shouted at her as she approached, and they pointed at the new notice that had been posted at the entrance to the playground on Jacob Obrechtstraat. When she gave them a friendly smile and sat sweet Sebastian on the carousel and turned it, the women shot her looks filled with hostility. Then, when she put him in the round sandbox he loves so much and sat down on one of the wooden benches, a murmur of deep shock passed between them. One of them had even run to call for help, so it transpired from the fact that after a short while, a policeman appeared on the scene.

He sees the picture of Van Gogh painting himself painting himself and realizes that in his new novel, he wants to also portray himself writing himself and longs to do it with the same precision with which Van Gogh painted, with the same sincerity, the same bungee jumps from which there is no return. To portray himself as a field of ripening wheat beneath storm clouds, to portray a band of crows circling above his head as if death has already come to him, to write his self until he too, like Vincent in his very last painting, will be nothing but twisted roots bare of bark and barriers.

The spring of Anouk's tears flows even more freely.

A policeman? a shocked Sonia says. Why a policeman? What crime was committed?

Meticulous in his uniform, the policeman approached the bench she was sitting on and Anouk was stunned when she looked at the face beneath the resplendent cap and discovered that the policeman was none other than Henry van Duren, who'd grown up here in the street and had played with her in their childhood in the same park and built sandcastles in the same sandbox in which Sebastian was now playing. I think, she tells Sonia, that they posted him here because he knows everybody in the neighborhood and knows which of them are Jews. . . . I said, Hello, Henry, how are you? she sobs and brushes a lock of honey-blond hair behind a pearl ear. But he just stood there and told me, over and over with a kind of brutal forceful-ness, that by law I must leave the park right away.

Oh, Sonia says, oh, my poor sweet, how embarrassing . . . And Anouk's beautiful face is once more washed by a new flood of tears under the brim of her fine white hat.

He didn't stop shouting and shouting, Anouk sobs, he said that under the new law he has to arrest me for this offense, but this time, just this once, he's prepared to believe that I hadn't seen the notice prohibiting me from going into the park, and that he wouldn't arrest me, but only on condition that I get up from the bench right now, take my child, and not come back.

Sonia puts a hand on her arm and tries to soothe her. This is a temporary situation, Anouk my dear, don't worry, the war will soon be over and you'll be able to go wherever you want, just like you used to.

My father will fix it with them even before the war's over, Anouk announces purposefully, and calms down for a moment, but then her head again starts moving from side to side, her bottom lip curls, a blue vein in her temple throbs, and she starts crying again.

But the humiliation, she sobs. I'll never recover from the awful humiliation that Sebastian and I suffered today.

And Sonia stands there with Leo in one arm and her free hand stroking Anouk's shoulder until the trembling and weeping subside slightly and her neighbor blows her perfect nose and announces: There are some Jews that I can understand why our neighbors don't want them in our lovely clean playground. But to throw out *Anouk de Lange*? To expel *me*?

And how often Vincent paints his own portrait. How he tries and tries to capture this thing called a face, this thing that other people see and think: Here's Vincent. The straight nose, the red beard, the windows of the eyes, once with a gray hat and once with a straw hat and once with a pipe, but always a stranger to himself, a stranger and an oddity. Perhaps his most accurate portrait, the one most faithful to the original, is the one in which he painted himself in the form of a bunch of wildflowers that had been torn off their roots and put in a vase.

In the afternoon Sonia picks Nettie up from school and sits both children on her bicycle—Nettie in the child's seat behind her and Leo in the carrier attached to the handlebars. The weather has finally cleared up after three days of rain, and since today is Nettie's birthday and Eddy is working late and won't be waiting for them at home, she pedals eastward to visit her parents in the beloved Old Jewish Quarter across the river.

Her heart fills with serenity as she reaches Waterlooplein, the Jewish market that is crowded day and night, and the pitiable and wonderful alleys, the alleys of her childhood. She passes between the stalls and carts whose owners are shouting their wares, takes care not to trample over the goods laid out on the ground, and finally turns right at the herring seller's barrel.

She gets the three of them off the bicycle, leans it against the wall of the house as she did when she was a child, and skips up the narrow stairs as she did when she was a child, though now her son is in her arms and her daughter is skipping gaily in front of them. A moment after she goes inside her mother is already grating pumpkin and making a mixture for sweet cutlets. Only God—whose existence Sonia has long since denied, but in whom her mother believes—knows where this woman obtains pumpkin at a time like this, and only God knows what else she puts into her latkes and what gives them their sublime taste. She stands patting them into round patties and they chat in Dutch spiced with a little Yiddish, they chat about Sonia's children and Eddy's work but don't say a word about the harsh situation or the increasing number of decrees or about the war itself. As they talk, Sonia's younger brothers, Isaac and Herz, come into the apartment. Her little sister, Trudy, sits on the floor with Nettie, teaching her a game of singing and clapping, and the two girls sing together in their thin voices, clapping each other's hands and laughing happily.

Only her father is silent, staring into space over the Gemara open on the table in front of him. An expression unfamiliar to her lengthens his face that has suddenly become old and sunken, and his fingers involuntarily stroke his beard that has become almost completely white. A moment before Sonia takes her leave, her mother prods him: *Nu*, Yoelisch! And her

father shakes himself and stands up to lay his hands on his daughter's head
and the heads of his little grandchildren and bless them with an ancient
blessing as his wife wraps up the latkes and says in her softest voice: Here,
maideleh, take this *mein tayereh kind*.

Evening is falling on the city as Sonia pedals home from Waterlooplein
with her daughter, her son, and the smell of the wrapped latkes that envel-
ops her like compassion. Evening falls and in one blow, short and sharp, she
is struck by the knowledge that this is not just another evening in the long
chain of evenings she has lived through in the streets of this city since the
day she was born. You'd better stop denying reality, she tells herself as she
wends her way on her bicycle through the crowds of other cyclists, in the
flow of carts and automobiles crossing the bridge over the river. Whether
you accept the facts or deny them, the life you were used to is over. Over
and done with.

And again Yoel goes up to the second floor of the museum and into the
first hall on the left and stands facing the painting by Jan Toorop, ready to
delve deep into its curvilinear design and in its depths seek the questions
for his answers.

32

On the eve of Yom Kippur, Bat-Ami packed vegetable cutlets, a pasta salad, and lentil soup in her plastic containers and they went to Galia's for the pre-fast meal. On their way back to Jerusalem from the mountain where Galia lives, they felt that they'd hit something and Yoel was shocked when they got out of the car and found the body of a beautifully bearded and horned billy goat that had apparently wandered off from one of the herds that graze in the area and he had killed it with his own wheels; with his own wheels he had cut off its magnificent life. What have I done? he asked, numb with grief. But Bat-Ami, who since her own traffic accident is frightened by the smallest incident involving cars, was overjoyed: It's atonement for all of us; killing a scapegoat on Yom Kippur eve is a good omen! And since Yoel was ashamed to admit his sadness over the goat, especially as Bat-Ami is the vegetarian half of their couple while he regularly eats killed animals, he pretended that he was only in a bad mood because the car's right-hand headlight was smashed by the force of the collision and the front fender was dented.

The sea in Toorop's painting rages toward him. He thinks about the Hebrew letters of the Hebrew word for sea, ‎יָם‎: a closed, vessel-shaped mem beside a detached, hovering yod. He thinks that the sea is a huge, finite vessel containing infinite waters. He thinks: I know nothing; I know nothing; I know nothing.

In one of their telephone conversations, Bat-Ami quotes what she'd heard on the radio that morning about the Dutch government's admission that on show in Amsterdam's museums are no fewer than one hundred and thirty-nine works that were plundered from their Jewish owners during the war. I wouldn't be surprised, she says, if that painting of the sea, the one you said you felt you knew from the past . . .

He sometimes goes to the painting twice a day. And sometimes he finds himself running to the Rijksmuseum for just a moment, even just a minute before closing time, just to hurry up the stairs to the second floor. And look.

In the space between the Van Gogh Museum and the Rijksmuseum he encounters the Scottish piper, and from day to day the brotherhood he feels toward him deepens, despite the tartan kilt and the red-tasseled knee stockings and perhaps because of them, and despite or perhaps because of the strident sounds the piper casts over the wide square as he walks round and round, blowing into his chanter and every now and then glancing from under the huge fur hat that almost covers his eyes, at the coins that people bend to drop into his open box on the lawn.

From day to day his soul also connects with that of the mandolin player who always sits on the low stone wall at the northern entrance to Museumplein, behind the crowds of tourists of all ages and races who have their photographs taken morning, noon, and night against the backdrop of the sculpted **I am**sterdam logo at the head of the lawn. The mandolin player is brown-skinned and has a head of thick gray hair, and Yoel doesn't know if he's South American or Italian, and he doesn't know if he knows that his soft playing isn't heard in all the surrounding noise, but he sees his permanent smile and how his chubby body, always packed into jeans and a denim jacket that are too small for him, sways from side to side as he strums his melodies to himself, and as he does he sees Yoel and smiles at him as if they really are friends.

Since the sky has finally cleared after three consecutive days of rain, the people allow their bodies to move across the museum square slowly and absorb the warmth of the sun's rays. Not far from here at the city high school where Anouk studied in her youth, and in whose big yard hundreds of bicycles are parked every morning, at this hour the farewell ceremony is being held for the seventy-four Jewish children whose deportation has been ordered by the Germans. The principal was dismissed after protesting against this order, and in another few weeks the whole building will be expropriated to house the occupying army's troops in the classrooms, the storeroom will be used for raising pigs, and dog kennels will be put up in the yard.

But on the grassy slope in front of the Stedelijk Museum, dozens of people, most of them young, are sprawled in the sunshine, their faces to the sky, not knowing that the past is still here, not imagining how close they are to the German police headquarters that Sonia always passes quickly and cautiously. It's good that in the covered walkway at the entrance to the Rijksmuseum there's a string quartet playing Bach's Concerto for Two Violins in D Minor. Yoel allows himself to be immersed in the crowd of passersby gathered beneath the stone arches and lets the music calm his soul, even though the Israeli tourist guidebook claims that it is only the rare acoustics in the thick-walled space that turn each musical performance heard there into a pleasure worth being born for.

33

Today they heard that from now on, all the Jews registered as such in the Amsterdam census would be obliged to carry identity cards stamped with the letter "J."

Sonia looks into Eddy's eyes. Let's ignore this order, she beseeches him. Let's decide that we're not handing in our cards to be stamped.

Her heart tells her to ask for this even though she doesn't know, because she can't know, what the future may hold for Jews whose cards will be stamped. Jews have been persecuted in the past, in Poland and elsewhere, but not in Holland. Jews were never persecuted in Holland. Jews never suffered any sort of discrimination in Holland. And Jews have always been law-abiding citizens in Holland. Jews have always observed law and order like every other respectable Netherlander.

Eddy looks at her as if seeing her for the first time. His eyes narrow at her behind the thick lenses of his glasses. What are you thinking of, Sonia my dear? How can we ignore the order? How can we decide that we're not handing in our cards to be stamped?

I'm begging you, she says.

It's out of the question, he states. He speaks gently but decisively. If we avoid having our cards stamped and then we're caught without the right documents . . .

It is evening and they are sitting on the fourth floor in Martin and Anouk's apartment. The two doors—that of the hosts and that of the basement apartment—are open wide so that Sonia and Eddy can hear if Nettie or Leo wakes up and calls for them. Martin puts out four glasses on the table and pours the home-brewed beer he bought from a source known only to him. Sonia hasn't seen such high-quality beer since Holland was occupied, but right now she doesn't feel like drinking.

I told you, she shouts at Eddy, I told you right from the start that we shouldn't have registered at the Jewish Council. Right from the start we should have ignored the orders and just got on with our life as usual.

We would have gotten into trouble, Eddy says.

Why would we have gotten into trouble? she replies heatedly. How would they have known we're Jews if we hadn't registered at the Jewish Council of our own foolish free will? And who could have known that now this damned "J" is actually supposed to appear on our cards?

Even Samuel Jessurun de Mesquita says that Jews shouldn't register and have their cards stamped, Martin says, quoting his revered teacher, the black in his eyes gleaming. De Mesquita says that the surest thing is to ignore all these separatist orders.

You see? Sonia's look tells Eddy.

But my father, Anouk interjects in the mollycoddled tone she uses, so Sonia thinks, whenever she mentions her father, my father says that so long as we all obey the authorities' orders, it will be better for us in the end.

So as not to ask her how her dear father knows all this, and to what extent the rumors about him being close to those authorities are correct, Sonia takes a sip of her beer and points at a large oil painting on the wall above them and the stormy sea depicted in it that seems so tangible.

A beautiful painting, she says admiringly after swallowing the bitter beer.

Martin laughs. It's obviously been a long time since you were last here, that painting has been there for ages.

Anouk joins in his laughter. Every morning, she says excitedly, when our sweet little Sebastian wakes up and I lift him out of his cot and bring him out of his bedroom, the first thing he does is point his darling little hand at this painting and say: Water, Mama, water!

That little one is certainly starting to appreciate art, Martin affirms with smiling pride. He particularly loves this painting, and the truth is, so do I. It should actually be in the shop, but I'm worried that as soon as it's there someone will buy it and we'll have to say goodbye to it. . . .

Anouk stands up to straighten her left leg that she'd folded under her bottom and then sits down again with her right leg folded under her instead. Eddy straightens his glasses on the bridge of his nose, examines the painting through his physician's eyes, and inquires gravely, as if trying to diagnose an ailment by its visible symptoms: What style is this?

It's by Jan Toorop, Martin replies, and pours himself another half glass of beer. It's difficult to attribute it to a specific style because Toorop worked in all the styles. He leans back, takes a sip of beer, gives the painting an affectionate look, and adds: Toorop called it *The Sea at Katwijk*.

Why Katwijk of all places? Sonia asks. The sea can look like that from any beach in the world.

Her question pleases Martin. You're so right, he says enthusiastically. I also think that the words "at Katwijk" don't refer to the sea but to the painter. The sea can look like that from any beach, but the painting shows how Jan Toorop actually felt when he was in Katwijk.

Eddy straightens his glasses again as he leans forward to take a closer look at the painting. But in this painting, he remarks, confused, you don't see the painter but the sea.

Martin smiles. Every painter evidently knows how to depict only himself, he says.

Sonia looks at the painted sea and sees not only the artist but herself. There she is in black, there in red, there she is borne from wave to wave, from wave to wave, moving in the infinite. Like the figures in the lithograph by M.C. Escher, Martin's friend from the time he studied with de Mesquita, that move in a building with numerous walkways and stairs and it's impossible to tell if they are descending or ascending, entering or exiting, and whether it makes any difference and why.

The bell of Our Lady of the Most Holy Rosary chimes ten times and Yoel writes Sonia rising from her chair and departing. We should go to bed, she tells Eddy. Don't forget that as respectable, law-abiding Dutch citizens we've got to get up early in the morning and go to have our cards stamped with that "J."

34

Ever since he'd replaced his famous cap with a black stocking cap and his tailored jacket with the shiny biker's one, he feels like any other passerby. Israeli tourists strolling around the Dutch capital no longer notice him, they don't ask him questions or compliment his writing, and they don't exchange remarks about him. Not only that, he'd stopped shaving and his features are changing from day to day so that even he finds it hard to recognize himself.

There is no doubt that something in this anonymity allows him to concentrate properly on his research. He can stand undisturbed even in the most crowded places, anonymous to the point of transparence, to take photographs with his small camera and simply to observe and listen and record in his notebook scenes, events, and thoughts. Anonymous to the point of transparency he enters the folds of the city, seeing but invisible, present but nonexistent. As if he is free of any external definition and open to the spaciousness of an inner experience, a heart-of- the-matter experience in which all is one and there is no division between one person and another, between reality and imagination, between time and time.

In the last few days, sometimes late at night, he has been hearing through the walls of his room loud young voices speaking and laughing in Arabic and arousing in him a yearning for the Middle East common to them and him. And in the afternoon the sun comes out between the clouds, and Sonia and Anouk take advantage of the temporary warmth to play with their children in the backyard. After the public park incident, banker de Lange swiftly equipped the yard with a small sandbox and swing, and now Sebastian is sitting in his private sandbox engrossed in filling a red tin pail with handfuls of sand while Nettie swings herself back and forth on the swing hanging from a branch of the sycamore, and Leo, shouting triumphantly, crawls up the five steps leading from the yard to the de Langes' back door as Sonia's long arms keep him from falling backward or sideways.

He comes back in the afternoon from a few hours of data gathering in the Jewish Historical Museum library, passes through the acoustic space beneath the stone arches just as the spring flutes of Vivaldi's *Four Seasons* hang in the air, and comes out into the square to the mandolin player who smiles at him while moving to the rhythm of his unheard strumming.

A little farther on, perched on scaffolding on the wall of a structure bordering the lawn, a few workers are busy putting together a huge portrait of Vincent van Gogh composed of the cut heads of sunflowers.

As part of this project, two beautiful girls stand there smiling at the passersby and handing out fresh sunflowers from pails. Yoel is filled with compassion for Vincent, who would doubtless be unhappy to see his flowered and unreal face on public display, but one of the girls approaches him and proffers a tall sunflower with a fleshy stem and a large yellow head, and Yoel hesitates momentarily but then thanks her and takes the flower. In his hotel room he fills an empty beer bottle with tap water, puts the sunflower in it, and stands it on the table next to the vainly switched-on laptop.

Sonia my dear, Anouk says in her spoiled-little-girl voice as she sits on the edge of the sandbox with one leg folded under her, maybe you've still got a nice hospital story left for me? One you haven't already told me, or one you wouldn't mind telling me again?

Anouk loves hearing real-life stories, especially stories of Sonia's experiences from the years she worked at the Jewish hospital. Good for you, she says to Sonia, that before you had children you learned a profession and worked in it. I haven't done anything, she grumbles, because with parents like mine it was clear I wouldn't have to work for a living. They sent me to learn dance, and truly, there's nothing that gives me greater pleasure than dancing, but nobody, me included, ever thought I'd suddenly work as a professional dancer. Her eyes sparkle as she toys with the notion that she'll go to work sometime in the future, perhaps as a chic saleswoman oozing style in the prestigious Hirsch fashion house on Leidseplein. There was even a time when I began taking private lessons to improve my French, she recalls, because the Hirsch saleswomen have to speak to the customers only in French, and no connections can help you get accepted there if you're not completely fluent in that complex language. But in the end, of course, I got pregnant with Sebastian and instead of learning how to speak French with customers in diamond-studded evening gowns I was consigned to bed with terrible nausea. I felt so awful I couldn't lift my head from the pillow and all my plans changed.

That's how it is, Sonia says, and Anouk goes on to say that a week or two ago Martin had told her that the Hirsch building and everything in it had been expropriated—plundered to its foundations, Martin said—so it turned out that in any case she wouldn't be able to work there until Amsterdam had rid itself of this unnecessary war and its sanity was restored.

Well, at least I've got this sweet little angel, she sums up with a sigh, and strokes Sebastian's sparse curls as he crouches over his pail, because without him what would I do with myself all day long.

Gently, Sonia takes Leo away from the steps he won't stop climbing. Leo protests but he seems pleased when she sits him down next to Sebastian in the sandbox and she sits down on the nice bench that de Lange has installed there. To comply with Anouk's request she tells her how, when she was a nurse in the Jewish hospital's internal medicine ward, she was passing from bed to bed administering the routine morning medication when she came to a bed whose occupant, a young man, paled as she approached and adamantly refused to allow her to give him an injection. All her importuning was to no avail; he simply drew his blanket up to his chin and wouldn't submit. When she asked why he was suddenly afraid of the needle today since the chart on his bed showed he had been given an injection every morning for a week, the young man lowered his eyes and confessed that it hadn't been him who'd been given the morning injections and that he wasn't the patient who'd been hospitalized for a week. He was a completely healthy friend of that patient, who'd agreed to take his place in the hospital bed for one night so the real patient could go out and have a good time.

The church bell peals five times and Anouk's laughter also rings out as she asks Sonia to tell her another story.

The church bell peals five times and from the scratched mirror above the tiny sink in the small bathroom adjoining his room in the Mokum Hotel a man who hasn't shaved for weeks looks back at Yoel. A man whose eyes look out from two narrow slits beneath his eyebrows and Yoel looks into these slits, moves his face closer to the mirror until his forehead touches the forehead of the man in the glass, and in the doleful depths of his eyes he sees the child he is seeking.

Sonia! Martin shouts agitatedly from the top of the steps descending from the de Lange apartment to the backyard.

Anouk turns her pretty head toward him. My dear! What are you doing home so early?

The Old Jewish Quarter, he says to Sonia. This morning. I've just heard.

What have you heard, Anouk shouts, Mar-tin?

Sonia quickly glances at Leo, who has found his way out of the sandbox and has crawled rapidly to the steps and now has his hands on the bottom one, ready to commence the climb again. Look after the children, would you, she says, her eyes moving from Martin to Anouk and back. I'll be as quick as I can.

Anouk puts on one of her disgruntled expressions, angry that nobody is telling her what's going on.

Don't go there, Martin pleads with Sonia. It's dangerous now and they're raising the bridges. . . .

But Sonia is hurrying up the steps and into the house. Without a word she passes the cook busy preparing the de Langes' dinner, rushes past Mrs. de Lange reclining in her armchair in the sitting room, and runs through the front door to the vestibule and out of the house.

She knows it's beyond her powers. She knows there's no point. She knows that her father, her mother, her brothers, her sister . . . But after a couple of minutes she is on her bicycle, crossing the avenue between the Concertgebouw and Museumplein, drawn eastward.

At night, from the balcony of his room, Yoel sees the dark, empty backyard of the house. Dim light is cast onto the five steps leading from the yard to the house and a breeze moves the swing hanging from the sycamore branch.

The psychoanalyst's piles of papers are scattered around her computer like a choppy sea, yet her chair is empty. The dancer, too, cannot be seen in his sterile white kitchen, but there is a bluish light on in the window to the right of the kitchen and there is the black-garbed dancer sitting on a white couch, apparently facing a TV set that cannot be seen from here, and curled up on his knee is the huge white cat that Josephine has to occasionally remove from the hotel, and then there's evidently a commercial break on the TV because now the dancer is standing up, the cat jumps from his lap and lands softly on the floor, and he exits the living room with perfect dancer's steps and a moment later appears in his kitchen window. Yoel is riveted to the elastic-like limbs of the subject of his observation, his precise, springy movements, his unblemished loneliness. But then a light comes on in an upper window and Yoel's eyes are drawn to the wall with the paintings, to the chest of drawers, and to the unidentified pet lying among the objets d'art this evening too.

From his place on the balcony Yoel examines the sharp-nosed animal and it examines him back. What, he wonders, brings a fox or jackal or even a dog to lie on a piece of furniture as if it's a decoration among other decorations? And suddenly he is hit by the realization that the thin, furry animal lying immobile on the chest of drawers, its head to the window and its tail folded along its haunch, always in the same position, is . . . a stuffed animal, a fine example of a taxidermist's art.

35

And before dawn breaks Yoel wakes up to find himself in his child-hood room in the apartment in Netanya. The blue wardrobe, the desk, and the shelves above it on which his storybooks are arranged beside the volumes of the illustrated children's encyclopedia and the old table games, are all familiar to him from way back when. And when he sits up in his narrow childhood bed the door opens and his mother comes in, young and vigorous and more beautiful than all the women in the world.

A sharp happiness fills Yoel's heart in that he is a child once more, that his mother is again young and healthy, but then she looks at him and in-stead of smiling and wishing him good morning, she is assailed by horror and bursts into terrified screaming. Who are you? she shouts into his face. Who are you and what are you doing here, and how dare you sleep in my child's bed?

He quickly goes to the window to raise the shutter and let more light into the room so his mother can see that he's her child, he and none other. But the shutter is too big and heavy for his small, weak child's hands. And when he finally manages to pull down on the shutter strap and open the window of his childhood room, he is stunned to see the almond tree that had grown over many years in the yard of his and Bat-Ami's home in Jerusalem. Like a gift of love, at the end of every winter this stirring tree would extend posies of delicate, sweet-smelling white blossom to their bedroom window, and Yoel turns his head and sees that he is indeed in his and Bat-Ami's bedroom on the second floor of the family's stone house in Rehavia. But a sense of mild amazement pervades him, for on one of the last occasions that he and Bat-Ami were abroad, her sister, who lives on the ground floor, called in a gardening firm to cut down the almond tree. He and Bat-Ami had returned from an exhausting literary trip and were shocked to find beneath their bedroom window only a mute stump. When they asked what had happened to the tree, his sister-in-law-neighbor had shrugged. It was choking the garden with its awful shed leaves, she hissed angrily. And anyway, it was a bitter almond, and who needs a tree here that just accumulates dead leaves and whose fruit is worth nothing?

And while Yoel stands at the window in Jerusalem seeking an explanation for why the almond tree is growing in their yard even though it's been chopped down, his eyes open and there he is in his bed in the Mokum Hotel in Amsterdam, and it's still dark outside.

What time is it? he asks aloud, and the church bell answers him with four metallic peals.

36

In the morning Sonia crosses Jacob Obrechtplein through a thin, incessant drizzle. Leo is asleep in his stroller covered with the hood, and she decides to go into Martin's shop and ask him about his father-in-law's connections with the Amsterdam Jewish Council.

Through the shopwindow she sees Martin moving paintings from one side of the shop to the other, from the floor to the display table, from the table to the window and back to the floor. The number of customers visiting the shop is dwindling daily, and Sonia can see how Martin is dwindling too. Especially since that rainy day when the police raided the neighborhood adjacent to the ancient Spanish-Portuguese synagogue and most of the Spanish-Portuguese community's families, including Martin's, were arrested and taken to the collection point for Jews at the Dutch Theater on Plantage Avenue.

At the time they have absolutely no idea about what is happening to the Jews taken to the Dutch Theater, where they are being taken from there, and for what.

There are rumors.

But nobody really knows.

In the meantime Yoel sits in the Jewish Historical Museum library almost every day.

He goes through books, scans documents, watches filmed interviews, and reads written testaments, while the librarians are only too glad to fulfill the noted writer's requests, provide him with more and more material, and whenever necessary translate information from Dutch to English for him.

On his way to and from the museum, as on his walks close to the hotel, he looks into the apartments he passes. In fact, he can't avoid looking into them: in spite of himself the big windows are exposed to him, revealing the lives of the people who live in the illuminated spaces beyond them, especially when they're the windows of ground-floor or basement apartments.

He looks into the apartments and sees that in each one there is a living room with seating and entertaining arrangements, and in each one there is a kitchen with a sink and faucets, a worktop, various utensils, and one sort of table or another and chairs for sitting around it. He observes these signs of life in wonderment, learning them like an archeologist trying to trace a lost culture through them or like a prophet seeking meaning and morals.

Up until the day they took his family, Martin thought they were taking only Jews who had recently immigrated to Holland or only poor Jews. That's what he understood from the information he gleaned from his constant listening to distant radio stations, but it transpired that his listening was flawed and his understanding inaccurate, for they had come and uprooted the wealthiest and most highly respected Jews too, privileged Jews of good lineage who had been rooted in Amsterdam since the Jewish expulsion from Spain. Martin's family was sent out of Amsterdam in one fell swoop, before he could exploit his father-in-law's influence to extricate them from the Dutch Theater.

All is not yet lost, he said after he heard that his parents and sisters had been taken out of Amsterdam; I'm sure that Papa de Lange will be able to bring them back. And Sonia saw the hope gleaming in his eyes and thought: And what of my family? Why didn't you suggest that I ask for help from the omnipotent Papa de Lange when it was perhaps still possible to bring back my mother, my father, my young brothers, and my little sister, Trudy?

In the end the banker was unable to save his beloved son-in-law's dear ones. Martin's parents and sisters were taken from Plantage Avenue to who knows where, and in all probability they're going through what her family had gone through or still were. And Martin, all that remained for Martin was to rearrange his beautiful shop.

When he hears the shop door opening he straightens up, startled over the large, heavy-framed painting he has just placed on the floor against the wall. Ah! he exclaims, smiling at Sonia with relief, it's you! She parks the stroller to one side, looks at the paintings all around, and tries to pluck up the courage to ask him what she has come to ask him about his father-in-law. You know I don't really understand these things, she says as her opening gambit, but ever since you explained to us the painting in the entrance to your apartment . . .

Martin nods. The Toorop, *The Sea at Katwijk*.

Yes, she says, yes, the painting of the stormy sea, and you told us that it's actually a painting of the artist's soul. Ever since that evening I've been thinking a lot about it.

Martin smiles sadly.

And what, she asks, pointing at the painting he has just placed against the wall, what does this one express?

They both step back and look at the large oil painting in which there is a table covered with a light silk cloth and on it shiny copper utensils, a torn loaf of bread, and a crystal decanter of dark red wine. You could say, he replies thoughtfully, that this painting expresses the same dilemma reflected in the Toorop work.

Sonia looks into his face and at the painting, and into his face again. A dilemma?

To be or not to be, he says, that is the question and that's the dilemma.

Everything is covered in water—or there's dry land, and on the land there's a table and on the table dishes and bread and wine . . .

And some of the old glow returns to his black eyes as he shows her more and more paintings, more and more psychological situations, more and more expressions of the dilemma of existence. But she is already incapable of talking to him about the subject that brought her here in the first place, she can't ask him about the nature of those famous connections his father-in-law has, that is, exactly to whom or what the banker is connected, and whether he does, as is said of him, hold a central position on the Jewish Council and is able to halt the disaster spreading among the Jews of Amsterdam like an epidemic.

His mother, the authoritative nurse who everyone in the clinic where she worked, even the doctors, respected and feared as she towered over them in her white shoes and the heavily starched white nurse's robe she always wore over a simple, straight-cut dress. During school vacation time he would sit in her white room and watch admiringly, shuddering, as she inserted sharp needles into people's arms and drew their blood into mysterious test tubes. And she didn't stop working when they were home either; she always had something to cook or mend or clean, especially to clean, and only on rare occasions he would see her standing immobile at the kitchen sink holding some dish she was in the middle of soaping, and it was as if her eyes were locked, through the window above the sink, onto the tiny patch of sea that peeked at her between the buildings.

To this day Bat-Ami loves telling anyone prepared to listen how one time, when his mother was already old, they had gone to the old-age home to bring her to their home for some holiday or other, and she had gone out to the car with them, pushing her walker as they carried her bags, when suddenly, when they had almost reached the parking lot, she halted and said, Oh, I'm sorry, I've forgotten something, and she simply left the walker on the path, turned round, and walked back to the building quickly, almost running, to fetch whatever she had forgotten.

It was only toward the end of her life that she confessed to him about the dream she had dreamed many times throughout her life in which she was crawling on her knees in a narrow tunnel, crawling and feeling her way in viscous darkness, and was unable to get herself out. And every time I have this dream, she told him with a shy smile, I wake up crying terribly. I always closed my bedroom door at night so you and Nettie wouldn't have to hear me crying like that.

Rain shrouds the city in a gray veil. Yoel is sitting in a Starbucks café at a small round table and watching the raindrops slide down the glass wall overlooking the street. He thinks about the innumerable small round tables identical to his own that are standing in innumerable Starbucks cafés all over the world. He thinks about innumerable cups of coffee identical to his own which at this very moment are steaming on these innumerable tables in front of the innumerable people sitting on chairs identical to his own beneath ceilings identical to the one over his head. And about the smiling young workers in their uniforms behind the counter who are completely identical to their colleagues who are presently serving the same beverages and pastries from behind identical counters in every city and country.

Perhaps there is actually only one single Starbucks that is incessantly distributed by copy-paste. And perhaps it doesn't matter who you are or where you've come from because the bottom line is that you're just another coffee drinker standing at the counter, moving forward as if on a conveyor belt to the ordering station and from there to the cashier, then waiting till your name is called and finally getting your cappuccino with the whitish layer of foam dripped onto your cup in the shape of a heart. The rain intensifies and Yoel would have liked to think that he is just another coffee drinker in another rainy city. But like the viceroy who goes in search of the king's daughter in Rabbi Nachman of Breslov's tale, he too must not forget the objective on whose trail he has embarked, and he too must look around incessantly and ask, Where am I in this world? Where am I?

Beyond the misted glass a tram climbs the narrow street paved with small brown stones that have become eroded and rounded with the passing years, and another tram goes the other way. The shiny trams glide soundlessly along their tracks, soundlessly, and people tread over the wet stones with rapid steps, their bodies wrapped in coats, hats, and scarves, leaning forward to shelter their faces from the heavy rain. Rabbi Nachman doesn't relate—either because he doesn't know or because it's not what's important—how the viceroy managed to find the princess and bring her back to her father's palace. But he ends the story with a promise: "In the end he found her," and Yoel knows that this is how his own story must end, the story in which he is the king, he is the viceroy, he is the lost princess, and he is the narrator.

37

There are tens of thousands of stolen bicycles lying on the bottom of the canals. It's so easy to pick one out of the thousands parked on every street and every corner, ride it to wherever you want to get to, and there drown it.

At the bottom of the Herengracht, too, there is an invisible heap of rusting bicycles at the particular moment when Yoel is standing on one bank and Sonia with her son, Leo, are standing on the other. Leo is sitting in his little seat on his mother's bicycle and pointing excitedly at the water where four flamboyantly colored ducks are squabbling loudly. Yoel sees Leo and sees Sonia and sees the ducks, which are apparently fighting over the favors of a brown-gray female floating nearby. The four males are paddling in rapid circles, pecking at one another, squawking and flapping their gleaming wings, while the brown-gray female swims calmly as if all this uproar has nothing to do with her.

Yoel calls his agent Zvika in Tel Aviv. He asks Zvika to inform his Italian publisher that he won't be able to travel to Italy next week.

But your new book's already on the shelves there, Zvika protests. And your lectures in Rome, Milan, and Florence were arranged a long time ago. . . .

I'm sorry, Yoel says, and he really does regret being unable to keep his word. I'm sorry, but I've no choice other than to cancel all the rest of the literary trips arranged for the next two or three months as well.

Zvika is stunned. You can't do this to me, he says, his voice strangled. You can't do this to yourself.

That's exactly what you told me, Yoel reminds him with a smile, when I refused to fly to Amsterdam. Remember? So I listened to you and went to Amsterdam, and now I can't leave!

What d'you mean, you can't leave? Don't tell me you've decided to stay there permanently.

Yoel laughs. Not permanently, just until I finish the research for the novel I'm going to write.

You're going to write a novel that takes place in Holland?

Yes, no, I don't know yet. But I'm gathering as much material as I can and writing all sorts of notes and comments. I don't intend to leave this place until I'm sure I understand my story here, and until I'm capable of coming home and sitting down to write that story from start to finish.

In midmorning, a short time after Sonia gets home from a walk with Leo, Martin comes from his shop to inform her that once again the police are planning a raid on the city's Old South to hunt down Jews. The raid will begin in the afternoon, he warns her, and Sonia presumes that he got the news from his clandestine radio stations. Not long ago he told her and Eddy that the enemy needed doctors, which meant that Eddy might be arrested shortly and sent eastward.

Before noon she quickly takes the children upstairs to the top floor and leaves them with Anouk, as she usually does in cases like this. From there she runs to the Jewish hospital to get Eddy, and they hurry to the closest and safest place of refuge: the Rijksmuseum.

They have to walk through the museum's galleries straight-backed and casually, their faces showing nothing but the pure pleasure of seeing the art treasures all around them. Sonia is particularly troubled on this occasion since today Leo is sick and coughing, he has a high temperature, and she can't trust Anouk's childcare abilities. Not only that, but so as not to rouse suspicion, Martin has stayed in the shop. It's hard for Sonia to imagine Anouk managing on her own with her spoiled little Sebastian and Leo as well, whose barking cough is shaking his little body, and with Nettie, who also looked a little pallid earlier and perhaps she too is harboring a virus.

But despite all this she links her arm with Eddy's, inclines her body as if she is leaning against his shoulder, which is lower than hers, and walks with him through the various galleries.

Ordinary, non-Jewish people are walking beside them and looking at the exhibits, breathing with equanimity, and Sonia tries vainly to remember what it's like to be ordinary like these people. What it's like not to be persecuted. What it's like going to the museum because you feel like enjoying fine art, and not because this is the only place where you have a chance of not being arrested, the only place where almost certainly nobody will ask you to present your papers and identify yourself.

Yoel searches the Rijksmuseum galleries until he finds Sonia and Eddy standing and looking, or pretending to look, at the interaction between the light and the objects in the works of the Impressionists. He stands behind them, looking at her arm linked with his and the way she leans slightly toward him as if leaning against his shoulder.

The sounds of the Scottish bagpipes insinuate themselves into the magnificent exhibition rooms from the lawn outside as Sonia and Eddy walk on, and Yoel sits down on the bench facing Rembrandt's vast *The Night Watch* and takes a folded notebook from his pocket. Relate a few scenes from Sonia's work at the Jewish hospital, he writes. Describe how she loved being a nurse, how she enjoyed exercising her strengths and skills to alleviate people's suffering. And the bounty of appreciation she enjoyed from the hospital during that period, and how she sterilized and bandaged and injected and cared so gently and precisely. And the patients' families for whom her steadfast presence was a source of confidence.

Young men she had known in her youth became her friends but did not fall in love with her, perhaps because they were deterred by her strength and sharp tongue, and even by that tall body of hers with its large, long limbs that seemed to be never-ending. But on one lunch break she went into the staff dining room and sat down, quite by chance, opposite the new internal medicine doctor who had just come to the Jewish hospital with his awkward way of moving and eyeglasses with lenses thicker than she'd ever seen. He was a head and a half shorter than her and spoke in the high chord that usually turned her off, but he was enthusiastically explaining to another doctor the importance of the cosmopolitan trend emerging in the world after the World War (the First World War, which they didn't yet know would be followed by another one) and the special role to be played by Holland, which, not by chance, had been passed over by that foolish conflict, in striving toward the unification of all nations and the abrogation of all the unnecessary borders—geographical, mental, and metaphorical—dividing them pointlessly. That was the first time she'd heard her own opinions voiced so cleverly and precisely by someone else, and with no less passion than her own, and she listened avidly to the words of the new doctor, who before long began listening to hers.

A great belief in humankind in general and the Dutch people in partic-ular was what brought them together during lunch breaks in the following days too, and through that winter they continued discussing the subject in the confines of the hospital and outside it as well, in cafés, in the park, in bed. When they decided to get married they believed that they had been granted the privilege of raising a cosmopolitan family in a world that would henceforth only become unified, a world that would break down the bar-riers of nationalism, separatism, and hatred, a world that would gradually be reformed.

As he comes out of the elevator into the corridor, Yoel meets Josephine coming out of his room after changing his sheets and towels. How good it is to meet someone who notices me, he thinks, how good to see a face lighting up on seeing me and lips smiling at me above a silver stud shining in the depression of a chin.

From their casual conversations in the breakfast room, where sometimes he is the only guest, he has learned that Josephine's family immigrated to Holland when she was a child, and that today she is alone after raising her two children on her own. At that moment he feels like asking her how one actually washes dreadlocks as long as hers, and how often, but instead he asks how she is, and after she replies that she's fine, he asks if she sometimes misses her beautiful islands. Josephine's thick black arms hug the bundle of towels and sheets she has taken from his room as she laughs. Miss them? No, never. But, she says gravely, her father, who all his life was a strong, sturdy man, was injured in a work accident last year and since then he's not quite right in the head. Most of the time he thinks he's in their old village in Curaçao, and lately he's started talking only in his childhood language, Papiamento.

Waiting for him on the Formica-topped table in his room, in a green bottle that once contained beer and is now filled with water, is the beautiful Van Gogh sunflower that also recognizes him, and it seems that its yellow face lights up when it sees him too. He confirms that Josephine has not moved his bag and exposed the stain of candle wax underneath it. On Saturday evening, after finally being able to count three stars in the sky, between the bed and the balcony door he had recited the evening prayer and the havdalah ritual separating the Sabbath day from weekdays, and when he crossed the two candles as he recited the blessing for the fire's light, he was concentrating so hard on not activating the smoke detector in the ceiling that he didn't notice the clear wax dripping from his flame onto the wall-to-wall carpeting, and afterward he was unable to get rid of the stubborn stain, not by scraping it with a knife and not by rubbing it with the liquid stain remover he bought in a supermarket the following day. So now he hides this mark of disgrace underneath his bag, suspecting it is liable to be discovered sooner or later.

Eddy's thoughts are with his patients waiting for him at the hospital and Sonia has to keep tugging his arm, to turn his head to the paintings on the walls of the museum and remind him that he's supposed to look as if he finds them interesting.

Now Yoel observes them from a distance after yesterday, while he was saying his morning prayer as usual in his hotel room, he discovered that from his balcony he can see the spires of the Rijksmuseum if there aren't too many clouds. Between the left-hand row of houses and the foliage of a nearby tree that almost hides them, the four pointed spires mark the horizon and he knows that somewhere beneath them Sonia and Eddy are walking around, hiding from their pursuers, and hoping for the best.

At that moment inside the museum Sonia feels that someone is following them, and when she turns to look she sees the inquiring eyes of a woman about her age wearing a fine fur coat. Sonia takes care not to display signs of fear or tension, and with all possible nonchalance she tugs Eddy in the opposite direction and they calmly walk into the next gallery, but a few minutes later the fur-coated woman and her suspicious look also come in, and Sonia stops at Van Veggel's *Madonna and Child*, pretending to inspect it slowly while deep inside she remembers how much she loved this statuette when she was younger and how she always noticed the hidden gold joining its two figures and always decided that this was the kind of mother she wanted to be when she grew up. Then she glances at the clock on the wall, makes a show of being surprised at the time, and says aloud: Look how late it is, we've got to run! And she pulls Eddy through the room where many more Virgin Marys are cradling their infants that they never had to leave in other people's hands, definitely not in hands like Anouk's and definitely not when the children were burning up with fever; she drags Eddy under the stone arches outside the museum, and from there not toward their street, where the police raid is apparently still at its height, but toward the Spiegelgracht, which is in the opposite direction. Don't look back, she warns Eddy, who is walking beside her. She tightens her arm around his and they cross the Prinsengracht, walk up the street with the art shops, cross the Keizersgracht, and walk away from where their home is, away from the coughing Leo and from Nettie, who is probably frightened lest she never see her mama again; lest she and her little brother have to stay forever with Sebastian's mother, who is trying to pacify the sick Leo, whose crying intensifies and Sebastian's mother is already crying with him.

Yoel is looking at the pointed spires of the Rijksmuseum marking the horizon in the narrow space between the trees opposite his room and the end of the left-hand row of houses. He looks at the spires and thinks about the museum he can see from the window of his home in Jerusalem: there facing him are the whitish cubes of the Israel Museum and the tapered white dome of the Shrine of the Book, at the right-hand edge of the bright panoramic view that spreads the width of the wide window of his study to the neighborhoods beyond the southern shore of the Valley of the Cross. There the horizon is marked by the western chain of hills of the Israeli capital, where on a clear day you can see the Beit HaKerem and Bayit VeGan neighborhoods, the mass of the Holyland Tower, and the forested hill whose summit, just before the big new Gilo neighborhood, is cut by the new separation wall. Here, facing the hotel balcony is spread the childhood landscape of Anouk Rosso, née de Lange, whereas the area spread before his Jerusalem window is the childhood landscape of Bat-Ami Blum, née Avni. How Bat-Ami loves telling him about her childhood in the wild, tangled thickets that in those days filled the Valley of the Cross, how she played there with her friends and how they gathered twigs for their bonfires and then sang sad Russian tunes around the tongues of flame and the baking potatoes, and how she and two other neighborhood children had laid claim to one of the many caves in the rocky ground and opened a "candle factory" in it where they melted candles they filched from their homes and tried to make new candles from the melted wax. We hoped to get rich from it. Bat-Ami chuckles. No wonder it was my first and last business venture.

Sonia's heart goes out to her children but she has no choice but to move farther away from them. They walk west toward Keizersgracht and Eddy suddenly freezes.

Don't stop, she urges him without moving her lips, I think we're still being followed.

But when she looks in the direction he's looking at she sees the crane of the truck parked between the buildings and the canal bank. She sees the arm of the crane raise a huge iron hook to an open window on the third floor of a fine house and the barge anchored in the canal and porters arranging on its deck velvet couches, carved wooden wardrobes, and other items of fine furniture that the crane continues taking, one at a time, from the open window. That's Sherman's house, Eddy whispers, and Sonia remembers that the director of the Jewish hospital indeed lives here, and at first she wonders why the respected director has chosen to move at a time like this, but then she notices how pale Eddy's face is and hears him murmur, They arrested him only last week, and she is alarmed, refusing to believe it: Arrested him? They arrested Professor Sherman? It was inconceivable that they would arrest such an eminent personality, an affluent physician who is respected in Dutch society and who lives, that is, lived until a week ago, here on Keizersgracht in that impressive house on the banks of the beautiful canal in the center of the city.

And the two of them stand and watch as the porters inside the house reach out of the third-floor window and catch the hook that had again been raised by the crane's arm and was attached to a heavy cable. A short time later the end of the cable emerges from the open window and on the hook are several large gilt-framed paintings bound together with a rope. The paintings are tied with their backs facing outward so it is impossible to see which paintings they are. The crane arm is slowly lowered, the bundle of paintings is landed on the barge deck, and the porters waiting there extend their arms to receive it.

Thieves, Eddy hisses. Disgusting thieves.

Sonia strokes his arm wordlessly. In a moment she will try to pull him away from there, and not only because she fears they are being followed. She will try to pull him away because she doesn't want to stay here until the workers finish emptying the house of all the valuables that the old professor and his wife have collected over all the years of their life. She doesn't have the strength to see him watch the barge sail away, loaded with all the Sher-mans' furniture and carpets and lamps, their dishes and art treasures, and their days and years and loves and hopes, and sail down the Keizersgracht on its way to the Amstel, then the IJ, from there to the Rhine and thence into the heart of Germany.

And Yoel leaves the room and walks, he walks amid all the unbearable beauty of this city until he stops on one of the bridges over the Keizers-gracht, leans on the stylized rail between parked bicycles, and thinks, If I had been an ordinary Dutchman among ordinary Dutchmen, if I had remained in the city where I was born and lived in it without fear, then perhaps I would have chosen—why not?—to live in one of these small houseboats moored along the banks of the canal. Perhaps I'd have bought myself an old fishing boat that was tired of sailing and adventures, and perhaps I would have remodeled that boat into a lovely little home: a home that sails above great depths while I lie on its bottom and feel the movement of the water beneath me, sit between its bulwarks and listen to the tumult of the abyss, stand on its deck and let my heart encounter the heart of the sea.

38

Leo rolls the red ball, chases it in a crawl, picks it up with both hands, and rolls it again.

Leo holds out a blue wooden building block. He smiles happily when it's taken from him. Then he opens his hand to ask for the block back, and then he holds it out again, and so on and so forth.

Leo mumbles his first words: Dada, Mama, [Net]Tie, [Than]Kyou.

Leo sits on the floor, his legs stretched forward and his feet crossed.

He looks at the colored wooden blocks scattered around him.

Puts a red block on top of a yellow one.

Claps his hands.

Late in the evening Yoel passes the Concertgebouw, hears the sounds of Beethoven's magnificent Ninth Symphony, and knows that inside the hall at this moment, during the war, that is, the last concert with the participation of Jewish musicians is taking place. He ascends the wide stone steps and waits by the closed doors until the final chord and the outburst of rapturous applause from the audience. The applause goes on for a long time as one at a time the Jewish musicians walk to the forestage and take a final bow. Then he hears the encore, excerpts from Bach's Brandenburg Concertos performed with a wonderful delicacy that does not leave a dry eye in the auditorium, followed by another prolonged wave of applause accompanied by calls for

another encore, which mandates a consultation between the musicians, and
then another short piece and more applause. As the Jewish musicians take
their absolutely final bow the audience gets to their feet and waves farewell
to them with their handkerchiefs. In accordance with the occupation authorities' decree, Jews will no longer be allowed to attend the Concertgebouw,
neither to play music nor listen to it. Even the names of Jewish composers
whose works are performed here will be erased.

Bat-Ami sometimes calls him *Eesh sheli*, in Hebrew—my man—and
sometimes she joins the two words and says *Eesheli*, but most of all she likes
to re-separate the words differently and call him *Ee sheli*: my island. For
even if he is indeed an island, he is hers. Even from across the sea she reads
him as if she has opened his soul with one of her numerous keys.

He is standing on his balcony and her voice is speaking to him from
the cell phone that is already burning his ear. He had returned from his
wanderings a short while ago, entered the hotel through the night entrance
at the rear, and climbed four flights of steep stairs. Now the backyards of
the two rows of houses are dozing down below, immersed in darkness, and
in most of the windows facing onto the yards the lights are off. Deep in
sleep is the third basement apartment on the right, the apartment he calls
"Sonia's apartment," and in its windows is only the reflection of the shrubs
against the backdrop of a swing hanging from a tree branch. In the psychoanalyst's unlit room the flickering of her screen saver illuminates the
piles of papers on her desk. The dancer's windows are in complete darkness
now, after he had earlier moved between the rooms of his existence in his
lithe movements as he washed and scrubbed and polished all the dishes and
surfaces in his white kitchen. Only from the upper left-hand window the
glass eyes of the stuffed animal still peer, and from between the tall trees
at the end of the right-hand row of buildings the gilded harp atop the Concertgebouw gleams, one moment hidden by the dark branches swaying in
the night breeze and a moment later revealed in all its glory, then hidden
again, and then revealed, and again and again.

As had been happening toward the end of each phone conversation since his arrival here, tonight too Bat-Ami suggests that she drop everything and come to Amsterdam to be with him. In all their calls so far he has refused her offer but the truth is that on this occasion it's hard for him: he so much would love Bat-Ami to come and look after him, look after him and protect him. He so much wants her to be with him, to be with him and alleviate the burden of his loneliness: the loneliness that has enshrouded him throughout his life like another layer of skin, and here in Amsterdam has become thicker and rougher, its weight restricting his movements.

What can he do when just as he replies to Bat-Ami's suggestion—You know what? Come then, but when can you get here?—the church bell starts announcing the arrival of midnight. The twelve peals of Our Lady sound from the end of the world all the way to its other end, and Bat-Ami shouts: What? What, hold on, I can't hear you! And at the finale of the chain of ding-dongs, which seems to be never-ending, Yoel says in his usual moderate tone, It's alright, Bat-Ami, everything's fine, there's no need for you to come to Amsterdam. I mean, thanks for the offer, but I think it's best that I continue along this road by myself, and Bat-Ami pauses a moment and says: Yes, my dear, yes, I understand. And after they wish one another goodnight and end the call, he switches the phone off and goes back into the room from the balcony, not before taking a last look at the stuffed animal that is still checking him out from the darkness of the left-hand window, still crouched on the sideboard and fixing him with its gleaming glass eyes as if trying to decipher him once and for all.

Jews Are Forbidden: To fish, travel on public transportation, drive a car, enter public places, join a club, go to school, enter a hotel, go to the theater, swim in a pool, appear without a yellow star on their clothing, buy vegetables at a non-Jewish shop, ride a bicycle, go shopping between three and five in the afternoon, go to a hairdresser, use a telephone, visit non-Jews, study at a university, leave their homes after eight in the evening, approach the municipal or state authorities unless it is through the Jewish Council.

We do not consider the Jews to be part of the Dutch nation. The Jews are the enemy with whom no armistice or peace can be made, says the Reichskommissar in the Netherlands in a speech. We shall smite the Jews where we meet them and whoever goes along with them must take the consequences.

And Martin. Martin continues his nightly scanning of distant radio stations.

Yoel knows only what he picks up through his five senses, but deep inside he is forced to admit that Bat-Ami picks up more than that. A few years ago, she decided to leave teaching and become proficient in some sort of parapsychological, physiological, spiritual therapy, and at first he feared she would get bored and change her mind, but since then, from day to day and by word of mouth, the list of women seeking this odd New Age therapy had grown, a therapy she's good at and about which he understands nothing. Her clients admiringly contend that she possesses the powers of a witch. And after one of them presented her, full of thanks, with a picture of a witch, additional clients and friends began plying her with drawings of witches, statuettes of witches, books about witches, and all sorts of items embossed with images of witches. Bat-Ami smiles when she sees how alarmed he is with all this witchery. They're just images of old women, she says, trying to calm him, at a certain age every woman gets a wrinkled face and a nice hump, a hooked nose and a hoarse voice, and every woman carries a broom. It's only you men who are capable of attributing negative magical powers to these sweet old ladies!

Once she was given a witch marionette. A loud handclap made it jump on its broomstick and its face light up while its contorted body emitted a malevolent witch's chuckle. He felt uneasy when Bat-Ami called him to come and see the grotesque show, and she, who of course had noticed his unease even though he smiled and said with forced amazement, What a present, what a present, had shrugged and taken her what-a-present, and that was the end of that. Until one summer night he got up from his desk very late when Bat-Ami was already asleep, and started, as was his wont every night, going from room to room and turning off the lights and locking the windows, and when he went into the room that was Bat-Ami's clinic he saw on the white wall near the window a huge dark brown cockroach, and he hates cockroaches, especially the ones that come up from the sewers. He detests them so much that he usually calls Bat-Ami to perform their execution, but in this case Bat-Ami was already asleep. And the disgusting creature that transmits bacteria and illnesses was resting on the wall, its long legs symmetrically arranged on both sides of its shiny body and its long antennae waving in the air like two human hairs taken out of their context. Yoel had no choice but to be lionhearted, take off a shoe, raise it, and with it hit the wall with all his might—and the moment he saw the cockroach fleeing down the wall and disappearing under the chest of drawers, he heard a loud discordant laugh and looked up and saw the marionette witch jumping on its broomstick, its evil face flickering at him in ridicule.

39

Morning and night the child Yoel would invent his absent father, his wonderful father. If the other children asked him about his father he would invent replies that later evolved into his first stories. But even to himself, without an audience, he would incessantly re-create his father. And even when he was grown up and accepted the story his mother told him, he would still imagine his father alive, that only by mistake his father was considered dead while in truth he hadn't been killed in that distant war but only wounded, or taken prisoner, and the mistake would soon be revealed and his father would return to the bosom of his beloved family.

You are hereby conscripted for forced labor under police supervision in Germany. You must present yourself for a personal and medical examination at the Westerbork transit camp.

You are to bring with you: 1 suitcase. 1 travel bag. 1 pair of work boots. 2 pairs of socks. 2 underpants. 2 shirts. 1 overall. 2 wool blankets. 2 sets of sheets. 1 bowl. 1 mug. 1 spoon. 1 coat. A towel and wash kit. Food for 3 days and all the ration coupons in your possession. Label the suitcase with your forename, surname, date of birth, and the word "Holland." Illness does not exempt you from reporting. Enclosed is a travel warrant to your destination by tram or bus. In addition, bring: details of your bank account, including confirmation of the state of the account and of savings accounts at the bank and/or other investments. Declaration of capital. Insurance policy details. Details of property in Holland or abroad. Details of safe deposits (the safe key must also be brought). Report on inheritances. Report on collections. Jewels and precious stones. Items of gold and silver. Other valuables. Gifts. Details of business partnerships. An exact report of real estate and mortgages. You must tear up the travel warrant when you reach your destination.

Along the canals the leaves on the trees are drying up, browning and withering. Yoel is walking and as he walks dead leaves fall around him. They fall in front of him, at his sides, onto his head.

In the evening Sonia reads Eddy's order and reads it again, and a third time, as if repeated reading will help her grasp what is written in it.

He has to report tomorrow morning. Tomorrow morning.

The attached travel warrant does not exempt him from paying his fare but only permits him to take a tram or bus even though Jews are prohibited from using public transportation.

Leo is crawling happily on the living room floor; he grasps one of their three chairs and hoists himself up onto his little feet. Then he starts tottering here and there as he pushes the chair in front of him with the chair legs making loud scraping sounds that he accompanies with triumphant squeals.

Nettie, who has recently discovered the magic of reading, is curled up in a corner of the couch with a fairy-tale book borrowed from her teacher's personal library. They had enrolled her for first grade in the Montessori school, but the school's doors are now closed to Jews. One of the Jewish teachers opened a temporary classroom in her home, and Sonia takes Nettie there on her bicycle every morning.

Eddy inspects the wooden suitcase standing in front of him. On the lid Sonia has written his full name in large, round, black letters. And beneath his name his date of birth. And beneath his date of birth the name of their beloved country in which they now have no place.

I'm sure there's no reason for concern, he says, perhaps to Sonia, possibly to himself. They're taking me because I'm a doctor, and they need doctors. They won't harm me.

Sonia cannot but worry lest something happen to Eddy's rare and expensive glasses with their thick lenses, without which he sees nothing. Do they have opticians in the Westerbork transit camp? If need be, will there be anyone who can repair glasses like them somewhere in war-torn Germany? And what will happen if he breaks his glasses or loses them, and he's unable to obtain new ones?

She leaves him with the open suitcase as he starts putting the required items into it with his ungainly movements. She takes Leo in her arms and hurries out, out and up the stairs to the floor above them.

Mrs. de Lange has been in a foul mood ever since Jews, even Jews like herself, were forbidden to continue employing non-Jews in their homes. The urgent knocking on her door troubles her, and the unexpected visit by the young tenant from the basement apartment does not exactly please her, even more so since this tall hyperactive girl appears to be distraught, and she is standing there with her blond infant, from whose diaper a nasty smell is wafting.

After apologizing for disturbing her and a brief exchange of courtesies, Sonia says, I'm looking for Mr. de Lange, I—

My husband isn't at home, the older woman interrupts her impatiently. What was it you wanted from him?

And Sonia doesn't understand why this is happening to her: why it's happening to her at all, and why it's happening to her with her landlady after all the time they'd been living here with not even a single meaningful conversation, but all her troubles and fears well up and then, her voice shaking and her tears flowing, she tells Mrs. de Lange, who is standing angry and impatient in her doorway, that her husband the doctor is being sent away from Amsterdam in the morning, and that she wanted to ask Mr. de Lange, that is to request—

Mrs. de Lange cuts her short again. I'm very sorry, she says, drawing out the first syllable of "sorry." But imagine, Mrs. Blum, just imagine that every Jew about to be sent away from the city came and asked my husband to prevent him being taken!

All at once Sonia regains her composure.

So it's true that your husband, that is, Mr. de Lange, can prevent Jews from being sent away?

My husband, declares Mrs. de Lange, cannot act on individual cases for the convenience and welfare of any specific Jew or family. While you, young lady, are worrying only about yourself, my husband is working tirelessly for the benefit of the entire Jewish community! That is the chief concern right now, that and nothing else!

And suddenly, as if she had heard her own words and was frightened by them, or realized that she'd revealed something she was supposed to keep secret, she angrily blurts out a few courtesies and slams the door.

Leo, who until this moment has been following the negotiation between his mother and their neighbor from his nest in his mother's arms in uncharacteristic silence, starts to cry. He weeps insult, he weeps despair, he weeps as if he understands that with the slamming of this door his fate has been sealed too.

Night falls.

Night falls and Yoel collapses exhausted onto his bed in the hotel room. For the first time since his arrival here he connects the TV on the table to the socket and switches it on, and to his surprise the cumbersome old set is filled with vitality and on its screen appears a game show in which two teams of adults are competing to spell words in Dutch. The studio audience is divided into two sets of fans wearing the color of their favorite team, and the tension soars each time one of the contestants tries to spell the word given to him by the panel of judges. All of them—the contestants, the judges, the host, and the audience—continuously joke and continuously respond to each other's jokes with loud laughter. Judging by the number of commercial breaks, Yoel understands that this is a program that enjoys high ratings. He too, even though he doesn't understand a word or the laughter, is riveted for a long time on the exciting game that is deftly moderated by a laughing, bubbling blonde, behind whom are beautifully arranged beds of tulips and windmills, and on the floor in front of her a large map of Holland is spread out.

Another commercial break, and the tournament continues. And again the host laughs uproariously, the contestants and the fans laugh uproariously, and it seems that the TV set is dancing with joy.

Sonia continues with her rescue efforts through the night. She doesn't leave Anouk alone. She doesn't leave Martin alone. She doesn't stop laying out her pleas before them, begging that they lay her pleas before the banker de Lange.

All Anouk says is: Tell Martin. Martin understands these things. All Martin says is: What can I do? I don't know what to do.

Eddy, whose suitcase is locked and waiting by the door, asks her to stay calm. It will pass, he assures her and tries to smile, it will all pass quicker than we expect.

When the TV spelling game ends, Yoel leaves his room, almost stumbles on the steep stairs, and slips out of the hotel through the rear door. He thinks about going into the neighborhood brown café but feels he needs a time-out from Jacob Obrechtstraat and cuts through Muntplein and Rokin to Dam Square and his usual table by the balustrade on the upper level of the Irish pub. He stays there for a long time, vainly trying to drown himself in beer, and on his way back he passes the house. A streetlight illuminates the wall of small red bricks and the climbing plant running up it, its branches bare, and he slows and looks down to the long window at sidewalk level. A dim light is on in the small basement apartment, and by this light he sees the kitchen sink under the window, he sees the draining board, he sees the table and the three simple chairs and tries to see Sonia, to see Eddy, to see Sonia and Eddy . . .

Don't go, she pleads all night long. And before daybreak, after Martin and Anouk had come downstairs and stayed awhile and climbed back up to their apartment, she makes one last effort. Don't go, my love, don't go, don't report.

I've no choice, he repeats.

You can hide, she begs. She repeats, as she's done a thousand times, the names of their friends who have already gone into hiding. Friends, who with the aid of one of the underground organizations active in the city, have already changed their identity and been granted protection by generous Christians, either for payment or gratis, so as not to be seen in public until the war is over.

All of them have ducked under the surface, she tells him. And it's with good reason, my Eddy, it's with good reason that people define hiding as ducking or diving underwater, because all you have to do in a situation like ours in Amsterdam is to lower your head and disappear for a while.

Eddy shakes his head.

She remembers with frustration how right at the beginning, when the city's Jewish residents were told to go to one of the branches of the Jewish Council and register as Jews, she had begged him not to comply with this demand and simply not register, and he had refused her pleas.

It's too dangerous, he tells her now too. They're liable to capture me, me and you as well. . . .

We've got nothing to lose, my heart. . . .

And we have to remember, he goes on, that all those Jews who break the law to try to save themselves are endangering not only themselves but the entire community. If you and I, Sonia my love, break the law, the authorities will punish other Jews because of us. Especially Jews like your parents and brothers, who are already being held by the enemy, and we are the guarantee for their fate. . . .

Don't report! she screams, leaping at the suitcase as if possessed, her hands tearing at the lock to open it and throw the contents of the case to the four winds.

Eddy jumps after her, trying to control her, and they struggle, hitting each other, scratching until they draw blood.

Finally they fall. Finally they fall to the floor locked in an embrace, their faces buried in each other's chest. Beside them stands the brown wooden suitcase bearing the name Dr. Edouard Blum, and his date of birth, and the word "Holland." And farther away lies a pair of glasses, Eddy's thick-lensed, silver-framed glasses that had flown off his face as they struggled.

In the early morning the water in the canals shines bright. Throughout the day flickers of radiant light will flow in the canals, their colors and shapes changing with the strength of the sun's rays and the position of the sun in the sky at any given hour.

Yoel reads Sonia's story from the scenes before him. He reads it like the viceroy, searching for the lost princess in Rabbi Nachman of Breslov's tale, reads the letter the princess wrote him, using her tears as ink, on a handkerchief she threw by the wayside.

I'll be alright, my dear, Eddy says, you'll see. He hugs her tightly, strokes her hair gently, don't worry, don't worry. I'll be working there as a doctor, I'll treat the people who need treatment, and I'll come back to you. I'll come back to you quickly, you'll see how quickly.

Sonia remains silent. Don't forget, she orders herself. The caressed head. The hugged body. Don't forget this feeling, take it with you to wherever the days ahead might lead you.

40

It's a beautiful day in Amsterdam, a beautiful day in the parks, a beautiful day in the streets and squares. On the canal banks the tree branches can be seen gleaming in a new light over the water, a light the likes of which has never been nor will ever be again.

Sonia tries not to worry too much about Eddy. In the early days Martin would update her on what he heard on his clandestine radio stations. Afterward he stopped updating her and she stopped asking.

In the afternoon she picks up Nettie from the temporary school and rides with both children on her bicycle: Nettie in the child's seat behind her, and Leo in the wooden carrier on the handlebars. She rides through the street running alongside Vondelpark, pedaling slowly beside the dense wall of trees delineating the green expanses that are now covered with crocus and iris blooms of orange and purple.

Her heart sinks as she passes the Jacob Obrechtstraat entrance to the park, as if this is the first time she is seeing the wooden notice nailed to one of the gateposts, and on it, in brutal black letters, the words: "Jews Are Prohibited."

She pedals southward along the border of the big park. Mama? her daughter's thin voice pipes from behind her.

Yes, my sweet.

Mama, why haven't we been to the park for such a long time?

Because it was winter, my treasure. It was too cold.

But it's not cold now, Mama, when can we go to the park?

Very soon, Nettie, we'll go very soon.

And only then Sonia realizes that the child has seen the notice, seen the notice and read the black letters. Since when has she known how to read those horrifying words? How many of those notices has she come across, my poor little gosling, at the various gates of the world she is only just getting to know?

After passing another entrance and another notice, Sonia puts a foot down onto the ground and stops. She stops by the bank of trees at a point where the branches are less dense. Between the unsullied foliage she can see into the park, as far as the lake in its heart and the crocuses flowering between the lawns surrounding it. Closer, by the park's central path, she sees the falling oak. It is a tree similar to lots of other trees in the park, but all the other trees have grown upward while this one has grown horizontally, actually lying on the ground. It seems that when it was a young sapling it was uprooted, then fell flat but continued living and growing after it had fallen: on its bottom side, its roots took hold in the soil and with them its branches, while on the upper side, the branches and roots grew skyward.

There's our tree friend, she tells Nettie. Do you remember us all coming to see it together with Papa?

The child nods excitedly, her eyes shining as Sonia mentions Eddy. When I was little, she says, and we came here with Papa, I thought that the tree was lying down because it was dead. . . .

Yes, Sonia replies, when you see it lying like that you might think it's dead. It's only when you take a closer look that you see it's alive.

Nettie looks at the tree from the distant observation point permitted for Jews like her. Its leaves are green, she says. It's a sign that it's alive.

Leo is quiet in the bicycle carrier; his blond eyebrows are furrowed and it seems that he is listening to the conversation between his mother and sister, listening and understanding.

Sonia recalls an emotional poem she wrote, in honor of this tree, when she was still in high school and still wrote poetry. She thinks the words of the poem were: "O, lonely tree, I am like you / To my heart you are so near / My branches buried, my roots exposed / My shout that people can't hear."

Or something like that.

As she turns her bicycle and her children in the direction they came from, to go home, she is surprised to see someone—a stranger in a dark suit—coming toward them rapidly, his expression grave. She is frightened by the thought that he is a policeman, but a moment later she sees that he is only an elderly citizen striding resolutely toward her and halting a couple of steps away.

He addresses her in an aggressive tone: Are you permitted to be here? It's hard for her to believe, but that's what's happening: A stranger. A stranger is asking her. A stranger is asking her if she and her two children are permitted to be by Vondelpark.

But, sir, she replies politely, trying to conceal her terror and even to smile, you can surely see that I didn't go into the park. I was just standing here with my two little ones, outside the prohibited area. . . .

You'd better get out of here right now, he says, raising his voice, otherwise I'll have to report you!

And Sonia pedals away, her daughter behind her and her son in front, she pedals alongside the wall of trees to Jacob Obrechtstraat, over which a dirty sky, the color of a muddy puddle, hangs low and embarrassed.

A thousand times a day Sonia puts a hand to her chest to feel the yellow cloth star pinned to each item of clothing she wears. If it weren't for the star, people wouldn't know she was Jewish, and the man outside Vondelpark wouldn't have attacked her and her children. When the law obliging all the Jews of Holland to wear the yellow star was promulgated, Anouk had told her: My father says we should wear the star not as a mark of shame

but as a badge of pride. Sonia intended to pass on that pride. But it transpired that every Jew, that is, everyone holding an identity card stamped
with a "J," would be arrested and punished if caught without a star. And
Anouk said that her darling father was prepared to save Sonia the trouble
of going to the Jewish Council offices and standing in the long line there,
by bringing her as many stars as she wanted to buy from the Council.

Sonia sent the required sum to the banker: four cents per yellow cloth
star. She did, however, decide that she wouldn't sew these ugly stars onto
her clothes, but only tack them on with a safety pin.

At night Yoel dreams that he'd been swallowed by a big fish. In his dream
he doesn't know how it happened, but he is lying on his side, his knees bent,
inside a pulsing space whose sides are soft, and it's clear to him that he'd
been swallowed by a big fish. Even though unlike his predecessors, from
the prophet Jonah to Pinocchio, this fact does not cause him distress. On
the contrary: being swallowed is sweet for him. He feels protected, feels
loved, feels a longing to remain inside this fish indefinitely, and when he
wakes up he can still sense that sweetness.

And every morning on her way to the home of Nettie's teacher Sonia sees
the Jews, every morning scores of Jews coming to Roelof Hartplein as
they had been told by the printed orders given to them, every morning,
men and women, the elderly and children, all in their best clothes, each
with a suitcase or a bag or a bundle made of a wool blanket with its corners tied together, the babies in the arms of their parents or siblings. They
all come from houses which until this morning were their homes, from a
life which until this morning was their life, they come to the square and
sit on the benches, rows and rows of benches placed there so they could
be comfortable as they wait in this beautiful big square in the center of
Amsterdam, at the biggest tramline junction in the city. And while all
these Jews are sitting on the benches, while they sit there looking like

people about to embark on an enjoyable excursion or a nice vacation in the bosom of nature, special attendants move among them speaking to them with exaggerated politeness, making sure they have everything they need and even serving them hot tea sweetened with sugar cubes so they will feel at ease and harbor no worries, no suspicion, no desire to cause unrest that might bother passersby and disturb the peace. And all this is arranged in an exemplary fashion, every morning, how can it be described, where are the words with which one can describe the expression of calm on the faces of those waiting there, the fur coats worn by many of the waiting women, their legs elegantly crossed as they sit in the rows of benches, their high-heeled shoes, the fashionable felt hats on the heads of many of the men, and the glances they steal every now and then at the train tracks and their watches as if they have control of their time. Where are the words to describe the children playing at their parents' feet, the confidence felt by children playing at their parents' feet, and the fact that not one of the adults has any idea of where they are going to, not even when a train comes to a halt and they get up off the benches, quietly pick up their possessions, stand in an orderly line, oh, how orderly, and climb aboard, helping one another up, helping one another to board and load the luggage. And they go on their way.

Roelof Hartplein is so close to Jacob Obrechtstraat, to the Mokum Hotel, Museumplein and the Concertgebouw. Yoel progresses only a short way southward along Van Baerlestraat and there is the square with all its tram stops and the wide expanse at the foot of the long rectangular building that the occupying forces converted into one of the main headquarters in Amsterdam, but before the war was the Jewish hospital's nurses' home where Sonia lived until her marriage to Eddy. One of the windows overlooking the square is the window of the room Sonia shared with her good friend Bett, it was through this window that she viewed her future, which at the time looked so enchanting, and now, from the safe distance she keeps at the edge of the square, she looks fearfully at the window and at what is happening below it. Where are they taking all these Jews? Where have her father, mother, brothers, and sister been taken to?

All at once Sonia knows for certain that what she wants—somehow, sometime, if only it will be possible—is to get to Palestine. In the world before the war she had never imagined she would want to go to Palestine, but right now there is nothing she wants more, if only because her beloved father had yearned for Palestine with every fiber of his being. He called it "Eretzyisroel" (Land of Israel), "Eretzhakoidesh" (Holy Land), and only God, who he called "Hakoidoshborchu" (The Holy Blessed One) and believed in with a pure heart, knows if he will ever reach the object of his yearning.

And she decides: when they go to Palestine she will change Leo's name to a Jewish one. She will name him after her father: Yoel.

On the fourth evening after the new order forbidding Jews to leave their homes after eight in the evening came into force, Martin knocks on Sonia's door after the little ones have gone to sleep. Thin, his eyes lusterless, he stands in the doorway and when Sonia sees him she is flooded with longing for Eddy and also with longing for Martin of before the war, the inspirational Martin who seems to have been taken together with Eddy, leaving behind only his degraded shadow.

Now Martin's degraded shadow comes into her apartment with hesitant steps, declines her offer of a chair, looks at her with an expression filled with defeat, and says: Sonia, I want to ask something of you.

What could you possibly ask of me, she thinks. Your family could have taken action to save my Eddy. Your family can still try to save me and my children. But I? What can I do for you?

He stands before her, his arms hanging helplessly at his sides. When she insists that he sit down, he sits on the very edge of one of their three chairs and waits while she wipes the table clean of the remains of her and her children's meager supper and sits down opposite him. He clears his throat, clears it again, and starts talking several times before he is able to continue. Once he manages to speak, it turns out that he has come to ask that she and her children dive underwater. He knows some people from the resistance, and of course Anouk's father must never hear of this, but he's already spoken to his friends about Sonia and the two children and they have promised to arrange an orderly diving for them. There are, of course, several matters that must be attended to—

Just a minute, she says, cutting him short. You've come here to suggest that I take my children, leave this house with them, and disappear to wherever we disappear to?

No, Martin replies quietly. Not you and the children together. You'll have to go into hiding separately, that is, the underground will arrange separate hiding places for the children. You've nothing to worry about, Sonia, finding a hiding place for the little ones is easier. Especially for Leo, with his blond hair and blue eyes.

Two thousand five hundred. According to the documents Yoel has studied, that was the number of Jewish children hidden by Christian families during the war. Two thousand five hundred Jewish children, most of them from Amsterdam. According to Dutch law only those children with a surviving parent were eventually returned, while according to reality only those children whose surviving parent managed to find where they had been hidden were returned. Many children therefore remained with the families that had hidden them.

Many of the hidden children were completely unaware that they were not the biological offspring of the people who raised them. Many are unaware of it to this day.

The ground dissolves under Sonia's feet. And what about you, she asks Martin, you, Anouk, and Sebastian? Do you mean to dive underwater as well?

This question greatly embarrasses Martin. He shifts on the edge of his chair, looks sideways, searching for words. In the end his answer is no, they do not intend to go into hiding. Anouk's father, that is Anouk's father's position enables him to take care of himself, his wife, and the three of them—Anouk, Martin, and the child.

I don't understand what you're trying to say—she slams her words at him with increasing anger—but perhaps you can explain it to me: your dear father-in-law is driving the Jews of Amsterdam from their homes and their lives, with his own hands he's sending them—

It's not him who is driving them out, Sonia—

He is, Martin, he is! First he urged us to register as Jews, then he made sure we all had our identity cards stamped, and he let them take Eddy and mark us with these yellow cloth stars to make it easier for them to take us all—

But he's only—

He's only what, she yells at him, he's only one of those responsible for all this? He only executes—who knows in what role, and who cares—the decisions of the contemptible, corrupt Jewish Council that collaborates with the enemy?

But, Sonia—

Not another word, Martin. I trusted Jozef de Lange, I listened to his instructions and advice, and now he's deporting all the Jews of Amsterdam—with his own hands, with his own hands—while he and his nearest and dearest—you—carry on sitting in your homes in complete safety. And all you can suggest to me is that I, who trusted his word, get rid of my children? That I abandon them God knows where?

Rage roils inside her until she is about to explode, or perhaps it isn't rage but desperation, and after Martin leaves she goes into the darkness of the little room filled with soft breathing. Nettie is asleep on her back, her face exposed and her arms outstretched as if in an expression of total belief in her mother's power to protect her from evil. Leo is lying on his tummy across the width of his crib, his legs folded under him and his cheek resting on the blanket she had covered him with earlier. He looks so small, so vulnerable, and in the hollow beneath his collarbone Sonia sees the artery in his neck rising and falling with each beat of his heart. Rising and falling, rising and falling.

41

He wanders the streets, wanders through the museums, wanders through his soul. And sometimes he looks at the beauty of Amsterdam, or at the profundity of works of art, and knows—for only a fleeting flash, but he knows—what he has been looking for all his life. Like the time he visited the Israel Museum in Jerusalem and saw Jozef Israëls's *Mother and Child Walking on the Dunes*, undated. And like on his last visit with Bat-Ami to the Museum of Modern Art in New York when he stood, as he had many times in the past, facing Matisse's *La Danse*, and unlike all the previous occasions he suddenly realized that there was no need to decide if the young girls in the painting are holding out their hands to one another or detaching them from one another, since both possibilities are one and the same. Just as it makes no difference if the girl on the left, who is falling from the circle of dancers, has stumbled, or has intentionally torn herself out of the circle.

Bett, Sonia's friend from her nursing days, comes to her apartment to rest after her night shift on the maternity ward. Bett works nights because she's unable to sleep at home: the police have raided her neighborhood twice and she's afraid she won't manage to escape a third time.

Her husband was arrested and deported, and they had handed over their only daughter for hiding beforehand. In the first days after sending the child away she couldn't stop crying, she told Sonia, but as time passed the well of her tears has dried up and her soul is parched. When Sonia asks her where the child is hidden Bett looks at her in surprise. It's the underground, she reminds her. They don't tell you what they're planning and certainly not where they're taking your child to. In fact, she goes on, as soon as they'd returned home without their daughter, she and her husband had changed their mind about handing the child over, and after an anguished night they'd decided to bring her home even if it meant death for the three of them. But in the morning, when they went back to the apartment where they'd left the child the previous evening, they were told that their daughter had been taken away and no one knew to where. The people we'd given her to the night before weren't there, she explains, and the new people claimed that they knew them only by their underground aliases, which were changed all the time.

One morning he is crossing the Amstel on his way to the Old Jewish Quarter, and here and there he sees tourists standing with an open city map trying to find where they are, and there before him are Sonia and Eddy and the two children at a different time, perhaps during the period when they were filmed in the wedding video that's in the museum. The four of them are standing on the big bridge and watching the huge barges sailing below them, their engines straining with their loads of flour, coal, and other goods, some sailing toward the inner port and from there to the North Sea and other continents, and others going the other way to the southern rivers and the expanses of Europe. Nettie is pointing excitedly at a long line of barges tied to each other like train wagons, and Leo is holding his little hands up to the seagulls gliding above, swooping down to the water and perching with folded wings on the mooring bollards.

And all his walks begin and end by the house. Tense and alert his feet measure the flagstones of the sidewalk that begins behind the concert hall and ends in the small market square in Jacob Obrechtstraat, or begins on the corner where, in the shop that today houses a real estate office, rare works of art were displayed and sold by a young man who loved art and loved people and believed in the presence of infinity within the finite and the limited, and ends behind the Concertgebouw, in a pleasant café whose walls and furniture are made of natural brown wood. He frequents the brown café quite often, sitting at a corner table that he thinks is suitable for a small group of young, vital, and opinionated people, and as he takes small sips from a glass of beer or a cup of coffee, he takes his notebook from his inside pocket and writes.

The old brown café on the north corner of our street, next to the Concertgebouw:
> A combination of neighborhood café and small, exclusive pub
> Dutch beer (Gulpener) with roasted hazelnuts and/or a hard-boiled egg
> People coming and going
> Lots of loud talking in Dutch spiced with bursts of laughter
> A wooden floor covered with faded Persian carpets
> A large aquarium with ornamental fish, corals, and marine plants
> A few wooden shelves packed with old books
> On the walls works of art, photographs, outdated concert posters
> Everything is in the old style
> Lace curtains frame the window overlooking the street
> A Victorian chandelier casts yellowish light

At one of the tables sits a young man with a woman who seems twice his age. Mother and son? Lovers?

At a corner table three men and a woman, most of the time one is talking and the others, including the woman, are listening, riveted

A bald man sits alone at the big round table in the middle of the café, going through the newspapers

———————

And how I miss Queen Wilhelmina, says Anouk. I hope that this awful war will be over by next summer and we'll be able to celebrate the queen's birthday as we do every year! I feel so important, almost as if I'm a queen myself, every time she visits the Spanish synagogue with her family, and how addicted I've been since my childhood to her processions here in the center of Amsterdam, with all the people celebrating and waiting on the sidewalks waving all those special colored flags they hand out only for the queen's procession and the balloons and the colorful paper windmills that turn on sticks. . . . When I was a girl I climbed up lampposts with all the boys, I wanted to be the first to see the queen arriving. . . . Remember, Sonke, how we all used to stand waiting, and how excited we'd be when the royal cavalry appeared on their gleaming horses, with their glamorous uniforms and helmets and drawn swords . . . I almost fainted I was so elated, and right after the cavalry came the army officers and the navy officers, and the wonderful royal band that played as they marched, and all the closed carriages carrying all the ministers and important people, oh, dear Sonia, I get excited just talking about it. . . . Do you remember? Do you remember the moment—just like a divine revelation—when the open royal carriage appeared carrying our beloved beautiful queen waving to us and returning our love? Oh, how I miss her, my dear Sonke, it's only in Holland that the queen is so close to her subjects, and how I pray that in the summer I'll be able to take my sweet little prince, Sebastian, to watch the procession and introduce him to the queen!

The entire interior of the café is still covered with the same old wooden beams. It seems that the scarred wooden tables and worn wooden chairs have also been here since back then, although it's possible that the original tables and chairs were confiscated for firewood in the winter of cold and hunger that beset Amsterdam toward the end of the war.

But there can be no doubt that the brown wooden counter is the same one. Back then did they serve the same roasted nuts with the coffee and the beer? Aside from the days of the winter of hunger, was there a bowlful

of hard-boiled eggs on the counter back then too? And the bartender—
a pleasant woman with broad shoulders and a smile that reveals horsy
teeth—was there someone like her here back then too?

And if there was, how did she get through the war years?

On more than one occasion, so he had read in the Jewish Historical
Museum library, Amsterdam's brown cafés were the secret hideouts of the
underground organizations active in the city.

It was here, in this brown café, that Sebastian burst onto the scene. That
evening, like many others like it before the war, the two happy couples
were seated at their usual corner table with beers and cigarettes and all
sorts of friends and friends of friends who came and went, and as usual
Martin was eloquently and enthusiastically propounding his ideas, while
Eddy smoked in silence and occasionally interjected with a concise remark
that undermined, in six or seven words spoken seemingly indifferently, the
tower that Martin had built out of hundreds of excited sentences.

Between making a comment of her own and taking a deep drag on her
cigarette and a resolute decision that it would be her last one that evening,
because she had to start considering the baby growing in her womb, Sonia
saw Anouk's lovely face contort in pain.

She gave Anouk an empathic smile across the table and asked, just
moving her lips soundlessly: Contractions?

And Anouk replied with a vigorous shake of her head. Why should I have
contractions? she said angrily. I'm just at the beginning of the ninth month!

Sonia shrugged and looked away, but soon after that, a short scream
escaped Anouk's lips and all eyes were turned to her in concern as she stood
up with a scrape of her chair and ran toward the privy in the café's backyard.
Sonia hurried after her. Wretched groaning came through the privy door.

Anouk, my dear, Sonia said to the closed door, are you alright?

I've got an upset stomach, came the choked reply.

I'm sure you know, Sonia said, that one can give birth at the start of the
ninth month, and even earlier. . . .

It's an upset stomach, Anouk groaned. Last night I ate some bad herring that Martin brought, and since early this morning I've had these terrible stomach cramps.

Maybe I can help you?

How can you help me? Can you rid my bowels of that damned fish?

All of Sonia's attempts to convince her that perhaps, just perhaps, she was in labor were in vain.

Anouk was in such great pain she couldn't walk. The three of them supported her all the way home, the two men carried her up the steep staircase, and when they reached the top floor she ordered Eddy and Sonia to go, and they went downstairs to their apartment to send Nettie's babysitter home and go to bed.

Less than an hour later they were awakened by the sound of Martin's fists banging on their apartment door, and when they opened it he was standing there paralyzed with terror, and Sonia ran upstairs in her nightgown and found Anouk curled up on the floor. While she bent toward her, the poor girl, who was soaked with cold sweat, continued screaming at the top of her lungs that she isn't in labor, she's not giving birth, it's only a badly upset stomach as I've already told you, why don't you understand ay ay ay what terrible constipation, aieee, and the gas pain, but Sonia, if you intend to carry on insisting that I'm having a baby then it's best that you leave me alone and don't do me any favors, aieeee. . . .

Quick, Sonia ordered Martin, who was so terrified he almost had a baby himself, we've got to be quick, we could deliver it here but I think the baby's too big, I think maybe the head can't pass through the birth canal and she needs an urgent caesarean section, and so Anouk was taken kicking and screaming to the Jewish hospital maternity department, suffering incessant labor pains as she sobbed: But I didn't plan to have the baby like this, not now and not like this! Four people had to hold her down so the obstetrician could examine her, and she didn't stop screaming with her ebbing strength that it's not right. And that she hadn't planned it like this, not like this.

The woman moving nonstop behind the brown wooden counter, preparing, serving, joking with her customers, and laughing, is the café's owner and its beating heart.

Her name is Vij, and Yoel has already made up his mind that when he writes the novel, he'll put her in this brown café during the war too. In the novel she'll be the age she is now. And she'll look like she looks now, including that laugh of hers and the short hair, the masculine trousers, and the apron whose strings go over her shoulders and are tied at the back, and also when he writes Eddy and Sonia and Martin and Anouk sitting here with their glasses of beer and nuts and hard-boiled eggs, that is, so long as she's able to obtain beer and nuts and eggs despite the war. He'll describe Vij as a proud, brave Dutch citizen who helps the Dutch underground and places her brown café at their disposal as a meeting and hiding place. And as the story develops, and Sonia will be in desperate need of help, it is Vij who will help her.

Now Sonia sees Anouk and Martin less and less. She has no interest in socializing with Jews like them who only worry about themselves in times of such horrifying rumors about the fate of the Jews in Germany and Poland and about what is happening here in Amsterdam to the east of the river.

Vij finds out that Yoel is a writer collecting material for a book about her country, and she enjoys teaching him a little about the Dutch way of life. She greets him with three kisses on his cheeks the way she greets all her regulars and the way, so it seems, that every Dutch person greets his friends and family. When he asks if they can't make do with less than three, Vij gives her toothy laugh and stresses that the answer is no: One kiss doesn't do the job at all, and you mustn't stop after two either. But there's no need for you to worry, she adds in a low voice, the Dutch are fastidious people who don't really like feeling someone else's spit on their face, so in most cases the kisses don't include actual contact between lips and cheek, they're just air-kisses given at a distance of a few millimeters away from the skin. And beware, she cautions him aloud, shaking an admonishing finger, you've got to kiss in the right order: Kiss number one toward the right cheek, number two to the left, and number three to the right cheek again! Any deviation from this order is liable to end up with a painful collision of faces!

Vij doesn't know that she's going to be a character in his novel. When the idea popped into his mind, he took out his notebook to get it down on paper before he forgot it. When he couldn't find his pen and asked Vij if she could lend him one, she laughed: What's the hurry? Have you decided to write her a love letter?

One day last week Sonia passed through the street and saw that the door of Martin's shop had been boarded up. Next day she went into the brown café where she still visits her friend Vij and heard one of the non-Jewish neighbors saying that it was the Jewish Council that had boarded up the corner art shop. Before the shop was sealed, the man said, they took out all the valuable paintings and all the rest of the rare treasures but promised that they wouldn't be sent to Germany as had happened in similar cases. The shop had been emptied under the personal supervision of its Jewish owner, the neighbor added. And it seems that the guy's got connections because they said that all the important objects would be put into storage and wait there for the owner until the war's over and he'll be able to reopen his shop.

Yoel emerges from the shower after again not managing to regulate the temperature of the water, and after the shower stall door again did not prevent the bathroom from being flooded. He stands barefoot in the water that almost reaches his ankles and looks into the mirror over the sink, and through the misted glass a strange face peers back at him. He no longer recognizes his own face, and he knows that it's not just because he's stopped shaving and his beard is growing day by day. He looks different because he's in the middle of an inner renovation, he thinks, like Amsterdam, in whose every street he sees scaffolding against old walls, cranes lifting bricks and cement, ladders rising from the ground, and construction workers climbing up them and coming down, their heads covered in high-visibility hard hats.

As Sonia rides her bicycle she hears the commotion of the waters storming and bubbling under the paved roads and sidewalks. She hears how, beneath the surface of the city, the primeval abyss is raging in a torrent and seeking to burst out and flood everything. Like every Dutch elementary school pupil, she learned about the history of the water that had covered Holland in the past. More than forty percent of this unique country's area is polders, areas that once belonged to the sea until they were taken from it, and since then have been drained by the Dutch by means of a complex system of dams and canals and windmills. A colored poster that was permanently on the wall in the entrance to her school proclaimed: "God created the world, but the Dutch created the Netherlands." For years this poster greeted the child Sonia every day. Her heart swelled with pride at being a daughter of the diligent and daring Dutch nation, the splendid Dutch nation, the Dutch nation chosen to be God's partner in the Creation and thereafter.

But now, she thinks to herself, the strength of the legendary boy who stopped up the hole in the dike is exhausted. Soon the hole will widen and the water will rise, the depths will again cover the land, darkness will enshroud it. Only the Divine Spirit will hover over the water, if there will still be, in this world, a Divine Spirit.

42

In the dead of nights Yoel stands on his balcony, his eyes on the basement apartment of that same house, and his heart is with Sonia, who remains awake and tense all night. If she lies down in her bed, she does it fully dressed, including shoes. She may fall asleep for a while, but even then, she hears every noise and every murmur. If her ears pick up any suspicious noise, she leaps out of bed before she is fully awake.

When they were already living in Netanya, she still continued this constant vigilance. At night, while asleep, if she heard even the least unfamiliar sound, she immediately leapt out of bed and stood in the hallway.

Only then would she open her eyes.

In the morning, Yoel dons a white shirt, walks the distance to the river's east bank, and goes to pray the Sabbath shaharit morning service in the ancient Spanish-Portuguese synagogue, the Esnoga. He is dazed and even somewhat overwhelmed as he enters the awesome, so solemnly splendid sanctuary, amass with pillars of marble, whose design, by the Jews who arrived in Amsterdam following the Spanish expulsion, was influenced by the First Temple. Its foundations are built on columns submerged deep into the water, and its wooden floor is covered with sea sand to protect it from the dampness permeating from below. Here, generations upon generations of the Rosso family came to pray. In one of these rows of ancient benches, a young Martin Rosso stood alongside his father and grandfather and uncles. Perhaps he returned here in adulthood, perhaps with his wife, Anouk, perhaps with their child, Sebastian, and certainly, at the very least, on Yom Kippur eve, when all the hundreds of seats in the synagogue's sanctuary and the women's section were filled, and in honor of the occasion, hundreds of wax candles were blazing in the huge brass chandeliers hanging from the lofty ceiling of the historic building that, to this very day, does not have electrical lighting.

Does this feeling—that this Spanish-Portuguese synagogue is familiar to him—suggest he was here in his infancy? Or does the place look familiar because when they are in New York for the Sabbath, he likes to go pray at the Shearit Israel Spanish-Portuguese synagogue on 70th Street off Central Park, which, just like the Esnoga, is an old and beautiful building established by Jews expelled from Spain and Portugal, built in exactly the same period and in exactly the same style as the Esnoga, and where the cantor and the heads of the congregation, just as in the Esnoga, honor the Sabbath services by wearing the same impressive cylinder hats?

Or maybe it is just the opposite? Maybe the reason that he always loved to pray in the Spanish-Portuguese synagogue in New York was because, in his subconscious, it recalls to him the Spanish-Portuguese synagogue in Amsterdam?

At the very same moment that the honored congregation members, led by the cantor and the rabbi in a festive procession, are returning the Torah scrolls into the Esnoga's lofty holy ark, when the splendor of the generations is framing the worshippers' top-hat-clad heads, and the grains of sand are scrunching under the soles of their shoes, Sonia and her children are returning from a Sabbath outing to where Jews are still allowed. She parks her bicycle on the sidewalk in front of the house, lowers Nettie onto the sidewalk from the seat behind, and lifts Leo, who has fallen asleep on the way, out of the front basket. When she enters the house's stairwell she meets Anouk, who is on her way out with Sebastian. Fresh and glowing, her honey hair curving next to her meticulously made-up face, wearing a polka-dotted spring frock, Anouk appears as if she is not at all aware of what other Jews in the city, at these very moments, are going through. Sonia cannot control the feeling of animosity mounting in her toward Anouk, and also toward little Sebastian, who is dressed in his cute little blue sailor suit and smiling joyfully as he descends the stairs step by step. He is the epitome of spoiled, she mutters to herself silently, wondering if he too is being fed these days, like her children, just with the bits of vegetables and lentils that the food coupons allow. She recalls that he is a finicky eater, and she realizes that he is merely a baby without sin, but she cannot find in herself the power to restrain the almost-loathing that engulfs her toward him. He is merely a baby, but she feels that every one of his movements comes at the price of her own baby's. He hasn't sinned, but his brown curls seem to bear witness to the danger threatening her blond-haired son.

Yoel lifts his gaze to the magnificent brass chandelier, imagining it brimming with burning candles during the Day of Atonement's Kol Nidre prayer and imagining Martin Rosso the child lifting his eyes to look at them from his place between his father and grandfather. He tries to find familiar notes in the melodies that the cantor and the congregants are chanting, the strains to which the carved doors of the holy ark are opened and the Torah scrolls draped in their exquisite vestments are placed.

Before he sits down again, he checks if the individual compartment under his seat can be opened. Built into each wooden bench in the Esnoga is a compartment that can be locked with a key, and Bat-Ami, when they were here together, was thrilled when she heard that most of these compartments have remained locked for many years. I wonder when they might have been locked, she had said to him. And when he asked her why she thought that was interesting, she said, What do you mean, why is it interesting? If there are compartments that haven't been opened since the war, maybe there are things hidden in them that the Jews left before they were arrested and taken away. Hidden until today.

Finally we meet! Anouk's voice rings out, totally void of fear. Sonia is forced to stop and stand in the stairwell, on the small landing between the house's main door and the stairs leading down to her apartment, Leo's somnolence weighing down her arms. Why have you been avoiding me and Martin recently, dear Sonia? We so much want to stand by your side during these trying days, and you are not letting us!

I'm fine, Sonia mumbles grudgingly. She looks at her neighbor and cannot help but think that even that yellow star sewn onto the front of her polka-dot dress looks like jewelry attached for decoration.

Leo's head is heavy on her weary shoulder, and Anouk is talking and talking and going on about how much she and Martin want to see her more and want to spend time together like before. That is to say, not really like before, Anouk corrects herself, because without Eddy it is of course not the same, but still . . .

I have to go down. Sonia smiles apologetically and is already stretching one leg forward toward the first step, when Anouk lowers her voice and says, You've probably already heard what happened to Garrett and Ulla Feinstein. Sonia stops and asks her what she means by that. She pictures pretty, introverted Ulla Feinstein, who lives with her husband and two daughters on the adjacent street. Her daughter, who had also been registered for the Montessori school, is Nettie's best friend in the temporary classroom operating out of the Jewish teacher's apartment. Because the girls are friends, the two mothers had begun to get friendly and Sonia liked Ulla.

Anouk strokes Sebastian's thin curls. He is pressed close to her legs, wearing his light blue sailor suit. Anouk clicks her pink tongue and says without batting an eye, They found them yesterday! Garrett and Ulla and their two children! In their beds! The gas valve in the kitchen was open—can you believe this?—and all the windows were fastened shut. Sonia finds it hard to breathe, but Anouk continues talking on in a sort of ecstasy: Garrett left a note, she reports. He wrote that he and Ulla had decided to do this because they realized what was about to happen here and believed that they were better off dying in the home they loved, dying together in their sleep, than to see themselves and their children experiencing that which the Jews in the countries to the east are going through.

Sonia's hands are burning. Under Leo's sleeping head, a stain of saliva mixed with sweat spreads onto Sonia's shoulder, but Anouk doesn't stop her rapturous chatter, even as Nettie is chirping from downstairs, Come, Mama, come! Even as Sonia is slowly, slowly descending toward her basement apartment, Anouk doesn't let up, and now she is leaning toward her over the banister. It's awful, she says, and her words spill over Sonia's head from above. It's just awful, how the Feinsteins, such intelligent people and so . . . so Dutch—just so Dutch, do you understand—could even imagine that here, in our beautiful homeland, here in our Amsterdam . . .

When the prayer service is finished, and the small congregation of worshippers goes out for the refreshments served at the kiddush, Yoel holds back inside the Esnoga's sanctuary. He finds it hard to leave. Immediately, a jolly, rotund Jew comes to his side, introduces himself as Kastiel, the synagogue's beadle, and proudly shows him the antique holy ark, the elegant velvet couch on which generations of Holland's kings sat when they visited, and the wooden floor beams that can be raised to reach the water canal underneath the building. Yoel is astounded to witness with his own eyes the quantities of water that are actually flowing underneath the building, whispering in the dark like in one's subconscious. He feels a sense of apprehension, yet he dares not ask his host how the congregation maintains the building's foundation columns, planted as they are in this water over these hundreds of years. Dares not ask if it is possible that these wooden columns may eventually weaken, may eventually even rot away.

As they leave, Kastiel closes the synagogue's massive wooden door behind them, inserts a huge iron key into the keyhole, and turns it twice. That's that, he says, passing a compassionate hand over the metal knob, which is covered with a fine network of scratches. I have locked it. Do you see? Now the synagogue is empty of living Jews, and the souls of the dead Jews are free to wander around inside at their will. In truth, the Esnoga belongs more to the departed than to the living, more to the souls than the bodies. That is why each time we living Jews want to open this door to enter, we first knock and scratch on the knob with this big key. This is our way to lovingly warn the souls that a living body is about to invade their territory.

Sonia breathes a sigh of relief when Anouk and her son go on their way and leave her to go down into the basement.

She doesn't know that after the prayer service in the Esnoga, Yoel will cross the wide street, enter the huge Ashkenazi synagogue, climb up to the Jewish Historical Museum with its historical display, and stand before the wedding scenes being screened in their never-ending loop on the opposite wall. He will wait until the image of the young woman holding the fair, unblemished baby in her arms flickers on the wall, and then he will say to her, *Shabbat shalom, ima yekarah*. A blessed Sabbath to you, my dear mother.

43

It has been years since there have been any small children in Yoel's life. Bat-Ami is correct, he thinks now, when she complains that he is missing the gene that allows one to discern human beings shorter than a meter. It seems that children tend to pass under his conscious radar, and it is no wonder that there is no boy—or girl—also in the latest novels he has written and published. His stories are always populated by mature adult characters who have long ago managed to work out their early lives and to distance themselves in all contexts from their immature early years and from all the helplessness and inconvenience wrapped up in living those years, which so many other authors, for some reason, tend to wistfully write about and return to in their works time and time again. Yoel is aware, of course, of his small grandchildren's existence, and is aware, of course, of the exuberance with which Bat-Ami and the girls discuss them, their nutrition and their eliminations. But he doesn't *see* his grandchildren, that is to say, he doesn't actually perceive them, until they have reached that age when they can communicate like real people. And even if he once did have a special kind of connection with his eldest grandson, Tal, so much time has passed since then.

But here, in Amsterdam, he cannot stop noticing all the little children. Especially babies. Especially babies and their mothers. He cannot stop seeing all the mothers riding bicycles with their babies: sometimes the baby is sitting in a little seat attached to the inner side of the handlebars, his back

pressed into his mother's bosom, the wind blowing into his face, and the
vistas opening before him at the pulse rate of the bustling city all around.
Then there is the baby carried on his mother's bicycle in a sort of triangular
basket made of wood or hard plastic and attached to the outer side of the
handlebars. He also sees babies and toddlers in the parks and museums, in
tramcars and in shops, in the hotel elevator and in the breakfast room. He
observes the movement of their miniature limbs. He observes the changing
expressions on their soft faces. And he marvels at their skill in manipulat-
ing adults to get what they want.

That's it, Anouk says to Sonia. Soon we will be going to America. Daddy
is already taking care of all the details, and it won't be long before we will
be sailing away from here. It is Sunday, and the bells of the church of Our
Lady begin to clang at a quarter to eleven in the morning. They clang and
clang and their thunderous clanging continues for many long minutes. Yoel
crosses the street to the church, goes up to the double gate, and peeks into
the majestically echoing nave. A tall priest in glistening liturgical vestments
comes out to meet him. He radiates cleanliness and peace, and every hair lies
on his head just so. With a broad smile, the priest invites Yoel to enter and
take part in the mass that is just about to begin. At that moment, three or
four blond children gleefully burst forth from the church, racing through the
narrow space between Yoel and the priest, who watches them with affection.

Cold. The sky is a muddy puddle and as he passes the house, he is suddenly
accosted by a piercing, wounding onslaught of hail.

He is cold. The ruddy ivy climbing up the front of the house is also
cold. Its two thin trunks twine together, clinging with all their might to the
shivering bricks, passing above the entrance level and terminating between
the second-story windows in an intricate knot of melancholic branches.

Sonia spends the early afternoon hours ceaselessly rearranging the apartment, while Nettie imposes her own order on her dollhouse, and Leo rolls
a red, slightly deflated rubber ball along the floor and then chases after it in
a joyful crawl. On their way home, they had been struck by a sudden onslaught of hail and Leo panicked. But with the same suddenness that it began,
the barrage has ended, the sun has come out from between the clouds, and
sounds of laughter and merriment are heard from the building's backyard.
Nettie gets up from her dollhouse, drags a chair over to the wall underneath
one of the back windows, and then climbs up and stands on it to better watch
Anouk as she pushes Sebastian back and forth on the hanging swing.

Mama, let's go out to the backyard.

No, Nettie, my sweet. Today we aren't going out to the backyard.

But Anouk and Sebastian are outside, Mama. There's no rain now.

Today we are not going out to the yard.

Oh, but, Mama. It has been such a long time since we went to play
outside!

. . . Fine, my child, okay. If you want to go out so much, bring me your
and Leo's coats, and your hats and galoshes, and we will dress up nice and
warm and go out. But we won't go into the backyard. Instead we will take
a little walk along the street.

. . . Mama?

. . . Yes, Nettie, my soul.

. . . You are not Anouk and Martin's friend anymore, Mama. Right?

The Dutch treat their birthdays with paramount importance, Vij says,
laughing, and points to the tray of cupcakes that today has been placed
on the brown counter next to the basket of hard-boiled eggs. Today is my
birthday, so all my customers must indulge me. When Yoel wishes her a
happy birthday, she ceremoniously selects and holds out to him a paper
liner with a chocolate cupcake topped with white icing and a cherry stuck
in the middle. Here, I especially recommend this one. And while he is
hesitating, considering whether to explain to her about the laws of Jewish

kashrut or simply to take the cupcake and not eat it, she shouts, Mr. Writer, what a bore you are! Do you think I have time to wait for you to decide to do me the favor of taking what you are offered? She immediately laughs, reaches out to pat him affectionately on the shoulder, and says, Hey, no fear! I'm just really blunt. This is also typically Dutch. And while he is still holding the cupcake in the palm of his hand, she tells him about Dutch forthrightness and how Dutch people have a habit of telling a stranger straight to his face exactly what they think about him or his haircut or about some outspoken phrase that the stranger just uttered. Yoel remembers his mother's direct, unconcealed frankness, how she always seemed to be insulting everyone and how he always thought that she did it to distance people from her and to ward off anyone who might be a friend. Nettie and he were also not safe from her tongue-lashings, and he recalls how distraught he had been the day he first brought Bat-Ami to meet his mother, who after listening to what her young guest said, commented: *Och.* I hope you are not really as silly as you sound. On their second meeting, she received a discomfited Bat-Ami with a sour expression as she declared: That dress really doesn't suit you. How lucky that his wife remained stoic all those years when her mother-in-law, almost every time they met, pointed out: You put on some weight, you know?

The cold seems to intensify the loneliness. To be alone in a strange city, especially in a city where the language is incomprehensible to you, is to be as alone as a human possibly can be. You are the most you. Just you. A man walking through a crowd. No one knows him. No one pays attention to him. No one notices that he is there. All around him the city's residents are talking in their stiff guttural language, their heavy language that sounds as clumsy as their traditional wooden clogs.

Everyone is talking to everyone, calling to each other and responding, asking and answering, shouting and whispering and laughing. Only he alone does not belong; only he alone is outside the circle of human brotherhood created by a common language; only he alone is alone. So transparent and voiceless that he often thinks that he doesn't really exist. Today he introduced himself to the reflection of his bearded face in one of the canals. I am Yoel Blum, he had said. The water was dark with drifting dead leaves, and a green-feathered duck floated idly by, dipping its beak here and there after bits and pieces of flotsam.

I am Yoel Blum, said the Yoel above the water to his underwater reflection.

I am Yoel. Do I yet live?

Suddenly, the duck dove into the murky stream and pulled out something, perhaps a fingerling that had survived among the waste.

He looks into the basement kitchens. He cannot pass without peeking in. He sees an oven, a stove, a sink, drying dishes, a stand full of knives, spoons and forks, cookbooks, a countertop, a bowl of fruit. He sees a table and some chairs. He sees that sometimes there are chairs for only one person, and sometimes for a couple or for a family.

Storekeepers, whom he addresses in English, answer him without seeing him. It seems that even the Jewish Historical Museum staff do not see him, even though they meet him almost daily and often help him in his studies and research.

Only when he returns from his wanderings back to the little square, walks past the real estate agency that once was Martin's art shop, turns into the passage under the faded sign, goes down the narrow stairs and into the Mokum Hotel's lobby, does he feel a little more like an actual person: here he has a name, here he has a face, here they speak to him. How happy he is when Achilles meets him with his grinning smile, tells him about some hidden layer he and his lover have discovered in the biography they are currently reading, or shows interest in the progress of his own work of writing. How comfortable he feels when Josephine stops in the middle of her kitchen or serving or cleaning duties to chat with him about the volatile weather or about her poor father, who thinks he is in their village in Curaçao, or about her son, whose medical studies in Hungary she is financing by working from dawn to dusk.

In his room, after opening the door which, again, has collided with the wardrobe door, he closes both doors, greets his sunflower, takes off his shiny jacket, and checks the condition of the havdalah candle wax stain hidden under the bag.

Then he goes out onto the balcony to greet the houses and the back-yards that can be seen from it and adds a greeting to their residents, both visible and concealed—to the dancer and to the psychoanalyst, to the families that he sees from time to time and to the taxidermied animal that never leaves its post on the bureau in the apartment on the left.

Sometimes he plummets into a night's sleep but later wakes up in un-explained panic and can't fall asleep again. When this happened in his childhood, he would summon his mother, who would instantly appear to protect him from all evil. When Bat-Ami started sleeping by his side, her self-assured breathing was what relaxed and soothed him. But now Bat-Ami is not here—in fact he misses her, he really misses her a lot—and that long-standing panic completely fills the tiny room where he lies alone in the middle of the night, in the middle of Amsterdam, in the middle of the universe. From time to time he hears the wails of fire engines as they pass outside, getting closer and closer and then fading away.

What will happen, he wonders, if a fire suddenly breaks out here at the Mokum Hotel? Everything here is made of wood: the floors, the elevator, the stairs, the furniture.

Everything is made of flammable wood. It will all turn into one giant conflagration.

How can a man like himself escape from a fire? Will he have to flee onto the balcony and then leap from the fourth floor to the cats in the yard?

And Sonia hears Eddy's voice. She hears him calling to her, hears him when her children are asleep after she has managed to survive another day with them. From vast distances she hears his voice rising toward her, from the very end of the world, and she has no doubt: it is Eddy's voice. He is calling to her, and she can hear him calling her.

She can hear him calling even as the church bell rings and rings.

44

And despite everything: the beauty. He walks along the street, and without any warning, the beauty floods him with an agonizing, heartbreaking elation. Every two or three days he phones Bat-Ami, and her voice allows the life force to flow into him, although he is not always successful at visualizing her face before him. He tells her about his experiences and about the people he meets. He tells her about his notebooks, which are filling up with the notes he intends to use to write his new novel. And he tells her about how he sometimes stands, simply just stands, in front of a particular painting in the museum or on the edge of a particular section of the canal or in front of a house on whose front wall a crimson shrub climbs, its falling leaves pooling like a red puddle on the doorstep.

He doesn't know how to tell her that this usually so punctual, usually so well-organized husband of hers now frequently loses track of the days. And that this lack of structure does not bother him, does not bother him at all, since he discovered that there is really no difference between past, present, and future. That there really is only one time. And that everything is one.

He admits to himself that sometimes he calls her only to see if she still recognizes him. To make sure he is still who he once was. To confirm that he is real.

Tonight he was walking around Jordaan, the artists' and students' area, between lit-up apartments with shutterless and curtainless windows as huge as shop display windows. All his life he has been imagining and inventing lives happening behind windows that are not his own, imagining and inventing, and here everything is visible and exposed; he can observe human beings like a zoologist studies a rare species of monkey or termite, learning how they prepare their food and put it into their bodies, investigating how they organize and clean their places of habitation and hunt their prey, following their courtship practices and how they raise their offspring, and perhaps even trying to comprehend their motives in all that they do, that is, to discover why human beings carry out these activities day after day and generation after generation.

Earlier that evening he left the Jewish Historical Museum at Mr. Visserplein, a square named after a Supreme Court judge who was suspended from his position during the war because he was Jewish, and walked to the Dutch Theater building. This is where the Jews of Amsterdam are taken to, this is where they are collected before being sent onward. He had already visited the theater complex several times, but this time he wants to observe the area from the outside and to get an idea of what the two-way boulevard looks like at night when the theater and the children's dormitory, one across the boulevard from the other, are deep asleep, and the trams are continuously moving along their tracks down the center of the boulevard, from east or from west and then back again, stopping at the tram stops adjacent to the entrance to the theater or the entrance to the dormitory, one on the north side of the tracks and one on the south, flickering their headlights as if to signal that all is well. He wants to know how all these appear when the dark cloak of night falls upon them: how they look in the gloom to those who have been forced here against their will, who have suddenly been plucked from the routine of a life to which they will never return. He stands and watches how Jewish families are being led inside. He sees the sentries, horrifying human robots, shouldering their long rifles at the doorway of the theater building and at the doorway of the dormitory building. He watches the boys and girls—small, terrified Jews—as they are rushed out of the theater and, in a faltering convoy, are driven across the street and into the dormitory. The children, he knows, would be housed in this narrow, yellow building under the attention of Jewish caregivers until, after a few hours or sometimes a day or two, they would be handed back to their parents and sent with them to the Westerbork transit camp. He knows that at night, under the cover of darkness, members of the Dutch underground would sneak into the children's dormitory. They would access the dormitory's backyard by way of its neighbors and risk their very souls to try to save even one boy or girl from their fate.

From within the dark canals the ducks sound to him, tonight, like squeaking rubber duck toys. Yoel walks along the street where the Museumplein art shops are. The square is deserted this late at night, the museums are closed and silent, yet from the depths of the arched passage between the Rijksmuseum's two wings emerge the boundless, soulful notes of a saxophone. He walks under the stone arches and there, on the sidewalk adjacent to the wall of the eastern wing, stands a lone musician in the dark, his tall, thin body wrapped in a long coat. He hunches forward and then arches his back with every breath he expels from his soul into his saxophone, its swan-like metal neck reflecting distant flashes of light, and the sound that emanates from it is the sound of complete loneliness.

Hunger has formed a crater in his belly by the time he enters the night door of the hotel. So immediately after ascending the four steep flights of stairs to his room, and separating the door from the wardrobe door, he must crouch down on the floor, attack the tiny refrigerator placed between the two incompatible doors, and pull out from its innards some smoked herring in a vacuum pack. He has no choice but to rip open the package and quickly devour its contents while still standing in his coat and scarf. Then he can calm down, but now the room is filled with the stench of dead fish that refuses to dissipate even after he has flung open the balcony door and gathered together the shreds of thin herring skin and the scraps of the package and sealed them into two plastic bags, a bag within a bag, and even after he scrubbed his hands and rinsed his teeth and mouth. At the end, he has no alternative but to descend the four flights of steep stairs, go out into the cold street, and throw the incriminating evidence into a public garbage bin. But the stench seems to seep through the inner plastic bag and then through the outer plastic bag, and then it wafts out of the garbage bin and the smell of death surrounds Yoel, diffusing itself around him in ripples that get wider and wider until it seems that the stench is filling Amsterdam from one end to the other and there is nowhere free of it.

In his dream he died too, but in the morning he knows he is still alive and that this is the morning of Sonia's separation from her bicycle. She didn't believe it when she heard that this, too, was to happen, but a few days earlier she saw the notice posted on the public bulletin board next to the Concert-gebouw, and she read with her very own eyes that all Jews must surrender their bicycles to the authorities. She stood there and read the instructions a second time and then a third time, and she still couldn't believe it. Now she is trying to convince herself that it is possible to live also without a bicycle. Possible. A bicycle is just a couple of wheels, like the wheels of a tram and the wheels of a bus, both of which she has been prohibited from using for a long time now, but nevertheless, she finds it hard to breath when she pedals her bicycle over to the Jewish Council headquarters on Obrechtstraat, and she chokes when she realizes that it will be a long time until she will again be able to do this most basic of activities, one that her body performs almost on its own, as if activated by some primordial instinct she has had since she learned how to walk on two feet and maybe even before then. And now, she and her bicycle are waiting, alongside many more Jews and many more bicycles, in a line that winds along the sidewalk in front of the Jewish Council entrance, so close to the entrance of the forbidden park. Everyone and everything are waiting silently. She also is waiting and silent, waiting and choking. And suddenly her body bends forward and she stretches out her hand to stroke, with trembling fingers, her beloved old bicycle: its wheels, its worn-out seat, its peeling silver-painted frame.

When she staggers out of the Jewish Council offices stripped of her bicycle, the sky is not the same sky and the earth is not the same earth. She is drowning in the air as in slime.

That same morning, Yoel is walking along the bank of the canal behind the Obrecht synagogue. He walks south and goes to the weekday-morning prayer service in a small synagogue near Beethovenstraat, which was founded by Jewish businessmen in a regular ground-floor apartment. Every time he comes here, he studies the apartment's structure and enjoys imagining how a typical Dutch family might conduct its life in an apartment identical to this one: in a kitchen like this one, in a corridor like this, in a living room like this one with huge windows facing the street. Most of the worshippers who stop here for morning service on their way from their homes to their places of business in the city's center are of the generation that grew up in Holland after the war. However, as expected, there are also among them a few Israelis who immigrated to Holland, and one of them tells Yoel, simply because he must tell somebody, that he returned just yesterday night from Jerusalem after sitting shiva for his father. May the Almighty comfort you, Yoel says to him in consolation, and the man continues to relate how he traveled to be with his ailing father just a little more than two weeks ago, and that for ten days and ten nights he didn't budge from next to his father's bed in the Jerusalem hospital. But finally he had to travel home to Amsterdam because he couldn't continue his absence from work, but the moment he landed in Schiphol, he received the message that his father had died, and so the very next moment, he turned around and got on a plane back to Israel. But when he arrived at Ben Gurion Airport, he discovered that he had missed the funeral. You must have been very disappointed, Yoel said to him, and thinks about Bat-Ami, whose father passed away years ago when they were in London.

They cut short their plans and immediately returned to Israel and, after landing, rushed as fast as they possibly could to Jerusalem, where they were told that the funeral had already taken place without them. And Bat-Ami, hurt and dripping with rage, burst into the circle of her mourning brother and sisters, shouting, What did you do to Daddy? Into what hole did you throw him like thieves in the night, hurrying so to cover the blood? But this ex-Jerusalemite, who seemed to be so totally Dutch already, so much so that the stubble on his unshaved face, his sign of mourning, seemed to be growing following a precise regimen, responds that he had no reason to be upset since it is well known that the custom in Jerusalem is to bury the dead the same day.

After the service, he goes into the Starbucks branch next door and orders a tasteless international cappuccino topped with the international heart made out of white cream, and he sits down at a small, round international table. It is almost eight o'clock in the morning, and through the café's glass front wall he watches Dutch high school students descending from the tram-cars and crossing the street on the diagonal. Many cyclists are zooming along on their bicycles on their way to school or work. Two strapping, sleek police horses are trotting along the sidewalk, and in the saddles are two gallant policewomen, their blond hair gathered into ponytails that exactly resemble the tails of their mounts. In the rushing river of bicycles, Yoel discerns a beautiful woman and watches as her little daughter, seated behind her, turns her head to watch the mounted police and their horses. He notices bicycles carrying varied loads, bicycles with an assortment of devices for carrying toddlers, bicycles whose drivers hold the handlebars with one hand only while their other hand presses their mobile phone against their ear. This natural, easygoing way of riding a bicycle belongs only to those who become familiar with bicycles from the moment of birth: erect of back and neck, hair flapping in the wind, they seem to have been created expressly for riding this two-wheeled vehicle. As if only for this is their body structured, are their limbs shaped, do their limbs bend. He sees how they dash across the intersection, cutting through car and bus lanes, cutting over the tracks of an approaching tram, and, in a wide arc, making their left turn. Only Jews are forbidden to ride a bicycle, only Sonia is now trudging along on the next street.

And like every time that he sits in this Starbucks branch, he sees a hunched old woman pushing a tiny dog in a baby carriage. When the old woman sits with her coffee-and-cake, she places the dog on the table beside her plate and serves him a saucer full of cream. When she shuffles to the counter, she carries her doggie close to her heart, and a tuft of its gray fur protrudes from behind her arm. Yoel looks at them and thinks that she is probably one of the older Amsterdam-born Jewish women who had been featured in the documentary film he watched last week at the Jewish Historical Museum library. If this is really the old woman in the film, then she is the same age as Sonia and, like Sonia, lived here, in the Beethovenstraat area, in the years before the war.

He sits and writes, trying with all his might to capture in words the impossible-to-say, looking for letters with which to compose his words but seeing only eyeglasses, a giant mountain of spectacles tossed and piled one on top of the other: spectacles of every prescription, spectacles of every size, spectacles with frames of every color and every shape, men's glasses and women's glasses and children's glasses, hundreds and thousands and tens of thousands, piled up and stacked, one on top of each other, one within the other. And among these countless spectacles, one particular pair, one specific pair which Yoel recognizes by their thin silver frame and by their thick lenses.

45

It is a radiant late morning, and the jolly, plump mandolin player is sitting in his permanent place on the fence outside the Rijksmuseum, except that today, a skinny, bald accordion player is sitting next to him. Together, they are playing—one on the mandolin, one on the accordion—a melancholy melody whose refrain, over and over, sounds to Yoel similar to that of "A Yiddishe Mama."

In the Jewish hospital, Sonia is attending to a woman about to have her seventh child.

When Eddy didn't return and the money he had left her ran out, she told her friend Bett about her predicament. Bett said there was a severe shortage of nurses at the Jewish hospital and that she thought they would be happy to hire Sonia to help out in the various units as need arose. Sonia told her that going out to work was out of the question, because she had no one with whom to leave Leo, but Bett, wonderful Bett, pointed out that she herself was only working the night shift at the moment, and there was no reason why she could not mind Leo the two or three days that Sonia worked. Sonia protested: But during the daytime you have to sleep, Bett. But she insisted: I'll sleep when Leo is taking his afternoon nap. And so, Sonia agreed to the arrangement because she had to make a living.

Thus, on this fine, sunny day, Nettie is in school, Leo is in the house with Bett, and Sonia is working in the delivery room. The patient, a devout Jewish woman from Amstelveen, arrived at the hospital after midnight with strong contractions at the rate of every three minutes. In the morning, when Sonia began her shift, the birth seemed imminent. But as the hours pass, the mother's contractions get farther and farther apart, fading away, as if the baby has reconsidered his plans and changed his mind about emerging into this complicated world.

The woman's heavy limbs move uneasily on the narrow delivery bed. Sonia thinks of her own empty pantry and that too many days have passed since the last time she went out to the farms outside Amsterdam to get food. She will soon have to take her life in her hands and head out there again, but in the meantime she just has to hope that today, between the end of her shift here and the beginning of Bett's, she will be able to pass by the brown café. Since Jews are now forbidden to buy fruit and vegetables in non-Jewish shops, Vij occasionally gives her four or five onions or potatoes from the café's limited supply. Sometimes she throws in a few apples or two or three carrots. Sonia is grateful to Vij and ashamed that she has become a beggar. The Jewish hospital has also deteriorated, becoming more neglected and impoverished than anyone could have ever imagined. Some of its departments are in a state of total neglect and destruction and other departments, those departments that continue to operate, are suffering from a severe shortage of medicines, basic medical equipment, and of course bedding and towels.

Again and again she asks herself why they complied in the first place. If we had not obeyed the orders, she scolds herself, if we had not gone of our own free will to register as Jews, Eddy might not have been taken. Perhaps we could have continued our lives as usual, perhaps we could have remained undetected among the city's non-Jewish residents without drawing any special attention. Perhaps.

Yoel greets the mandolin player, nods to the doleful accordion player, and enters the museum. He goes past the classic portrait paintings and death

stares at him from each and every painting. It stares at him from the portraits of Dutch noblemen with white lace collars, it calls out his name from
the portraits of women with puffy cheeks powdered in bright pink and
with hair tucked under traditional cloth caps, and it flashes at him from
the portraits of babies and children. I am death, death announces to him
from the paintings. I am the death of every human being, the death that is
conceived in him from the very moment of his creation, that accompanies
him into this world and walks with him wherever he goes.

I'm not having any contractions at all, says the woman whose baby refuses
to be born. She sits up on the delivery bed, defeated.

I will go call the doctor, Sonia says to her.

On her way from the delivery room to call the gynecologist for the
woman whose birth seems to be fading, she sees police bursting into the
hospital building. She cannot believe that this is what she is seeing. She
cannot believe that what she sees happening is really happening, that it is
happening right here and right now, and that she is part of it. But after a
terrifyingly brief time, which is also the longest time she has ever experienced, she finds herself in a group of thirty or forty Jews, some doctors
and nurses, some patients who are mobile, and this group is being led out
of the hospital building and into the sun-drenched street. Among those
being taken is the gynecologist, the one she was on her way to call for the
poor mother.

They are all being marched forward by eight or nine immense, faceless
policemen, who with hollers and rifle blows are shoving them, frightened
and hunched, with a yellow cloth star on each and every chest, along
Obrechtstraat and toward Van Baerlestraat. Some patients find it difficult
to walk this fast. Sonia is doing her best to support a young patient who un-
derwent abdominal surgery just yesterday and is too weak and too frail to
manage on her own. It is difficult for Sonia to think about what is happening to her and to understand that this is actually happening to her, because
her thoughts are entirely on each step she is taking together with this pale,

trembling woman who is leaning on her and on wondering whether they will survive the next step.

Yoel feels a need for fresh air and he closes the briefcase in front of him, rises up from his chair, and leaves the study room in the Jewish Historical Museum library and the museum building itself. He walks rapidly, but the suffocating feeling won't leave him, and when he passes through Rembrandt Square he can hear the dead painter calling to him from inside the stone monument, begging him for light. But he cannot fulfill this request because in the meantime the police are shouting and striking at Sonia and the others as the column of prisoners from the Jewish hospital stumbles along the avenue under the blazing sun.

The column falters and deep in Sonia's consciousness she is punctured by the certainty that there is something, something specific and defined, that she is supposed to be thinking now. But she does not know what it is, she does not know what this thing she is supposed to be thinking about is, this step and the next step are the only things that fill her head at the moment, and her terror of the police, and how all this can possibly be happening. How can this be happening? And now here they are in front of the Concertgebouw, Van Baerlestraat is jammed with pedestrians and people in motor cars and in trams and riders in horse-drawn carriages and crowds of cyclists, and all these people, all of them, are just living their lives as usual and going about their business as though this strange little herd of doctors and nurses and patients is not being marched among them, right here on this actual sidewalk, people who in the space of one moment were torn from their freedom and their identity. From within this herd, Sonia tries to make eye contact with any of the passersby, but there is not even one pair of eyes that is willing to acknowledge her. And suddenly she knows what she should be thinking of. Like an arrow, swift and sure, the knowledge pierces through the clutter of thoughts-non-thoughts that encompasses her like a fog: She has two children. She has two children, and these two children have no one else but her.

The police encircle the column trailing along the sidewalk, separating with increasing annoyance the detainees from the commotion on the street. Sonia surprises herself too when she apologizes in her heart to the feeble patient whom she had been supporting, releases herself from the girl's desperate grip, turns sharply sideways, and walks in the opposite direction, against the direction that this group of captured Jews is being marched. *Halte!* comes a sharp shout from behind her, as one of the police guards realizes what she is doing and stops in his tracks. But she continues walking. The world is filled with the baboom-baboom of her heart as she moves away, and again they are shouting to her, demanding that she stop, but she can only think: I must get back to Nettie. I must go back to Leo. And she continues to walk, careful not to break out into a run or to quicken her steps, even when she hears the cocking of a weapon behind her. *Halte Halte Halte* but Sonia holds her head high and says to herself, Do not look back. Her heart threatens to burst, but she just keeps saying, Do not look back, do not look back, and walk slowly, yes, like this, not like a Jewish prisoner escaping for her life but like any normal Dutch woman going about her own business or taking a pleasurable stroll toward the museum.

And now she has merged into the crowd, her back already looks like all the other backs on the street, and she walks slowly and hears how the policemen's shouts falter, lose confidence, subside, and finally die. A few more steps and she has merged into the other pedestrians, merged completely, and as she walks, she reaches under her shirt, into the hollow between her chest and her left shoulder, opens the safety pin, and removes from herself the yellow cloth star.

Yoel feels pain in the hollow between his chest and his left shoulder. Could it be his heart? He does not recall how he returned to the Mokum Hotel entrance, but when he descends and enters the lobby, all sweating and panting, there is a woman with her back to him standing by the reception desk. The first thing he notices is her hair, which is similar to Bat-Ami's hair, and her small, spotted trolley suitcase, which is similar to Bat-Ami's small, spotted trolley suitcase, and the next moment this woman really is Bat-Ami, whom he could not have imagined how happy he would be to see, turning her smiling face to him and shrugging her shoulders in a kind of apology, one hand holding the suitcase handle and the other a transparent plastic pot with a beautiful mauve orchid.

It seems that Sonia has lost her mind after she extricated herself from the line of Jewish prisoners. Or perhaps the sane and reasonable woman she had been up to that moment was still obeying the police's orders and allowing them to lead her to wherever the column was being led, while the woman who escaped and returned to her two children is some other woman. Because just before dusk of that day, when she looks through the tall window in her kitchen, she identifies the banker's confident legs walking along the sidewalk as he returns home, and she bursts out of her basement apartment and rushes, frantic, to the entrance, waiting for him to enter the stairwell and close the door to the street behind him. And then, suddenly dropping herself to the floor, she is clutching his ankles and pleading, Save us, please, sir, save us, save my babies. But he just stands there, just stands there and his stony figure doesn't budge. It doesn't move until the door of the main apartment opens and his wife screams, Leave my husband alone. You're crazy, Mrs. Blum, leave my husband alone! And immediately after, there's also the sound of the door on the upper floor opening and the staircase rings with an urgent shriek of "Mar-tin," and Martin quickly descends to detach the claws of the woman from his father-in-law's ankles, to stand her on her feet that have turned into rags and to lead her, gently but firmly, down the stairs to where her children are waiting for her.

Bat-Ami meets the wonders of the Mokum Hotel. She is introduced to the yawning Achilles and his invisible love. She gets acquainted with the breakfast room, the groaning elevator, and the main entrance that closes from seven to seven. She goes into the little corner room on the fourth floor, detaches the front door from the cupboard door, and places the mauve orchid on the Formica table beside Van Gogh's sunflower, which, miraculously, has not yet withered.

Bat-Ami: Oops, the wardrobe door has opened again.

Yoel: How is it that you brought me an orchid? You don't like orchids.

Bat-Ami: But you do.

When she asks how he possibly manages to write with all those ringing bells cutting off any lines of thought every half hour, he realizes that he must have become so used to the chimes that he no longer hears them. But come and see what I have here, he says to her, and takes her out onto the room's balcony to show her the backyards, the windows, and the figures.

Yoel: And now. Look into the left window, above the dancer's window. Do you see that animal sitting on that bureau?

Bat-Ami: It's stuffed, isn't it?

Later she meets Josephine and tells her she's beautiful, and their first conversation ends with a warm embrace-plus-three-kisses-to-the-cheeks. Her first meeting with Vij also quickly reaches the three-kiss stage. From the brown café she walks alongside Yoel to the Albert Cuyp Market, walks with him along the market stalls, and eats a vegetable salad and falafel balls with him at the Maoz counter. I am not at peace with this novel, he tells her, and I fear that, like me, my readers will not understand how this issue is connected to an Israeli writer of my generation. The tahini could stand improvement, she replies, wiping her lips with a napkin.

When darkness falls, she walks with him along Rokin to Dam Square and sits with him with a beer at his regular Irish pub, at his usual table. If this is a subject that you are concerned about, she says, there can be no doubt that it is connected to you. And if you feel it, your readers will also feel it. And late at night, she returns with him to the Mokum Hotel through the back night door, climbs with him up the four flights of steep stairs to the room, and smiles indulgently as the room door and the closet door again insist on colliding with and wounding each other. She moves his tote bag to make room for her suitcase and discovers the puddle of wax stuck to the carpet.

Bat-Ami: It's not very clean here.

Yoel: The candle dripped when I made the havdalah.

Bat-Ami: So why don't you remove it?

She connects his iron to the power outlet, spreads a sheet of newspaper over the stain, and passes the iron on the paper back and forth as if she were ironing the main headlines. After five or six passes, the wax parts way with the carpet and clings to the paper, leaving the carpet wax free.

Yoel: You're a witch. There's no question.

Bat-Ami: You should talk! Will you perhaps reveal to me the spell by which you changed my husband, an upstanding, clean-shaven gentleman, into a wild motorcyclist who spends his time in pubs and hangs around with stuffed animals?

46

Sonia never again returns to the Jewish hospital.

 People are constantly being taken, arrested, disappearing. Yesterday, on the central boulevard, between the concert hall and the museum square, a man who tried to escape from a different column of Jewish detainees was shot dead. It could have been me, Sonia thinks. Maybe I actually didn't escape from the column. Maybe my bullet-ridden body is the one lying on the sidewalk with that dark, almost black blood oozing out of it and spreading under passersby's feet and between bicycle wheels that are passing and passing.

Bat-Ami stays with him in Amsterdam for only three nights and three days because he did not ask her to come, and when she came, he did not dare ask her to stay.

 He introduced her to the house where his story was taking place, and she was touched as if Sonia and her children were actually there, inside. Look, she said, pointing to the climbing ivy, which just this morning had begun pushing out fresh, tiny red leaves on its bare branches. Just to think, she had whispered, her eyes moist, just to think that Sonia also, this morning, sees these new buds . . .

 They went into the Rijksmuseum to visit Jan Toorop's painting and into the Van Gogh Museum to visit Vincent and finally, also, into the museum of modern art to see an exhibition of works by avant-garde artist Kazimir Malevich. Avant-garde, shmavant-garde, said Bat-Ami, wrinkling her forehead as she pondered the scattering of geometric shapes through which the Russian artist had chosen to express himself. But Yoel stood before the piece *Black Square on White Background*, and knew that this is the way he yearns to write.

Reddish leaves are budding on the ivy climbing up the front of the building, and Sonia wants to think that this new growth is a sign of good things to come, but at midmorning there is a knock on the door and it is Bett, who has come to say goodbye. Her face is ashen: This is it, my dear Sonia. I am about to dive. I've sold my jewelry, including my wedding ring, and used the money to buy a forged identity card and arrange the details of my dive. She lets out a nervous giggle as she shows Sonia the document where her photograph appears under the name and personal details of another woman, a Dutch Christian, who, according to the birth date, is a number of years older than Bett. They found me an address in Utrecht, Bett continues, and Sonia knows that in underground jargon, "address" means a hiding place. She sees the fear in her good friend's eyes. She sees the brown coat, which is too large for her and which she keeps on even as she sits down with her in her apartment. She tries to imagine how it feels to be someone who has been stripped of her husband and of her child and is now being stripped of everything she has ever known, even her name and birth date. It seems the woman in the large coat is not even the real Bett, and that the person sitting here across from her is actually that strange Dutch woman, the Christian, whose name appears on the identity card Bett bought with her wedding ring. The only reason I am diving, whispers Bett, is to stay alive for my little Hennie. But what if someone who hides me panics and turns me in? And how do I know that sooner or later, I and the person hiding me won't be betrayed by someone else? How did I get into this situation, Sonia? How can it be?

After the two friends stand facing each other and sharing the silence for a while, Bett moves slightly back to look into Sonia's face: Do you think we'll see them again, Sonia? Do you think I'll ever again see Hennie and Yop, and that you will find your Eddy?

Realistic writing—to describe things exactly as they look. Surrealistic writing—to describe things not the way they look but the way they actually are.

I think I understand your mother a bit better now, Bat-Ami says to him. Her toughness, her obsession for order and cleanliness, and why every time I tried to embrace her, she thwarted my plan: "Don't come close to me. I *haff* a cold."

On Sunday Bat-Ami said her goodbyes and flew back to Israel, to her patients waiting for her, but the day before, that Shabbat, Yoel made a point to take her to the Spanish-Portuguese synagogue and introduce her not only to this noble community's dead but also to some of its living members. I already have a sense of belonging here, he heard himself proudly saying, as he walked her to the stairs leading to the women's section. Her face beamed out toward him, and during the entire service he realized how happy he was that she was at the Esnoga with him and found it difficult to restrain himself from frequently raising his eyes to the balcony to verify that she was still there. After the prayers, he waited for her at the exit, excited and impatient to hear what she would have to say. Moments later, he saw her coming toward him from the exit of the women's section and for the first time in his life he noticed that she did actually walk with a slight limp, the almost imperceptible limp of a person with one leg slightly shorter than the other. And a wave of sorrow washed over him when he realized that she is right when she says that the years and life events have changed her, and she is right when she alleges that his obliviousness to these changes—to the point where he refuses to even acknowledge the limp she got from her car accident—is because he does not really *see* her. From within this wave of sorrow he stretched out his hand to greet her as she moved toward him in the ancient synagogue's courtyard, he stretched out his hand to the faint limp that only a loving eye notices, he stretched out his hand and gathered his wife to him in a sort of clumsy, side-long embrace. And Bat-Ami smiled at him, slightly amused and slightly puzzled, but willingly folded herself into his embrace.

That night she sat in his room in the Mokum Hotel, on the bed that might have been a wide single bed or a narrow double bed, and read everything he had written since his return to Amsterdam.

These are just sketches, he warned her when she picked up his pile of forty-page notebooks. It's not even a first draft of a novel, just some scribbles, a sporadic collection of reminders and ideas, some wild experiments from which I might, just might, be able to, eventually, create the book that I believe I want to write.

Alright, alright! She waved her hand at him. Please don't distract me. So he sat down on the chair, sat down next to the sunflower in its bottle and the orchid in its pot, and watched her read, searching for clues in the fluctuating expressions on her face, his heart leaping every time she smiled or moaned or even simply turned a page, and relaxing each time she finished reading one notebook and opened another.

He looked at her figure, sprawled on the bed in her baggy pajamas and blue-framed reading glasses, and he thought about their embrace today in the Esnoga's courtyard and wondered if, years before, he really comprehended the significance of that serious car accident on this woman, his wife. Had he really, but really, comprehended how critical her condition had been then? How the doctors had already almost given up? He had stayed, of course, at her side in the hospital. He had done everything that was expected of him. But he did not scream. He did not go to pieces. He did not tear the heavens to shreds with prayers for her recovery. He probably hadn't even admitted to himself that he might lose her, just as he had never admitted to himself that he loves her. Yes. Not merely feels attached to her but loves her. Loves.

47

T oward evening Sonia climbs the stairs to the house and she is bereft of strength and emotion, so hollow she feels the wind whistling through her with every breath. She goes up the stairs of her house and each and every step rises before her like an insurmountable wall. When she gets to the second story, she furtively passes the apartment of the banker and his wife, whom she has not seen since that day when she extricated herself from the column of prisoners taken from the Jewish hospital to who-knows-where.

Yoel is alone again. The rain is ceaselessly falling onto the sad canals, pedestrians are struggling against the merciless winds, and on the street corners, trash bins are collecting the skeletons of umbrellas that the winds bent and broke.

In the museums, death reappears to him from each and every masterpiece. He sees the death of the subject, the death of the painter, the death of the observer. He sees the finality of all things.

Was Rembrandt van Rijn successful in capturing the secret of his own enigma in even one of the eighty self-portraits he painted throughout his life? Did Vincent van Gogh, who painted self-portraits in winter and in summer, in his youth and in his maturity, with and without the pipe, the hat, the ear?

And what unacknowledged mystery is solved for Yoel in Marc Chagall's self-portrait, which, for some reason, he often visits on the Stedelijk Museum's first floor, where Chagall is sitting in a typical Chagallic setting, painting a self-portrait in which his head floats above a neckless body, and his hand, the hand with which he holds his palette of colors, is a hand with seven fingers.

Now she mounts the stairs. The stairs are slippery cliffs and she climbs up them to the top floor and knocks on the door.

Anouk opens the door, and the freshness emanating from her smacks Sonia in the face. *Och!* Finally you're here, Sonia dear! Come. Come in.

Sonia does not enter. Where is Martin? she asks.

Anouk hurries inside to call her husband, and Sonia tries to steady herself.

She looks at the painting by Toorop, which is still hanging on their living room wall, its waves still breaking.

Sonia.

Martin is standing in the doorway and she tries to say something to him but her voice is lost. Martin . . . those people you told me you know . . . the people from the student underground . . .

He looks at her intently.

From his place next to his improvised desk, Yoel also looks at her. He looks at her and at Martin and at this specific moment of theirs and sees everything that preceded this moment, everything that followed it, everything that could have happened had this or had that.

I am asking you, says Sonia to Martin. I am asking that they hide my children.

Leo is nudging the red rubber ball. He screams with joy and crawls on all fours after the slowly rolling underinflated ball. He grabs it between his two hands, sits on the floor with his legs crossed, utters an enthusiastic da-da-da-da, and again, with cries of joy, pushes the ball. He crawls after it quickly, then sits down again, looks up in wonder, calls ma-ma-ma, and when he smiles toward her he reveals two tiny emerging incisors.

Yoel stays in his room for entire days. He sits and writes, goes out to the balcony, and then comes back in again and sits and writes some more.

When he is sitting and writing, he sometimes hears the bagpipes of the plaid Scotsman from Museumplein, which is strange, since for a while now, he has not laid eyes on the man himself and was certain that he had gone back to his country.

His heart sinks each time he hears the rising-falling wails of a passing emergency vehicle. That's it, he thinks, here come the police to arrest Anne Frank.

There are long hours when he doesn't hear a thing.

Toward evening, he forces himself to drink a glass of water, to run a comb through his knotted hair and his Robinson Crusoe beard, and to take himself out for a walk the way one takes out a dog. While he is walking, his eyes wander to the windows he passes, into the apartments, some of which he is already familiar with their rooms, their objects, and their tenants. Are you alright? Bat-Ami asks him on the phone. And he answers, of course I'm alright, and smiles to himself sadly without telling her that at this very moment he is passing by the apartment where there is always a jar of tubes of paint waiting on the windowsill alongside another jar with six or seven paintbrushes in various sizes.

He usually takes himself out for his walk at the hour of the day when many cyclists are making their way home from work or school, alone or with their children who have finished school or day care. Yoel sees a father and his teenage daughter riding next to each other, sees a pair of parents, each of whom is transporting a child behind them, sees a family cycling together on bicycles of different heights.

As he is walking one day on the bank under Obrechtstraat, he feels that someone is watching him and he raises his head, and his eyes meet the grief-stricken, weary gaze of a large water bird with a long beak and mussed-up and faded feathers standing close to the water on long, thin legs. For a moment, Yoel and the bird are kindred spirits, united in body and soul. An elderly cyclist passes in the opposite direction, pedaling steadily while talking to a boy mounted behind him, a boy who may be his grandchild and whose face perhaps slightly resembles that of Yoel's eldest grandchild. Thoughts of Tal send the faintest shiver down his spine, and his winged comrade also shivers slightly and lowers its beak. But it does not move from its place or change its focus, even as Yoel photographs it for a memento.

One day he is walking by the house when the mother arrives with her two children, and when the girl gets off the bicycle's back seat, he sees that she is crying, and her mother stands at the edge of the sidewalk and pulls her daughter to her while stroking the head crowned with thin blond braids and saying comforting words. It seems that something happened to her in school. Maybe her little friends betrayed her, or maybe somebody—a boy, a teacher—insulted her, said something that hurt her tender soul and will never be forgotten, not even after many years.

He sits in his room and writes, sits in his room and writes, sits in his room and writes.

Sometimes he talks to himself out loud. Scolding, praising, listing urgent duties.

And sometimes it happens that he will suddenly utter Dutch words into the silence: *Goedemorgen.*   *Gracht.*   *Ik spreek geen Nederlands.*

Leo crawls on all fours around the narrow apartment, pushing his little wooden car with one hand.

Leo pauses, abandons the car, picks up an unidentified crumb between his thumb and forefinger, and lifts it up to his eyes for a good look.

Leo continues his wanderings and finds his mother's net basket on the floor and in it are three potatoes. He yanks at the edge of the basket and knocks it over, sits back on his diaper-padded rear end, and peers at the basket, which is now lying on its side. Then he takes a potato that has rolled out of the basket onto the floor and crawls, one hand holding the potato, to the next room, to his crib. He pushes the potato between the bars of the crib, lays it down, and immediately turns around and crawls swiftly, with rapturous cries of da-da-da, to convey the remaining two potatoes.

Yoel wanders all the way to the De Pijp area, passing Etty Hillesum's house, and south of the city market he goes into Sarphatipark, another large public park that Jews were forbidden to visit during the war. He walks on a thick carpet of rotting leaves, while looking down at him from the center of the park is the statue of Samuel Sarphati, the Jew this garden was named for, who was a doctor and businessman but primarily known as the designer of Amsterdam. Once he leaves there, Yoel searches for the synagogue on the road above the market, where three or four other Jews hid in the niche of the holy ark during the war. He hunts along the street a number of times, back and forth, until he notices a Star of David engraved on an iron plaque at the top of a staircase of a narrow building, and beneath it, in Hebrew letters worn with age, are the words: "Arise, be our help, and redeem us for Your mercy's sake."

Sonia walks along Market Street, as they instructed her.

She is dressed in long, dark clothing and a black hat, as they instructed her. She pushes the baby carriage in front of her, as they instructed her.

In the low wooden carriage sits her son, whom she loves.

A few days ago, a member of the student underground came to her apartment, a short girl who introduced herself as Katya. Katya stayed with her and the children for a bit as she observed the children closely.

The next day, another underground member, a man, came and informed her that they had an address for Leo.

He gave her instructions and told her that Katya would be her liaison.

And now it is happening.

Leo sits in the carriage, his back straight. It is hard for him to move because he is wrapped in his checkered coat, and under the coat he is wearing three layers of clothes, and under the three layers of clothes he is wrapped in three diapers. Other clothes and diapers are folded on the bottom of the carriage, as many as she could hide under the blanket he is sitting on. Surrounding him, stuffed between his body and the carriage sides, are his decorated tin plate, the orange tin cup that he is used to drinking from, the underinflated red rubber ball, and the small wooden car. Leo loves outings, and even now he is watching the world with interest and delight, his eyes swallowing up the market street sights—its stalls and colors and the multitude of people filling it, all of them preoccupied with their own affairs.

Sonia pushes the baby carriage in front of her. She pushes deep within the market, near the food stalls that are at this hour ensconced by busy crowds, and suddenly, at the right of the carriage, she catches sight of Katya, the short underground activist who had visited her just a few days ago. Katya's appearance is not supposed to be a surprise for Sonia, because this is exactly the way they told her it would happen.

But she is nonetheless surprised.

Katya, that Katya is perhaps not her real name, walks next to Sonia. She is also wearing long dark clothes and a black hat. Katya does not resemble Sonia, if only because she is especially short and Sonia is tall, but, nevertheless, their black clothes create a certain resemblance.

Katya walks next to Sonia without looking at her, and Sonia continues pushing the carriage in front of her and walking straight ahead. She walks into the throng without turning her head to the left or to the right.

Sonia's mind is empty of all thought.

As they are walking, as the two of them are walking side by side without looking at one another, Katya reaches out a hand, a small, thin left hand, and rests this hand on the carriage's metal handle. Sonia, as she has been instructed beforehand, removes her right hand from the handle.

Another few steps, and Katya also places her right hand on the carriage's handle.

Now the carriage is being pushed by Katya's two small, short-fingered hands, and just one of Sonia's large, long-fingered hands.

Sonia commands her left hand to let go of the handle. It lets go.

Now only Katya is pushing Leo's carriage.

Sonia continues walking next to Katya without holding the handle of the carriage at all.

This whole process did not take longer than ten or twenty seconds.

When they reach an intersection, Sonia turns sharply to the left. Without the carriage, without her baby, she turns into a side street and disappears into the crowd.

Katya continues walking straight ahead. Pushing the carriage in front of her.

Taking Leo away.

Sonia walks a few steps. And then a few more. Then she collapses and falls to her knees, screaming soundlessly.

Once, at the end of a family picnic in the Jerusalem Forest, they had returned to where they had parked the cars and near the Subaru's front right wheel lay a starved, injured Siberian husky. What a beautiful dog, exclaimed Bat-Ami, even though the dog was nothing but skin and bones and dirty fur. Who knows what dangerous ticks this dog may be carrying, what germs, Yoel warned, but Bat-Ami put the dog into the back seat of the car and brought her home and fed her and bathed her and took care of her, and Zohar immediately declared that she wanted to adopt the dog. Then, after four or five days, Bat-Ami took the dog to a veterinarian to scan for the electronic identification chip that must, by law, be implanted in every dog so she could find the dog's legitimate owners. The veterinarian carefully passed his scanning device behind the dog's ears and along the back of her neck and finally declared that the dog didn't have an electronic chip. But Bat-Ami did not let up and insisted that he keep looking. She had no doubt that this beautiful, clever dog belonged to someone who was missing her, and she wouldn't allow the vet to give up until he had scanned the entire length and breadth of the huge Siberian husky's body—every single millimeter. All the while, the dog was lying on the examination table without moving, her blue eyes looking at Bat-Ami with gratitude as if she understood everything, until finally the chip, the size of only a grain of rice, was discovered in one of her hind legs, where it had wandered under her loose skin, and the vet checked the registration on the veterinarian's association website and gave Bat-Ami the owner's details, so that very same day Bat-Ami dialed the telephone number that the vet had given her and the man who answered the phone almost choked when she told him that she had his dog. They've found Blue! he shouted to his background voices, and Bat-Ami heard the voices changing into cries of joy, and the man told her that the dog had been stolen from them over a year ago when they were hiking in the north, near Rosh Hanikra, and they had already given up any hope of ever seeing her again, and when he asked if he could come and get her, and Bat-Ami asked when he wanted to come, he sounded as if he didn't understand the question. We live in Gush Etzion, he said, we are leaving this very moment, and a light-colored Ford Transit stopped outside the house less than an hour later, all its doors opening in one fell swoop, and a religious family—a father and mother and seven or eight kids—poured out of the van, all of them crying with joy and hugging the dog, who was leaping excitedly on each one in turn, and hugging them, and laughing out loud too. Yoel had never imagined that dogs knew how to laugh like this.

48

There is a stretch of time, a short one as long as eternity, when Sonia continues taking Nettie to the temporary class in the Jewish teacher's apartment. Sonia hasn't slept since she gave up Leo into the hands of the underground. She does not sleep and she does not eat. In the mornings, she leaves the house before daybreak to clean the brown café. I won't agree to anything that may endanger your life, she had said to Vij when the woman implored her to hide with her daughter at her place. But I am willing to work for you for whatever you are able to pay me. Until the sun begins to illuminate the day, she has time to wash and dry all the wooden tables and wooden chairs, to lift the wooden chairs and place them upside down on the tables, to place all the previous day's empty beer bottles into the wooden crates, to take out the trash, to wash the glasses and plates and ashtrays, and to scrub the wooden counter and the wooden floor.

Slowly, the brown café is flooded with glowing sunlight. When the sun has risen, Vij arrives, and the two women peck at each other's cheeks three times and look into each other's eyes and say, Now, another day begins. Then Vij places some money into Sonia's hand and puts some scraps of carrot, onion, and parsley, and sometimes also an apple or two eggs, into her basket. Housewives are already opening their apartment windows when Sonia passes on the street, shaking out their bedclothes, beating carpets. When Sonia enters her house, her little girl is already awake and dressed. Don't give me away, Nettie's eyes beg her. Don't give up on me too. Look how independent I am; look how easy. Look how I don't bother you. Don't give me away to strangers like you gave away my baby brother. Sonia plaits some fine braids into Nettie's hair and they leave on foot. Hand in hand, they go forth into streets that have become the streets of a strange city.

On the road that leads to the market there is a store with colorful wooden toys in the style of bygone days. Yoel goes in, wanders between the jam-packed shelves, and studies the toys. With great care, he plays the music boxes with the rotating mechanisms, touches colorful cubes, and pushes along wooden trains whose cars can be dismantled and rebuilt. Then he pulls the strings of the hanging Pinocchio doll, and it moves its wooden hands toward him and looks at him above its long nose as if they have once both met.

He didn't want to visit the Anne Frank House. It was enough for him to see the line that stretched from the famous building's entrance on Prinsengracht all the way along the bank of the canal, every day of the week, every hour of the day, and in every type of weather.

But Bat-Ami, when she visited him, said that it was impossible for him to write a novel about the war years and about hiding Jews without seeing Anne Frank's house from within.

This isn't even Anne Frank's house, he told her. It is the factory building in which the Frank family tried, but failed, to hide.

So what? Bat-Ami asked.

In fact, they emigrated from Germany and lived in a different neighborhood entirely, he tried to explain to her. They lived on a lovely boulevard not far from Sarphatipark, and up until the time that all the Jewish children were expelled from their schools, Anne had studied in a Montessori primary school. The same school, you know, that Nettie was registered for and had started in grade one. The one you and I passed on Shabbat when we returned from services at the Esnoga.

They arrived at the Anne Frank House in the late morning, when the line stretched out to the sidewalk, turned ninety degrees to the left, and filled the entire length of the street parallel to the canal. Most of those waiting looked young and not Jewish, and the weather was fickle: one moment it was raining, and umbrellas in an array of colors soared above the line; the next moment the skies cleared, and the umbrellas were folded. Yoel shivered, perhaps because of the cold wind, and watched the falling leaves whirl over the people's heads.

Look at that, Bat-Ami said to him, pointing to a sign warning those standing in line about the dangers of pickpockets. It's really a fabulous idea, she said, and grinned.

Instead of standing uselessly here in line, you can make good use of your time to do a little pickpocketing. But Yoel found it hard to smile. His thoughts were weighed down because of the gravity of the events that were happening at this very moment to Sonia and her children as well as to poor Anne Frank. When Bat-Ami showed him that her cell phone was suggesting that she connect to the Anne Frank House Wi-Fi, he became totally confused: If the Frank family hideout is connected to the net, why don't those hiding use it to tell the world of their plight? Why are they not using the internet to call for help?

They were nearing the head of the line. On either side of the building's entrance, photographs of Anne Frank's life and quotes from her diary were being screened. "*A day will come and the war will end,*" said one of the quotes, "*A day will come and we will again be people, and not just Jews.*" Here, too, he hears the neighboring church's bell clanging away. Yoel knows that the Frank family members hiding behind these very walls, which he and Bat-Ami are standing next to at this very moment, can hear the bell's clanging every quarter of an hour. And he knows that they will continue hearing it until each and every metal bell in Amsterdam had been appropriated to feed the German arms industry.

Anne dreams of becoming a great writer. Through the almost completely sealed front office window she watches dirty children playing along the canal and expresses her desire to reel them to her with a fishing pole, to bathe them, and to mend the rips in their clothes. She enjoys the sights of the cars, the boats, the rain. She finds a funny dimension in the squeals of the electric tram's wheels, and she affixes to every woman who passes on the street a résumé and a husband.

Reluctantly, Yoel purchases a ticket and follows Bat-Ami into the stream of visitors who are ecstatic to have finally reached the head of the line. He follows her from room to corridor and from corridor to a steep stairwell and from a steep flight of stairs to another room and another corridor, at whose end is a camouflaged cupboard and behind the camouflaged cupboard a door that opens into another, even steeper, flight of stairs. Day after day, men and women and children follow this route. They all go up and go down, and they all look into the rooms of the house and into the very depths of Anne's soul.

At the end of this pleasant tour, the hordes of visitors arrive at the museum's modern and spacious souvenir shop, where they can purchase a copy of that mega-bestseller, *The Diary of Anne Frank*, in the language of their choice.

They can also purchase a fresh, new notebook, one that is exactly the same as the checkered-covered notebook that Anne used for her diary. They can write their own bestselling diary in this notebook, especially if they get lucky and become entrenched in the middle of some war that breaks out and allows them the opportunity to hide away under similar remarkable and inspiring conditions. In addition, the shop offers a variety of Anne Frank House miniatures alongside other typical Dutch souvenirs, such as miniature windmills and wooden clogs. It is almost as if the entire story of the young girl's imprisonment in this awful place, her exposure by a Dutch informer, and her arrest by the Dutch police, who sent her to her death, is nothing but an elaborate myth that should somehow make the

Dutch people proud. Yoel tries to imagine what Anne and her family feel when they see the museum's ultimate offer: a do-it-yourself kit for a charming dollhouse that is none other than a perfect replica of Anne Frank's house with all its rooms and stairs and passages, both visible and secret. What does Anne feel when she sees boys and girls assembling the colorful cardboard model and playing with it, not to mention the captivating computer application—free on the Anne Frank museum website—where users can, to their amusement, virtually meander through the house's convolutions, virtually go behind the revolving bookcase, and then virtually climb up into the annex and hide.

In the middle of the night, Sonia once again awakes from a brief nap in a panic. It was Eddy's voice that woke her, and this time he not only called her name. This time he also said something to her. But what? What did he say?

49

In the morning Achilles looks tired and especially unkempt. Yoel goes into the dining room and finds the back door open and the tabby cat standing on the buffet table and modeling the shape of the Hebrew word for cat—חתול—with its head in the tray of sliced meat and its upright tail the perfect model of the lamed letter. Yoel takes for himself a small bowl from the stack of small white ceramic bowls next to the wrinkled apples and the yogurt at one end of the buffet. However, on the bowl's rim, a thin black line curves, and because he cannot be sure whether it is a crack or a hair, he returns the bowl to its place and leaves.

It's getting too dangerous. It's getting more dangerous from day to day and from hour to hour. Many Jews already have nothing to eat, and the synagogues, including the Obrecht synagogue, are serving as soup kitchens. They are also selling yellow fabric stars at a subsidized price. Very soon, Anouk reveals to Sonia secretly, very soon we will be leaving for America. Sonia does not respond to her words because she doesn't feel like reacting and because she doesn't have the strength to talk to Jews who collaborate with the enemy.

Yoel would have liked to write about the architectural significance of Amsterdam, about the implication behind the labor invested in the rows of tiny reddish bricks, about the stylized cornices above the windows and the artistic embellishments that adorn every single building. But early the next morning, Sonia is walking along the street, and across the road the police are evicting a Jewish family from their beautiful art-nouveau-design house. The members of the banished family are trying to walk proudly to the truck that has come to take them away, but the wailing little children, the heavy suitcase, the elderly grandmother who is having difficulty walking, delay them, which annoys the police, who end up shouting and forcefully dragging them away. Sonia knows she cannot wait a moment longer, and one evening, that same short, young girl, who may be Jewish and may not be Jewish, and for whom Katya may be her real name or her underground alias—who knows?—comes to her door.

Sonia cannot control herself. She falls on Katya with animal-like howls: My baby! Where is my baby?

Your baby is in a safe place, Katya tells her unsmilingly. I don't know where he is, but as we promised you, we have given him to a good family in a village.

When she notices Sonia's trembling, her expression warms slightly and she adds: With his blond hair and blue eyes, you can be sure that this family won't have any problem presenting him as one of their own.

Nettie can see how Sonia is trying to keep herself from falling into pieces, and Nettie knows. Nettie lies in her little bed. She lies next to her brother's empty bed and listens to the conversation between her mother and the woman, and she knows.

The next day she is also handed over.

In the Museumplein, tourists are continuously being photographed in every possible variation next to, on, and around the sculpted **I am**sterdam sign. They crowd around the amateur acrobat street performers and enjoy leisurely impromptu concerts in the space beneath the stone arches. They are constantly photographing themselves and their loved ones, and Yoel thinks of the countless photographs in which he has been immortalized in the background as a bearded figure in a motorcycle jacket. From morning to night, the plump mandolin player sits on the fence and happily strums away. One day, a teenage boy and girl are standing in the crowd. They stand face-to-face in the rain, a shared umbrella over their heads. As Yoel approaches, the boy is saying something and the girl (in a purple coat, an orange scarf, and cheerfully colorful pants) is listening to him, trying to use her umbrella to hide her eyes, which are dripping tears.

As noon approaches, Sonia tightens Nettie's light-colored braids and pretties them up with some pink ribbons. She places the girl's satchel on her shoulder. The satchel has been emptied of books and notebooks and has been packed with some clothes. Together, the two walk through the cold streets, across the boulevard, over the stone bridge, alongside a brick wall, and then pass over another bridge, a smaller one, connected to the canal's bank. Young laborers are running along the bank, pushing flat-bottomed cargo barges. They are holding long sticks in their hands and using them to push the schuyts along in the water. Beyond the third bridge, the street is crowded with girls and boys who have just been let out of the municipal school and mothers who have come to take their young children home, and Sonia and Nettie are swallowed up between all the mothers and children. Presently, a woman on a bicycle emerges from the crowd, and sitting on the bicycle behind the woman is a child swathed in a plaid cape. A few more minute pass, and Sonia also leaves.

On foot. Alone.

50

Of the approximately one hundred and forty thousand Jews of Holland, only about thirty-eight thousand survived the war years. Including children. Sonia, for example, has purchased for herself a false identity and found shelter and employment at the old-folks home in the city's northwest. She feeds weary old people, washes shriveled bodies, and changes soiled diapers with clean ones. She does all these things quickly and quietly, without thinking about anything or feeling anything. Between shifts, she sleeps in the home's attic, on a tattered straw mattress that she shares with the caregiver who works the other shift. It seems as if entire eternities have passed since she lived in the de Lange house. Entire eternities since she was Eddy Blum's wife. Entire eternities since she was Nettie and Leo's mother. She doesn't know where they are. She doesn't know if they are being properly cared for. And she doesn't know if she did the right thing or if she should have perhaps kept them with her, no matter what the consequences. Now she is sitting in the old-folks-home dining room ladling spoonful after spoonful of thin pea soup into the mouth of a gawping old woman. Now the other caregiver is supposed to be resting on the mattress in the attic, but here she is, entering into the dining room, coming close to Sonia until she is almost touching her, and whispering into her ear, You are a Jewess. Don't think I don't know that you are a Jewess. Sonia freezes for an instant but immediately recovers and dips the spoon into the bowl, recovers and raises the greenish liquid to the wrinkled mouth that opens to receive it like a baby bird.

I have no idea why you suspect me, she says, but if you like, I can show you my papers and you can assure yourself that you are wrong.

Your papers? The girl lets out a snort of disdain. What are your papers worth? You are Jewish, and I'm not sure that I'm willing to risk my life for you.

The church bell fills the air and Yoel counts five rings and goes out to the room's balcony. It rained today and now the sky is covered with layers of dark clouds. They say tomorrow there's going to be a storm, Achilles had told him earlier, but Yoel doubts the ability of a Dutch storm to be truly stormy. He stands on the balcony and sees that a drizzle has started and the birds are already gathering together into the trees for their night's sleep, gathering and quietening, and only one chirp, croaky and anxious, repeats itself, getting croakier and more fretful, becoming more agitated and distressed the stronger the rain gets.

Here and there a man or a woman appears in the windows facing the balcony, fragments of lives are revealed. But the psychoanalyst is not there, only her computer screen saver is alive and breathing in her abandoned room, and in fact, Yoel has not seen her today, or yesterday, and it's hard to say that he is not concerned for her welfare. The electric lights have not yet been turned on in the windows on the left, the dancer has not yet returned from work, and the stuffed animal is merging with the growing darkness. But there is a warm glow from the lower apartment on the right, and in the window Yoel can see the end of a light-colored sofa, a section of a book-stuffed shelf, and some moving figures.

What are they doing there inside? Talking, laughing, living. Maybe the mother is watching cartoons on television with her children, maybe they are stacking blocks into a tower or putting a puzzle together, and maybe the baby is hanging onto the chair on which the little girl is sitting preparing her homework, hanging on, rising up, and standing on his feet.

Did the little girl cry again today when she got home from school?

Now, perhaps, the girl has asked for a drink. Her mother makes mugs of hot chocolate for the three of them, and then she opens the radiator taps and turns up the heat because it's getting cold outside. Then the apartment door opens and her husband, the lenses of his glasses all fogged up, returns from work and he swings the children up in his arms, up to the ceiling and up to the sky, and calls them and his wife by endearing nicknames, and his wife, laughing, gets up to also fix him a cup of hot chocolate. The apartment is warm and cozy, and they will spend a relaxing evening until it is time to bathe the children and put them to bed. Tomorrow is a new day. They say there's going to be a storm.

Night. Sonia is lying, dressed and alert, on the straw mattress in the old-folks-home attic. Her body burns with fatigue, but she does not allow her eyes to close. Perhaps the other caregiver, the one whose shift it is now, has already gone and informed the police. Not because she is mean, but because she is a law-abiding Dutch citizen, and because she wants to live. When the decrees against the Jews had just begun to gather momentum, Amsterdam's laborers had gone on strike and demonstrated in the city streets for a few days to protest these decrees. But today, Amsterdam is a place where anyone hiding a Jew or helping a Jew in any way is risking his life. The building is deep in slumber, but Sonia can hear coughs, sighs, and the shuffling of old feet from its many corners. Outside the rain is pouring down. The wind is beating the windows. They say there's going to be a storm soon, and by all the signs, Sonia predicts that this will be a severe one.

After midnight there comes strong knocking at the main door, strong knocking and orders: Open! Police!

That's it, it's all over, Sonia says to herself. They've come to take me away. It's over. She jumps up from the mattress, quickly does up her coat and her shoes, and at the same time thinks Nettie and thinks Leo and asks herself if there is a chance that she can escape or hide. She hears the other caregiver opening the main door. The police shout, and from their shouting she gathers that they are here to arrest a couple who just recently came to live in the home, a man and a woman.

Sonia had been awed by the respect and tenderness that these two elderly people have expressed toward each other, and now it turns out that
they are Jews and that the police have come to this old-folks home to take
them away to the place where they take old Jews.

Sonia hears shouting, and the sounds of dragging and shoving, and
wailing and sobbing. She hears and she wants to die, to die she wants,
to die.

How, before it was cut down, those branches of the almond tree in their
yard in Jerusalem (bare, save for the smattering of bitter fruit still clinging
to them) used to beat against their bedroom window on winter nights,
scratching against the windowpane as if asking to enter.

Before dawn, the other caregiver ascends into the garret. You must go
down now to work, she mumbles, embarrassed, when she sees Sonia
dressed in a coat instead of her pressed white work uniform.

Sonia replies: I have to leave.

They say, the girl warns her with genuine concern, that there's going to
be a huge storm today, and Sonia looks her straight in the eye, says thank
you, and immediately picks up her skimpy bundle and descends, almost
sliding, down the steep stairs.

The office of the old-folks home's director is still empty so early in the
morning. She passes it. If he were here, she could have asked him for her
final salary, but she cannot allow herself to wait until he arrives.

As she leaves the building, a barrage of hailstones smacks her face.

It's only since I have begun taking part in these meetings, said Raphaels
when they were again chatting in the synagogue after Sabbath service,
only since I have spoken to other Jews who were also hidden in their
childhood, that I have become aware of the anger hiding within me all

these years. It turns out that all of us—anyone who was passed from hand to hand, from one parent to another at a young age—suffer, even today, from similar problems, and especially have difficulty forming emotional relationships.

After their latest conversation, Raphaels invited Yoel to visit him in his home in the northwest of the city, and they've arranged Yoel's visit for today. At breakfast, Josephine tells him that public transportation has been canceled for the day in anticipation of the forecast storm, but this meeting at Raphaels's is important to Yoel, and he decides he will take a cab. He bundles himself up well and goes out to discover a reasonably benign autumn day outside, opens the top button of his coat, and says to himself, storm, shtorm. These Dutch people exaggerate, probably because, other than the weather, they have nothing to occupy themselves. He goes to the taxi station at the Concertgebouw, gets into the first taxi in line, and the driver, a bearlike man with grim eyes, sets out.

For a long time, the taxi navigates the half-empty streets. Here and there, the wind is generating large and small whirlwinds of leaves or trash. The distant neighborhood where Raphaels lives was built after the war and reminds Yoel of an Israeli kibbutz, maybe Nettie's kibbutz in the Bet She'an Valley: rows of low, single-story houses, plonked down on the edges of wide lawns, separated by tiled paths and surrounded by green woods as far as the eye can see. The house numbers have been arranged in some impossible-to-understand method, and for almost an hour the taxi meanders among the houses until they find the number they are looking for. A fierce wind batters Yoel as he steps out onto the path. Droves of dead leaves are galloping from one side of the lawn to the other. Behind the rows of houses there are only a few people out walking their dogs, riding bicycles at the woods' edge, or jogging. The taxi driver, his sad eyes peering through a small crack that he has opened in the window next to him, holds out his business card and promises to return here later to take Yoel back to Obrechtstraat.

Sonia drags one leg after another with great effort, pressing against a wind that is growing stronger from moment to moment and threatening to push her over once and for all. How strange it is to return here, after all this time to pass through the arched space at the entrance to the Rijksmuseum. How strange to come back and cross the green square and Van Baerlestraat to the Concertgebouw building. Both strange and dangerous. It must have been force of habit that led her here from the old-folks home even though she has nothing to look for here: de Lange won't help her, and Martin and Anouk also won't lift a finger. Maybe, she thinks, maybe she can carefully slip into the house and go down into her apartment to take a few small things. Maybe she can sneak in for just a moment, despite the tremendous danger of approaching the house of a Jewish Council member who is collaborating with the Jews' persecutors.

Since handing Nettie over for diving and stripping herself of her identity, she had been certain that a day when she can return home and have her children back cannot be far away. In her imagination she sees herself alongside her two children welcoming Eddy, and sometimes she dares imagine the four of them setting sail for Palestine.

But she has never pictured a situation like the one she finds herself in now. And she never imagined that so much time could pass with no end to this nightmare. With no end to this nightmare.

From a distance the house looks strange, and only when she gets closer does she realize why: all the front windows are open wide, and the wind is raging through them to the rear windows, which are also open wide. Through the open windows she can see that the house's interior is bare of furniture and objects.

Completely stripped. The heavy velvet curtains that once hung in the central apartment's windows are gone. Mrs. de Lange's elegant chandeliers are gone. All the paintings are gone; all the interior walls exposed. When she bends down to the long, low window at sidewalk level and looks into her and Eddy's apartment, nothing looks back at her except empty space, the gloom of a grave.

Sonia stands on the sidewalk, paralyzed. The wind is whistling within the walls of her heart. Her mind refuses to absorb what her eyes are seeing, but when she finds the strength, finally, to make herself move and to draw nearer the house, her heart leaps within her when she notices that despite it all, the entrance is awash—like last autumn and like all autumns—with the reddish leaves of the ivy ascending the front wall.

But then she notices the iron chain that strange, evil hands have wound round the door handle and fastened with a heavy, unequivocal lock.

The entrance to Raphaels's kibbutz-like house is blocked by some sort of large, thick rubber strip, and while Yoel languishes in the cold wind and wonders how to surmount this obstacle, Raphaels himself appears at the door, smiling from ear to ear and shouting syllables that the wind immediately snaps up and sends in the opposite direction. Finally he motions to Yoel to go around the house and enter through the huge window that he opens for him from the inside, and inside the house he welcomes him joyfully and introduces him to a smiling woman by the name of Regina, who has been his neighbor for decades, but just lately, thanks to those meetings he told Yoel about, he found out that she is also a Jew who had been hidden as a child. It's simply amazing, he says with a laugh, and adds with a kind of exuberant joy that about an hour ago the storm blew off his roof, and that thing that is blocking the path to the house is simply a part of the roof.

The man is wearing a bright yellow turtleneck sweater and looks totally different from how he looks when they meet on Shabbat at the synagogue. It turns out that of all the professions in the world, he spent the majority of his years as a railway engineer, and when he retired, he allowed himself to devote himself to his great love: miniature electric trains. In fact, his entire tiny apartment is crammed with model trains of every type, and pressing on this or that button gets them going, together or individually, along lengthy tracks that pass over hills and between water canals, alongside cities and villages, and through tunnels and over bridges. At the moment, he is in the middle of setting up a miniature zoo next to one of the tracks and he invites Yoel to help him construct the monkey cages while his neighbor

Regina is creating a nice little pond for the water animals. Raphaels never married; neither has his neighbor. It's better this way, says Regina, as she leans over a grove of tiny plastic trees. Many of us Jews who were children during the war chose not to have families of our own.

Raphaels: Tell him. Tell him the story about your name.

Regina: I am not sure if the gentleman is interested in hearing it.

Yoel: Of course I would like to hear it, if it is not too great an imposition for you.

So, while the three of them are hunched over a world that Raphaels has created, and while outside the storm is shaking up the world that God has created, Regina relates the story of her war-year tribulations and how she found herself, after the war, in a Jewish orphanage where the people who had hidden her brought her to when nobody came searching for her at their place. She had no idea who she was, no idea what her name was. Yoel connects minuscule plastic branches to minuscule plastic trunks and thinks how awful it must be not to know who you are, how awful not to know your name. But one day, Regina continues, actually one evening, when I was all alone in the orphanage garden, I heard a voice. Are you following me? Yoel looks at her and nods, and she continues. I am not a mystic, and I don't believe at all in mysticism, but the fact is that I heard a voice, and this voice said to me, Chaya Malka. Chaya Malka Goldmintz. She pronounces this name that the mysterious voice called out to her in a whisper, as if she is revealing a deep, dark secret, and then she is silent. Amazing, says Raphaels proudly. No? What do you say about that, Mr. Author? And Yoel answers: What can I say . . . And was this really your name? And Regina: After the phenomenon repeated itself a number of times, meaning I had heard, over and over again, the same voice calling me by this same name, I went to the orphanage director and told him that I thought I had discovered my name. The director checked and found that a Jewish family by the name of Goldmintz, who had a daughter named Chaya Malka, had lived in Holland before the war, and so on and so forth. All the details were consistent.

The storm intensifies. A furious wind is whipping the world and Sonia tries to look onward, but the wind only allows her to look down, and she is pushed to the corner of the street and is pressed, so weak, into the back door of the brown café. Perhaps she fainted there. Or perhaps she just slept for a bit. But Vij finds her and groans, *Oh jee*, a wicked steamroller rolled over you, my poor child. You are unrecognizable.

Vij wants to take her into the café. To warm her up and give her something to eat and to drink and to hear what she has gone through since she gave away her two children and dived. Sonia hesitates to go in, hesitates to endanger this dear woman, wants only to ask if she knows where the de Langes are, where they went with the contents of their house, and what they did with the contents of her little apartment.

It is really strange, says Vij. The two heads of the Jewish Council are still living with their families in their homes as usual, but de Lange and his wife, along with Martin and Anouk and the little one, simply disappeared from here one day. It was quite a while ago. Just a little bit after you dived.

Maybe they found a way to get to America, Sonia wonders out loud. Anouk was always saying this is what they would do.

I hope that's the explanation of their disappearance, even though you know, Sonia dear, that they have arrested Jews who you wouldn't believe—Martin would be crushed if he knew that they arrested and took away Samuel de Mesquita, his respected teacher whom he admired so much, along with his charming wife, who had nurtured a greenhouse of cactuses in their house. Escher, the artist, who still comes by here sometimes when there aren't any German soldiers around, told me that after the couple was taken, he succeeded in getting into their house and saving some wonderful works by de Mesquita, some of which were almost completely trampled.

Sonia follows her friend's quick, precise movements as she checks the condition of the beer fizzing in the row of small barrels in the café's back room. These days I serve mainly homemade beer, Vij explains apologetically, because on the one hand, they have almost totally halted the supply of factory-made beer, and on the other hand, every evening all these officers show up and expect me to pour them rivers of drink. The day before yesterday I used up my sugar supply and I have no idea where I will find any sugar for my next batch of beer, not to mention that it is only through a miracle that I manage to get the yeast and the malt on the black market.

It's amazing, Sonia says, how they probably did manage to organize for themselves a way to leave here for America. . . . But what about all the things that were in the house? Did you simply just come one day and see that the house was empty of people and contents? And why would they take with them what belonged to Eddy and me?

Vij straightens up behind her barrels and looks at her. The truth is that it was strange, she says. A few days after they disappeared, one of those huge modern cranes appeared, the ones the police use to empty out the homes of the Jews. From morning till night that crane rose up and came down, rose up and came down, and from morning till night they removed and removed from that beautiful house all the furniture, all the books, all the paintings, everything. . . .

The three of them are sitting and drinking tea next to the white-and-blue-delft-plate-filled cabinet that seems to be mandatory even in an apartment as small and as crowded with trains as Raphaels's. Regina elaborates on her decision not to have a family of her own, on the difficulty of trusting others, on the fear of loss. Raphaels says that he feels exactly as she does, that for years he tormented himself for never marrying, whereas today he understands what a miracle it is that he has actually chosen life after what he went through in his childhood. He phones to check when they are coming to fix his roof, and when he is told that weather conditions force them to postpone the repair till tomorrow, he expresses concern for his beloved trains, which by then will have been exposed to the dampness seeping through his roofless ceiling.

Toward the end of their visit, Yoel rings the taxi driver who brought him over and the driver promises him in his cumbersome heavy English that he is setting out now and should get there in about twenty minutes. Soon after, Yoel takes leave of Raphaels and Regina and goes outside, and the wind blasts him with amazing force and he must summon up all his strength to remain on his feet. The trees in the woods are bending to and fro, the storm has already broken and knocked over three or four massive trees, and one huge tree is lying across a lawn, its crown spread on the ground like a hand with extended fingers.

It is only with great effort that Yoel reaches the curb between the houses and struggles to walk to the corner where he has arranged to meet his sad-eyed driver.

But twenty minutes pass and the taxi does not appear. Yoel is chilled to the bone. Rain mixed with hail is pelting him and the wind is thrashing him as he clutches his coat and his hat and his scarf, pacing back and forth on the sidewalk and trying to imagine what Sonia must be doing in this piercing cold. What.

Another twenty minutes pass and the taxi still doesn't arrive, still doesn't arrive. In the woods behind the houses a broken trunk lies on a slant and a group of boys are climbing on it like on a bridge to nowhere. Yoel takes his cell phone out of his sodden pocket and dials the driver again. Except that this time, the driver doesn't answer. He just hears the automatic voice mail saying something in a spirited guttural Dutch. Yoel dials again and again hears the recorded announcement. The cold is getting worse. In the distance a man is running along a path with a large dog, and right behind the man and his dog, without warning, another tree falls. Yoel looks up, his body frozen inside his clothes and the layers that all the rain in the world has seeped into. At any moment, a nearby tree could fall on his head and kill him, and how miserable it would be to end the story of his life with such an awful metaphor.

Late at night Sonia studies the house from the outside. The storm has abated a bit, and she steals along the back of the road and squeezes herself between the fences into the neglected yard, and she creeps silently between the bushes and the red-brick wall, checking the handles of the low windows and pulling at the bars. Finally she climbs up the five steps in the back and presses on the door handle at their top. To her surprise, the handle responds and, despite the heavy lock that is also chained around it here, she manages to open a narrow gap. She crouches under the iron chain, squeezes between the door and the frame, and now she is in the de Langes' kitchen. The dark is so thick at first that she can actually feel it—and then, in one fell swoop, the absolute desolateness of five stories of empty house strikes her in the face like the breath of death. I expected more from you, Martin, she says, and the echo of her voice bounces back to her from the wall. But she immediately regrets this. What power, actually, did Martin have? What could he have done for her and her children? And had she been in his place, would she have given up the chance to escape and save herself and her family? Nevertheless, when she descends the dark stairs into the barren, yearning space of the apartment that had once been hers and Eddy's and Nettie's and Leo's, she cannot deny the seething rage almost blowing her up from inside herself when she thinks that perhaps, at this very moment, Martin, Anouk, and Sebastian are enjoying themselves in some other place, a free place, a place where they are allowed to breathe without fear. Don't hate them, she advises herself. Especially, don't hate their annoying baby, who is lucky not to have to part from his parents for even one day, while at the same time my children . . .

And she fumbles her way back up the stairs to the banker and his wife's apartment on the three middle floors, then continues to the apartment on the building's top floor. The lives that were lived in this house unfold before her eyes; the words that have been spoken in it flutter around her like transparent butterflies. People lived here, people spoke and loved and laughed, but now they are all gone; they are all gone. Only she is here. Only she.

If this is indeed her.

Like a ghost she floats from floor to floor, from apartment to apartment, and from room to room. The house has been desecrated, shaved, exploited of any signs of the human existence that flowed in it, and she drifts through its empty spaces, scanning, feeling, calling out the names of those who had lived here until she can no longer, no longer, and she stumbles into the niche where the beds of her two children once stood, and there she collapses, there she allows her body to drop, limb by limb, onto the wooden floor. Her eyes close.

And to think that Bat-Ami has lived her entire life in that one stone house in the middle of the Rehavia neighborhood in Jerusalem. Her father, who was a Torah scholar and a land merchant, built the house before she was born, and he was also the one who planted the cypress and pine trees that surround the house and isolate it from the world to this very day. When Bat-Ami and Yoel married, her father gave them a small apartment that adjoined the house, and when they became parents to the three girls, he upgraded them to a large front-facing apartment. Later, Bat-Ami inherited this apartment, and her two brothers and two sisters inherited the apartments to the left, to the right, and below.

Thus it has transpired that Bat-Ami has never experienced residing permanently in any other place, and all her life has been spent in this one house. Maybe this is the reason she renovates the apartment so often, and every few years, as if to move without moving, she hires a renovations contractor and has him tear down most of the interior walls of the apartment and move the rooms from one place to another based on the design of some wonderful, up-to-date architect which this time, she always promises Yoel, will improve the quality of their life beyond recognition, will give them plenty of light and air and will expand their minds. Yoel is reluctantly forced to suffer long weeks of hammering and drilling, and chaos and bedlam, until one day he comes home to find a new apartment: the space where the kitchen used to be is now the new hallway, the former hall is now a new bathroom adjacent to the new bedroom, and in the area of the former balcony, a modern, upgraded kitchen now gleams. However, Bat-Ami and her squad of dusty handymen are strictly prohibited from touching his office for any matter whatsoever. His private territory is strictly off-limits for them, and since Bat-Ami abides by his wishes every time she destroys and rebuilds the apartment, Yoel knows that he will always be able to sink into his familiar armchair that is positioned next to his familiar desk that is standing between his familiar bookshelves, and he will always be able to look out from his familiar window and see the familiar trees and concentrate on his work.

In the end he returned to his hotel in another cab that Raphaels ordered for him after he had waited for the first cab for over an hour. This time, the driver was a cheerful Indian immigrant who chattered, nonstop, all the way and who said "too many" and "too much" instead of "many" and "much." Once, maybe they had been in Hong Kong, he and Bat-Ami had had a driver who spoke exactly the same way, and they couldn't stop laughing and delighting in the "too many tourists" that he had driven and the "too much money" that he earned in his job. But now this seemingly charming mangling of the language depressed him. The man went on and on about "too many canals" and "too many museums" but Yoel felt nameless and homeless, and stormy Amsterdam looked like something after an apocalyptic destruction, all fragments and gashes, its roads covered with fallen trees that have surrendered and will never rise again.

The next day when he went down to breakfast, Josephine and Achilles told him how worried they had been about him yesterday. Many pedestrians had been injured during the storm, Josephine told him. One tree broke and killed a woman who was walking in the city center, and another tree fell on a houseboat and it was a miracle that the residents weren't injured. A taxi driver was a lot less fortunate, she sighed as she arranged the slices of sausage on the buffet table. A taxi driver? Yoel jumped. Yes, she said, a taxi driver was crushed and killed when a tree fell on the taxi he was driving.

Later, Yoel also heard the news from a yawning Achilles: there were two killed in the storm—a woman and a man; a tourist and a taxi driver.

He did not dare ask which taxi station the dead driver was associated with. Or where the tree fell on him. And at what time.

51

Little by little, in the last months of her life, his mother's consciousness had dimmed. Little by little, his mother departed from him. Sometimes when he came to visit her in the nursing ward of the rest home, he found her drowsing sitting up, her head slumped on the back of the armchair and her mouth turned upward like the beak of a thirsty bird. Soundlessly he would approach her. Silently he would sit in the chair next to her. Sometimes he would find her book of Psalms in her lap and he would read the verses and find in them new meanings. And sometimes it happened that her eyes opened and stared straight ahead until they homed in on the figure sitting next to her, and then her wrinkled face glowed at him with a smile, and her voice, now softer than ever, murmured to him: Eddy. My Eddy. And sometimes more animatedly: How I have missed you, my Edika.

When she was hospitalized, he did not stray from her bed day or night, did not stop fretting whether they were doing everything possible to relieve the intense agony tormenting her body, her tall, broad body whose huge strides had conquered the earth and all the seas, and even now clung to life with some mysterious force, refusing to leave this world and refusing to let the soul depart. When the struggle was almost over, just a moment before the curtain came down, a moment before she left him entirely, he saw her lips moving as if she was trying to tell him something. So he bent down at her side, between the bed and the monitor on which the rhythm of her heartbeat and the levels of oxygen in her blood had nearly leveled out, and brought his face close to hers, trying to catch this last utterance that she so wanted to bestow on him, but he could find no meaning in the two syllables that he heard her whispering over and over again and he thought that perhaps she was trying to call him, and the letters of his name were getting all mixed up.

He contemplated this over and over again in his mind throughout the entire seven days of mourning, reconstructing these last moments to everyone who came to console him. Nettie and Bat-Ami tried to hint to him that he should change the subject, that he should talk about his mother's life and not just about the moment of her death, but again and again, as if obsessed, he heard himself repeating this story-not-story to the ever-changing procession of comforters, as if he expected one of them to solve the mystery for him.

And yet now he is recalling the movements of her tongue and the sounds that faded in her mouth, and he understands that the name his mother was trying to call out, in her final breath, was Le-o. Leo.

At night Sonia huddles in the desolate, silent house in which even the chimes of the church bell are no longer heard because all the bells of all the churches in Amsterdam have been confiscated and are gone.

Over the following nights, Vij smuggles in to her a blanket, a piece of soap, bits of food. Sonia looks at these gifts and wonders why her kind-hearted friend thinks that a dead woman would want to cover herself, that a dead woman would wish to bathe, that a dead woman is able to chew and swallow.

Vij says to her that she has managed to contact the Dutch student underground group. I've informed Katya, Vij says, that you aren't working in the old-folks home anymore, and from now on, any messages to you can be relayed through me at the café.

On the days following the great storm, the row of trees east of the Museumplein are standing totally bare of leaves, and broken branches are scattered over the lawn that has been colored a grayish brown by the murky runoff.

Even though the psychoanalyst has returned to her post and to her patient reports, Yoel is still worried about her. He can't see her face, but he does see the sad angle at which the delicate nape of her neck is leaning, the disappointment locked up in her shoulders, and the curve of her back that expresses a yearning that cannot be contained.

He takes care to avoid passing the taxi stand at the Concertgebouw so that he will not have to search for the bearish figure of his driver and will not need to determine if he survived that day of the storm and if he is alive or dead.

And each and every morning he battles with the three knobs that adjust the shower, trying in vain to control the water temperature. Shivering with cold, frustrated—perhaps even furious—his body hunches under the cracked shower head where the water—one moment a barrage of ice, one moment a cascade of fire—spills and splashes onto him until he gives up and exits, defeated, into the murky sea pooling on the bathroom floor, in which dead body cells, especially hairs whose lengths and colors testify that they are not his hairs, are floating around the soles of his embarrassed feet.

The days pass. No matter what happens, the days always pass. Winter returns to Amsterdam, the daylight hours diminish, snow covers the beautiful streets and evokes memories of families gathering in their homes in the evening, warming themselves next to charcoal stoves and eating Dutch pea soup or a dish of sauerkraut with potatoes and sausage. And then again comes spring, and again summer, and again.

On the television in his room, Yoel zaps between tepid American dramas, pausing occasionally to watch a Dutch television show in which a bearded man—not wildly bearded like himself but with a beard that is well groomed—helps his ever-changing guests to research their ancestors. Yoel has no idea what the people searching for their family roots are asking and doesn't know what the bearded man answers them, but he enjoys looking at the ancient manuscripts with brown letters curling on yellowing parchments and enjoys when they compare old landscape drawings of different Dutch places to contemporary photographs of the same sites. He doesn't understand their language, but he is somehow fascinated by the authoritative host, who sits with his guests on soft armchairs before a table heaped with archival documents and in front of piles of firewood logs. Yoel guesses that they are mainly focusing on the Dutch Golden Age, when their country was a powerful and influential empire, and he understands that every scrap of information they acquire fills them with satisfaction. Sometimes he even recognizes familiar words in their conversation, such as "ancestors" or "archive."

And now Sonia imposes on herself an automated routine. Every day she arises when it is still night and goes to clean the brown café; with sunrise, she is again concealed inside the house. She is not living, but she is keeping herself in a state of not dead. You have children, she reminds herself with every breath in and every breath out. You have children. You have children. One day, a man from the student underground comes and instructs Vij to arrange an emergency night meeting between Sonia and Katya. They meet under the Muntplein clock tower, and Katya says, Come with me. Come with me and don't ask questions. They walk quickly, a tall, broad-shouldered figure and a small, thin figure, hugging the buildings' walls until they climb onto a tram. Sonia cannot remember the last time she rode a tram. It is late, and the car is almost empty except for a few tipsy German soldiers, and Sonia does not breathe. Katya sits next to her and says to her, Come, we must look like two girlfriends on their way back from a nice party, and now I will tell you something and you will respond with a nod and smile. Okay? But just with a nod and a smile! Someone informed on where your daughter was, and there was a raid, and your daughter was caught and taken to the Dutch Theater and from there to the children's home on Plantage Avenue. We will find her another address, but in the meantime we have to get her out of the dormitory. We have to get her out of there before it is too late, and therefore, you will take her now with you, and hide her with yourself, until we find her a new place.

Sonia responds with a nod, with an outward smile and an inward prayer. What can she do except to pray inwardly? We have to try to get her out of there, Katya says to her, to the glances of enemy soldiers sitting next to them in the tram's car. We have to try. Do you understand what I am telling you, Sonia? We have to try, even if there is only a slight chance that our people will be able to get the child out of the dormitory tonight, and an infinitesimal chance that you will be able to safely get to your house with her. Sonia nods and smiles, nods and breaks into pieces and smiles.

A short while later, Sonia finds herself standing all by herself at a tram stop on the tramway in the middle of Plantage Middenlaan. To her right side is the entrance to the children's dormitory and to her left, across the street, the door to the Dutch Theater. Both buildings are packed with women and men and children who are due to be sent tomorrow morning to the Westerbork transit camp and from there to Poland, meaning that tomorrow morning they are about to be sent to whatever happens to those who are sent to the Westerbork transit camp and from there to Poland. She sees an armed sentry standing at the entrance to the theater, and when she turns her head, she sees an armed sentry standing at the entrance to the dormitory. Once every few minutes, a tram stops at the station, once at the station in one direction, and once at the station in the other, and every tramcar conceals one of the sentries: the tramcars that stop at the station to her right hide the tense, nervous sentry at the entrance to the dormitory, and the tramcars that stop at the station to her left—the tense, nervous sentry at the entrance to the theater.

And Sonia is waiting. Katya has disappeared somewhere, and Sonia has been waiting a long time. And now two tramcars are stopping at the very same instant at the two stops, concealing, for just a fraction of a second, both the doorway to the theater and the doorway to the dormitory, and in that fraction of a second, when both sentries are hidden, somebody appears next to Sonia and presses into her bosom something warm and shivering that turns out to be her little Nettie, and at once the mother and daughter are in the electric tram leaving the station and there is no way to describe it. No way.

Again he stops writing before sundown, lifts himself up from his chair, and takes himself out for a needed walk like a man taking out his dog. A twilight wind welcomes him with its perpetual caress as he emerges from the hotel's entrance, and the beauty—the stylized buildings, the flower boxes, the glowing water under the stone bridges, and, above, the treetops against the background of the sky—the beauty is unbearably painful. He walks along Obrechtstraat, goes down to the Vinkeleskade, and tries to think only about the similarity between the Dutch word "*kade*" and the Hebrew word "*gadah*," both of which mean "riverbank," or "quay." And about the fact that it requires at least three adults holding hands to encompass the giant trunk of each of the trees growing along the bank, their dense branches shading it along its entire length.

He walks slowly and sees the water flowing along the wide canal, reflecting the sparkle of the sunbeams that gently dip into it. He walks slowly and listens to the birds getting ready for their nightly slumber in the treetops. Cyclists pass him nonstop: dozens of cyclists pedaling their way home from another day at work or study, boys and girls riding from school in pairs or in groups, and young children mounted on their parents' bicycles or riding alongside one parent on their own bicycles. They are all chatting with each other while pedaling, talking and laughing and asking questions and answering and exchanging experiences and thoughts in their language, which sounds to him like a jumble of mud and gravel. Some of the utterings that the cyclists toss from one to the other are suspended in the space between their bicycles, remaining there even after the utterers themselves have glided forward on their way. And Yoel observes the syllables hanging between heaven and earth and thinks about bygone days when he must have understood Dutch, not to mention also have spoken it, even a little. Now these words are foreign to him, but this doesn't add or detract from anything because none of the speakers are trying to converse with him, nobody knows him and nobody notices him as he walks along, seeing but unseen, among the speaking people, the real people.

I am Yoel Blum, he says silently, in Hebrew, to a cyclist who bends forward toward the handlebars of his bicycle to kiss the head of the little boy riding in front of him.

I am Yoel Blum.

The branches of the trees bow to him gently.

Nettie tells her things. Oh, what she tells her! How can such a small child tell her mother things such as these that she is too young to comprehend? Things about the autumn-winter-spring-and-summer when she was in a totally different world, in the hands of totally different adults, in places that she knew not what they were. How can she describe the events that were responsible for her arrival at the children's home on Plantage Avenue, about the children that she had time to make friends with there and the babies she witnessed being smuggled out of the children's house: one in a knapsack and one in a laundry basket. The caregiver, who conveyed her out in the middle of the night through a back window of the house, to the man, waiting in the yard, who passed her over the fence to another man who smelled just like Daddy does and brought her to her mother.

It is only when he gets back to Obrechtstraat, crosses the small square, and enters the Mokum Hotel that he can feel real. Sometimes he loiters in the lobby doing nothing, waiting for Achilles to appear at the door next to the reception counter, and sometimes he wanders the hall searching for Josephine's short, beaming figure. Just to meet someone, just to ascertain that he is visible, that he is present, that he exists.

This morning Josephine told him that her daughter, an economics student at the University of Amsterdam, won a municipal kickboxing contest
and received a trophy. My daughter will remain here, she told him, and
for the first time he saw her without a smile. But I, after my dad leaves this
world, I am going back to Curaçao.

I am tired of the cold here.

Days come in which Sonia and Nettie are hiding together inside the
empty house. Depending on each other, resuscitating one another, keeping each other alive. Nettie is still of tender years, but she is no longer a
little girl. Maybe, Yoel thinks, maybe she is, after all, telling her mother
just a bit of what she went through in the many long months of separation. Sonia does not pressure her, but he should probably write and tell
about how she was passed from hand to hand and from place to place
until she got to a family that introduced her to everyone as a Christian
child from Rotterdam who was orphaned as a result of the bombing. He
should write about how her non-Jewish appearance allowed her to enjoy
relative freedom and even to attend the local school with children of her
own age, but that in the house she had to deal with disconcerting harass-
ment, the manifestations of which she was too young to understand. And
how this abomination was revealed to the members of the underground,
who then transferred her to another family hiding other Jews, and how
she stayed there until the police raided the place and all those in hiding
were arrested.

On the one hand, Yoel is drawn to develop Nettie's story. On the other
hand, he is aware that the time has come to proceed with his notes to the
next part of the story. He understands that his desire to detail the particu-
lars of his sister's dive is for no other purpose than to postpone the end and
delay having to deal with the story's continuation: the part he is most afraid
of writing, the part that is impatiently and restlessly waiting right behind
the part in which Sonia and Nettie were snuggling inside five deserted
floors of a house that once was their home.

He gazes at the multiplication table printed on the back cover of his notebook and accepts that he will have to make do with only a succinct account of the mother and daughter, who are at this moment holding each other over the whirlwind of hunger and cold and despair. They are barely nourished by the morsels of food that Vij manages to get them from time to time, and they never turn on any form of light in the house. At night, through the low, wide kitchen window above their heads, they see on the sidewalk the walking legs of more and more Jews being taken from their homes. And after all their lip biting, the day comes when they are also taken. Their hideout is exposed. The iron chain on the front door is severed, and they are both led along Apollo Avenue to the Green Police headquarters next to Beethovenstraat and sent north to the Westerbork transit camp and Yoel rises from his seat, goes out to the balcony, scans the house across from him window by window and floor by floor, and then he goes inside, closes the closet door and opens the door to his room, and a moment later he is outside, hurrying along, panting. He veers into the bicycle lane and is almost run over, passes under the arches of the Rijks exactly when the violins reach the crescendo in Brahms's first symphony, and keeps going, passing the galleries and the antique stores of Spiegelgracht, crossing Prinsengracht and then Keizersgracht and Herengracht. The entire city is pounding in his head, all its water is flooding his heart, and he breaks left and heads down the Leidseplein and escapes into the open spaces of Vondelpark, where traces of the great storm are still evident. The fallen tree is alright, but the wind had wrecked quite a few upright trees, and in various corners of the park, municipal work teams are still laboring to saw off giant limbs that have been severed and to load the sawn-off chunks onto a truck with a huge yellow crane.

Soon everything will be fixed up and cleaned up, and the park will look as perfectly perfect as always, the way it also looked when Sonia and her children were prohibited from walking in it or even looking into it from the outside. A woman with a beautiful face and amputated legs drives along the path on a sort of tricycle that she pedals with her hands; another lady is leading two large dogs on leashes, ordering them in harsh Dutch. There are also a group of Israeli cyclists on red rented bikes, a man sitting withdrawn on a bench off to the side, huge pigeons pecking in the lawn, and an azure dome of a sky in which a jet plane is stretching out along its breadth a long, white unmistakable contrail. And still his head is pounding but he has no choice. And here he is back in his room, sitting again at his narrow desk, and the orchid is watching him with compassion. And it is not without a sigh of relief that he opens a new forty-page, single-line notebook and begins to write the next part of the story.

FOURTH NOTEBOOK

52

Hi, Nettie.

Yoel! How are you? Are you back from Amsterdam?

No, Nettie, I am still here. I want to ask you something.

One moment, I'll just turn off the radio. What do you want to ask me?

If you remember how I was on the train, on our first trip together.

How you were on the way? In the train itself?

Yes.

You . . . you cried, Yoel.

How long did I cry?

The trip took more than two days, and you . . . you cried for more than two days. You cried the entire trip.

And did Mother try to calm me?

You didn't let her get near you. They took us in a cattle car. All those people were on the floor of the car, and you moved away from Mother, and also from me, as far as you possibly could. . . . You were so small, and so miserable, and you simply crumpled yourself into a corner, pressed against the car's side panel, and cried and cried nonstop. . . .

Did I say anything?

You called: Mama! Mama!

I called Mama. . . .

Yes, and Yoel, you were just so hungry and thirsty, and . . . well . . . you had made in your pants, and you smelled dreadful . . . but you wouldn't let yourself be touched, you wouldn't even let anyone get close to you. And if Mother or I tried to stretch out our hand to you or even to just move a bit in your direction, you started to shriek so terribly that everyone looked at us as if we were murdering you or something. . . .

So Mother . . . Mother didn't touch me? What did she do?

Nu . . . what could she do? She just sat as close as she could to you. And most of the time you weren't the only one crying. Mother cried too.

This part of the story he decides he will begin with the dramatic scene on the train platform at the Westerbork transit camp. Not from Sonia's first days in the camp, and also not from the shocking moment when she meets Martin and Anouk. It will be the scene that takes place on the train platform, not on a Tuesday, the day of the human transports destined for Poland, but on a different day, when the train heads for Germany, to Bergen-Belsen, as a result of a rare deal in which dozens of Jews are to be sent from Bergen-Belsen to Palestine in exchange for German citizens who live in Palestine under British rule.

This is the moment. Now it is happening.

Sonia is standing on the platform. Next to her stands Nettie, and at their feet their few belongings are bundled into a ragged blanket whose four corners have been sewn together. Sonia's eyes are torn open after she hasn't slept or eaten a thing for a number of days. She has been waiting and is still waiting for her son, Leo, whom the messenger from the underground is supposed to bring from the village where he was hidden. She is waiting for Leo so she can take him, with Nettie, up into the train, its engine already belching smoke, its passengers anxious to leave for Bergen-Belsen and from there to freedom, to Palestine, to life. Martin had promised her that Leo would be delivered to her the day before yesterday, but Leo was not brought then, nor was he brought to her yesterday, nor was he brought to her at any time during the long night that was between yesterday and today.

And he wasn't brought today.

HOUSE ON ENDLESS WATERS

Come on, people shout to her from the train. Come up. Don't miss your chance to live.

Sonia doesn't answer. Sonia pays them no attention.

Suddenly two Jews jump out of the car behind her. One lifts up Nettie in his hands and the other picks up the bundle and pulls at Sonia's arm.

Come. Come quickly. The train is pulling out!

No, she cries. I won't go without my son.

At least save the girl, shout out countless voices.

The train seems to be starting. Black smoke billows from the locomotive's smokestack, there is a sharp whistle, and the German soldiers are rushing back and forth to make sure that all the doors of all the cars are fastened.

The two Jews let go of Sonia and Nettie and rush back into the car.

But here comes somebody else. Someone is dashing up to the platform at a crazy sprint.

It is Martin.

Who does he carry in his arms.

It is his son. It is Sebastian.

In the morning, that same hunchbacked, Jewish-looking, elegantly dressed old lady, her lips painted bright red, enters the café on Beethovenstraat. This morning too, she is pushing in front of her a baby carriage holding a tiny gray dog, its long hair gathered above its button eyes and fastened with a ribbon. And today, too, she parks her carriage alongside the inner tables, gathers up her furry baby, and goes to the coffee counter.

She must have known Sonia, Yoel thinks as he watches how, toward eight o'clock, the avenue is filling up with vehicles and people. The trams stop one after the other and high school students, their faces a testament to freedom, health, and youth, descend from the cars and cross the street to the school. Countless bicycles stream in front of the café, a river of bicycles, including tandem bikes on which parent and child ride together and bicycles with accessories attached to carry all kinds of loads, and of course countless bicycles with all sorts of varied contraptions for carrying children. With what confidence the cyclists move, how much trust they must have in man and the world and how relaxed their bodies are on their wheels, their backs always upright, their clear gaze straight ahead, the long hair of young female drivers streaming charmingly. Here they are, zooming across the intersection; here they are, easily cutting across the transportation lanes and the tram tracks in endless nonchalance, turning in a wide arc toward the intersection and cycling on.

Hello, Bat-Ami.

How are you, my darling? Where are you?

I'm on the balcony.

Ah, really? And how is your neighbor the dancer?

The dancer has not yet returned from his dancing job. Just his cat is at home, evidently immersed in the writing of a novel.

And what about the psychoanalyst? Is she still engaged in her psychoanalytic labor?

A psychoanalyst's life is indeed a hard one.

And the life of a stuffed animal?

That too. But, my wife, I just called to say I love you.

What—

I love you, Bat-Ami.

Are you . . . I don't . . . Sorry for my bewilderment, *Ee sheli*, my island, but I don't recall you ever saying this.

I love you. I am sorry that I've never said this.

Martin hands her his son. Take him, he says breathlessly.

Sonia looks at the boy. Her ears are ringing from the roar of the train, from the voices of the people shouting at her, from the rocks exploding inside her. Her eyes mist over.

Take him, Martin chokes. Take him and we will bring you your son. . . . We'll bring him to Bergen-Belsen next week. . . . A girl and a boy are registered in your papers, and a boy is written in ours—

And as he utters these impossible words, he thrusts forward his free hand and raises Nettie onto the car whose door is still slightly ajar. In the blink of an eye he shoves in the cloth bundle and Nettie is screaming, Mama, Mama, get on. And Sonia is nothing but a lump of ash that people are pulling and lifting into the train, and in her arms is the boy, in her arms is little Sebastian Rosso, who gives her one look and immediately bursts into tears.

Night. Dam Square. On the way here, he went into a women's clothing store on Kalverstraat, because for the first time in his life he was overcome by a sudden urge to buy Bat-Ami some clothes. He stood in the store, facing the loaded hangers, but he realized he had no idea of her size and had no idea which items on display were to her taste. He almost chose a sort of zebra-striped jacket for her, but then changed his mind and gave up, continuing on his way. From his post at the top of the Royal Palace, the statue of Atlas is collapsing under his sphere and it seems that he can no longer bear his burden. The stone lions flanking the monument are watching with worried, stony eyes as hordes of young people, many of them Israeli, walk around the square with meaningless gaiety. And Yoel turns into his alley, goes into his Irish pub, and sits down next to his table adjacent to the upper-level railing.

Does Anouk agree, he asks himself while sipping from his first green bottle, does Anouk agree to this crazy exchange that Martin has conceived. Does she even know about this spontaneous transaction, he asks with his second green bottle. Does she even know what he is going to do. And how does she react when he comes back from the platform without Sebastian. What does she do when she realizes that her baby has been taken from her, that her baby is now with Sonia on his way to the unknown.

———————————

And all in all, what did Zohar want? Zohar, his youngest daughter, whose life, so she said, had flopped somehow but still, she went on to say, she thought she deserved a chance to be a mother. And how Bat-Ami had sent him to buy those bromeliads; Zohar was then working in the Botanical Gardens nursery, and only now—idiot that he is—does he realize that Bat-Ami sent him not to buy that silly plant but to speak to his daughter, who was then at the beginning of this single-parent pregnancy of hers and needed her father's support. And he just stood there as Zohar was preparing the flower pot, and instead of asking how she's doing and if she has morning sickness and if she is scared to death of becoming a single mother at a not-very-young age, instead of all these appropriate questions, he asked her—idiot that he was, idiot, idiot, idiot—if she was in touch with Gidi, who had left her ages ago after years of a bad relationship. And this poor woman, who had started working in the nursery because she couldn't make a proper living as a hydrotherapist, or perhaps because, at that time in her life, she needed to work with earth more than with water, said to him, With Gidi? Why would I be in touch with Gidi? Her voice choked, and she turned away from him, probably so that he wouldn't see the tears as she dug little holes with her trowel to sink the little plantlets into. And instead of letting the topic go, he continued: Do you have any idea where Gidi is? Because he had no idea what he was supposed to talk to her about, and with the same choked voice, she replied that Gidi was living in Italy and working there as sort of a ship's captain, that is to say, he sails rich people's yachts, and anyway, he has already found something (he remembers that she said "something" and not "someone").

When she finished planting the flowers, she added some more handfuls of crumbled soil and some fertilizer, and smoothed the earth around the reddish plants as if she were preparing a soft bed for a baby.

The later it gets, the fuller the pub gets. When Yoel is on his third bottle, all the levels are already packed full of human bodies, music, smells, and conversations. And then the third bottle empties and there are two boys at his side who are asking him, in broken English, if he is Israeli. When he answers in the affirmative, they change to Hebrew and introduce themselves as Ido and Tomer, who have recently finished their matriculation exams and are now spending a bit of time in Amsterdam before their enlistment into the Israel Defense Forces.

We wanted to ask you something, says Ido or Tomer. And Tomer or Ido explains, We're here with another friend, and this friend of ours claims that you are Yoel Blum the writer. The truth is that we're pretty sure he's wrong, because you really don't look anything like Yoel Blum the writer. . . .

We even searched the internet. Ido or Tomer laughs and points to his smartphone. We found pictures of Yoel Blum the writer and we could see that you are definitely not him.

And why is this friend of yours so certain that I *am* Yoel Blum the writer?

Because our friend is the author's grandson. In his opinion, you are his grandfather.

It was only on her third or fourth day in Westerbork that Sonia discovered, to her shock, that Martin, Anouk, and Sebastian were in the camp. She had heard the name de Lange mentioned as one of the Jews appointed to decide the fate of all the other Jews, but it didn't occur to her that it was Jozef de Lange, the banker from Amsterdam. The banker, she believed, had surely long since fled and settled far, far away from Holland with his wife, his daughter, his son-in-law, and his grandson. But now it turns out that all the family members are in the camp, that is to say all of them except for Mrs. de Lange, who had fallen ill and died a short time after she had been expelled from her house. Sonia and Nettie were housed with the rest of the women and children in barbed-wire-surrounded barracks, in a building in which three stories of sleeping pallets lined the lengths of the walls. Yoel feels nauseous when he writes about the moldy wooden pallets, known to every Hebrew reader from stories of other writers. But what can he do if

Sonia and Nettie are there now? And what can be done if the words "Soon we will be in America," that Anouk says to Sonia when they meet in Westerbork, cannot conceal the harsh reality? My poor mother will not merit to see America. Anouk continues talking as her finger vainly searches for a strand of honey hair to move from cheek to behind ear. But Martin and I and Sebastian will get to the shores of New York very soon.

Sonia had been horrified earlier when she was summoned to report with her daughter to the Jewish living quarters of those who had positions in the camp. And how surprised she had been when she arrived there to find her former neighbors.

Anouk had lost her freshness, her body had wasted away, and her hair had become ragged and faded, but she and Martin and the boy were protected. They were protected.

It's all thanks to my father, crowed Anouk. My father saw your name on the list of new prisoners and told us that you and Nettie had arrived at the camp. When we asked to see you, he arranged it so they would summon you here to visit us! And Sonia cringed inwardly, because she knew that Anouk's indulgent father was collaborating with the Germans, helping to organize those efficient worklists that they of the Dutch transit camp were so proud off, and in the framework of his job, he had a decisive influence also on preparing the weekly lists of Jews to be sent on the trains to Poland. The camp's veterans had already explained to her that the train to Poland left the camp every Tuesday at ten in the morning, meaning that the list of deportees was compiled the night between Monday and Tuesday. De Lange, they told her, is one of those who must verify that the number of people on the train exactly match the quota. If a Jew on the list escapes the transport, de Lange has to immediately improvise and choose someone else: another man or woman who will replace the defector.

Yoel turns his head in the direction that the two bashful youths are pointing and within the huge multitude crowding the pub he sees Tal, a handsome boy with brown hair shorn almost to the roots. Tal waves his hand at him and Yoel rises slightly from his chair, waves back, and wonders what is expected from a grandfather meeting his grandson under such circumstances.

We'll leave you two alone, says Ido or Tomer as Tal approaches, but Yoel hears himself protesting loudly, almost shouting, No! Why should you go? Sit. I'm asking you to stay and sit with us. Here, I am already ordering a round of this excellent beer for us all! And Tomer and Ido, startled at his vociferous insistence, quickly sit down. In the meantime, Tal has come over and they both sort of extend their arms to greet each other, but they don't hug, not really. That is to say, the boy places a tentative hand on his grandfather's shoulder, and the grandfather slaps the boy's shoulder a few times, and they both say to each other:

What's happening? What are you doing here?

No, I don't think your mother told me that you were going to Amsterdam before your enlistment.

No, Grandma didn't tell me that you were working in Amsterdam on a new book. Or maybe she actually did say something, but I didn't pay attention.

And that's it. That, more or less, covered the topics of conversation at their disposal. The three young boys sit at his regular table, sip the beers he ordered for them with tiny sips, and glance at him with awe. Yes, they find the city beautiful. No, they haven't really visited any museums, in fact they're not really touring a lot. They mainly came to have a good time between matriculation and the army. Yup, that means mainly spending time in the coffee shops. No, not, God forbid, hard drugs, but you probably know that most young people come to Amsterdam for the coffee shops. In another day and a bit we will be heading back home, so . . .

It's all thanks to my father, Anouk said, and it's true that thanks to Jozef de Lange's status, Martin managed to slightly ease the tribulations of Sonia's and Nettie's lives in Westerbork. Sonia capitulated despite herself: she couldn't forgive de Lange for his part in Eddy's tragedy, in her own tragedy, in the tragedy of the Jews of Amsterdam, and Martin, too, was to her nothing but another miserable collaborator. But it seemed that the more she made her hard feelings known to him, the more he went out of his way to do things for her. The family's status bestowed on Martin extra privileges, and due to them he was able to keep his radio and listen to Western stations. So he often came to Sonia in the evenings, the time when only those with special permits were allowed to walk around the camp despite the curfew, to check how she was and what she needed, and to pass on to her reports about the military forces' movements throughout Europe and the prospect that the war was finally reaching its end.

53

The first transport of Jews destined for the exchange had left a short while before Sonia got to Westerbork, and since then, four or five additional exchange transports had gone from the camp. At first, so people told her, the exchange prisoners didn't even go in a freight train but in a real passenger train, with seats. The camp commandant permitted the deportees' friends to escort them to the platform, where they parted singing "Hatikva."

Martin told her that another deal would probably take place, and in the meantime, the things he heard while listening to the Western radio stations become more and more encouraging. Victory could already be seen on the horizon, he told Sonia, even though in anticipation of the war's end, the enemy might resort to extreme measures of despair, and it is best to be careful. And so it was that the number of Jews sent out every Tuesday to Poland grew, and everyone witnessed the elderly, the children, and the sick being shoved into the cars to the barking of dogs and the commands of soldiers, and everyone understood that these people were certainly not on their way to do labor. And another train went out, and the countdown of the days and hours until next Monday began again: who will live and who will die, whose name will be on the next transport list, and how to avoid the list, one more week, and another one, and remain in Westerbork in the hope that each additional day on Dutch soil might be the day of rescue. Only those with official tasks and their families passed the days with the complacency of someone who does not fear their fate. And how selfish and despicable this complacency was to Sonia, how selfish and disloyal and despicable.

One day, Martin informed her that another exchange was about to take place. A few hundred more Jews would be sent from Westerbork to Bergen-Belsen and from there to Palestine, and this time—his voice quavered—this time I have successfully arranged for you and your two children to be on the list.

She was frantic. What about my Leo? How will my Leo get here? But Martin calmed her. I've already taken care of that, he said. The student underground will bring the boy to you one of these days. Soon. In fact, the underground liaison has already set out to the village where Leo is hidden.

And Sonia's soul blossomed with excitement after all her unbearable yearning for her son, who was being raised by Christian parents as if he were their own, her son, who surely didn't remember her anymore and surely was calling someone else "mama" and speaking in a rural dialect that she herself does not understand.

And when she asked, But what about you? Why don't you also get yourselves on the list for exchange, Martin explained to her that the fact that they were on the list of camp officials prevented them from joining another list. But there was no need to worry about them, he reassured her, because their privileged status protected them, and in due course, they, too, would leave.

A letter that arrived a few days later from the Red Cross confirmed that Sonia Blum, Nettie Blum, and Leo Blum were included in the next exchange deal between citizens of Palestine who were now on German territory and German citizens who were living in Palestine. The letter revealed the departure date of the exchange train, and, as if divulging a top secret, Martin told Sonia that he and Anouk and Sebastian would be coming to

Bergen-Belsen in their wake, with other job holders, on a different additional train that would leave Westerbork a week later.

From the moment she was told that Leo was on the way to her, Sonia didn't sleep and didn't eat and barely breathed. She didn't know if the underground emissary had safely reached the village south of Amsterdam and, if he had arrived, had found her little boy there. And if he had found him, if he had successfully gotten him out of hiding, and whether Leo, who had certainly forgotten her by now, would agree to return to her. And what. And how.

His phone rings in the middle of the night, in the middle of a fascinating dream, just as he is about to discover in this dream some vital secret that the ringing erases without a trace. Yoel wakes up in a panic: There's a fire! I knew a fire would break out. How will I escape? But then he comes to his senses and answers the phone and the caller identifies himself as Tomer, Tal's friend.

I hope I didn't wake you up, says Tomer. I got your number from Tal's mom. She said it would be okay if we called you.

Has something happened to Tal?!

We started out the evening in this coffee shop, Tomer explains, and someone invited us to a private party, and Tal was really thirsty and drank a lot of this juice they were serving there, except that after he lost consciousness we understood that it was an alcoholic drink, and the combination of marijuana and alcohol—

Tal lost consciousness!?

Yes. I mean sort of lost. Or passed out. At any rate, our hosts called for an ambulance and now we're in the emergency room, and the doctor says he will be just fine. The problem is that someone needs to pay the bill here, and besides, we have to vacate the room we rented tonight and our plane is supposed to take off in a couple of hours, and to tell the truth, Tal is really out of it, he can't stand on his feet, let alone fly. So we called his parents, and Ronit told us to ask you if you could . . .

The bell of Our Lady of the Most Holy Rosary rings out a lonely peal as the writer Yoel Blum bursts out the back door of the Mokum Hotel and runs to the Concertgebouw taxi station, and as he is running, he reminds himself that he might meet the taxi driver who was crushed and died, but he keeps running and rushes into a taxi driven by a middle-aged lady. Any other time, he would have made conversation and asked her what a woman, especially one of her age, is doing in this kind of work, especially at this time of night. But tonight he is thinking only about Tal. Tal is in trouble. Tal needs me. The Saint Luke Hospital is in the city's west, and on no other than Jan Tooropstraat (Jan Toorop Street). Ido or Tomer is waiting for him at the main entrance of the modern white building and takes him into the emergency department, where Tomer or Ido is waiting for them and says that Tal vomited his guts out just a moment ago, and Yoel sees that Tal is lying motionless, his eyes closed, his arm connected to an intravenous drip.

After a while, his grandson's two friends part from him with firm handshakes, tell him that they will leave Tal's bag with the landlady, and go on their way.

Yoel talks to the doctor, pays for the ambulance and for the treatment, and bright and early in the morning, he is helping the unsteady teenager to exit the taxi that has brought them from the hospital to Obrechtstraat. Since the hotel gates will open only in another hour and a half, he takes his grandson in through the back door and supports him up the steep steps, that is to say, he actually lifts him in his arms and for part of the climb heaves him onto his back in a fireman's lift. He has no idea where the strength to do this came from, but he carries his heavy load up the four flights of stairs and along the length of the fourth-floor corridor. The moment that he staggers into the room, Tal begins to twist and to retch once more, and Yoel rushes him over to the lavatory and cradles his cold forehead with a supportive hand while he vomits and vomits.

Then come the long hours during which the grandfather sits on the only chair, his back to the narrow table where he usually writes and his eyes on his grandson, who is fast asleep. Beyond the glass door the night is retreating slowly. A pale dawn is outlining the buildings and the trees against a reddish-gray background and the houses' windows look into the little room like numerous eyes. The room is the same room but now, in the sagging bed (which might be a narrow double bed or a wide single bed) lies a person whose life is still not worn down and frayed but is laid out before him, fresh and clean and full of possibilities. Yoel listens to the boy's breathing. The substances coursing through his blood are probably what are making him snore and sound troubled. He looks at the body covered by a thick blanket and dressed in the warm fleece tracksuit that Yoel himself pulled out of the closet at the break of dawn and helped his dazed grandson put on after he had also helped him remove his soiled clothing. How can it be that this tall, sturdy body lying here is that of the lithe child who used to leap into his lap and shower him with such sweet hugs? And why did Tal love him so much in those far-off days?

Every hour or two the teenager's eyes open and stare, lost and lifeless in the room's expanse, and Yoel hurries to the head of the bed, supports his grandson's shorn head in the hollow of his elbow, and holds a glass of water to the parched lips. Tal takes a little sip, says a few incoherent syllables as if he is trying to ask or answer, and immediately his eyelids flutter closed, his head drops into the pillow, and he sinks again.

All that long train ride. That child's wailing. The mother's sobbing.

The end of the war is complicated and dangerous and they reach Bergen-Belsen only after a night, and a day, and another night, and another half a day. All those meant for exchange are imprisoned in a compound called the star camp, named after the yellow stars on the chests of all the prisoners locked up there.

Sonia's spirits fall when she learns that there are Jews who have been waiting here for their exchange to take place since last autumn.

From the moment they step down from the train, poor Sebastian Rosso clings to Sonia like an infant monkey to its mother. He allows her to take off his soiled clothes, scrub his body clean from the filth that has stuck to it, and dress him anew, but otherwise he is pressed to her bosom, his skinny limbs locked around her neck and around her waist, and he won't allow her to detach him from her for a moment. At night she, he, and Nettie squeeze together on the pallet, clutching one another.

Additional human transports arrive and depart daily, but a train with Martin and Anouk Rosso and Leo Blum does not appear: not after a week and not after two weeks, and not after three weeks either.

54

When did Sonia realize they would never show up? Tal asks.

The grandfather and grandson are strolling leisurely in the hotel's immediate vicinity at the request of the grandson, who has read his grandfather's notebooks and asked to see the front of the house, Martin's shop, and other settings around which the story happens.

Little by little, Tal wakes out of the fog in which he had been scattered. Slowly, slowly, he wakes up and reclaims reality together with Yoel, who had never imagined that he could spend so many days simply being with someone else, simply being, without feeling the need to write a word, without clouding the fact of his existence with even a touch of guilt over the fact that he is watching his grandson instead of creating, sitting next to him instead of working, breathing free air that was not earned with labor.

Like Rabbi Shimon bar Yochai and Rabbi Elazar, his son, in the Galilean cave, so Yoel and Tal hid away on the Mokum Hotel's fourth floor, concealed from the world pulsating on the other side of the walls of their room, but seeing it in sharper resolution than ever before. And like a worried aunt, Josephine came up to them three times a day, carrying pitchers of fruit and vegetable juices she went to the trouble of preparing in the hotel kitchen, and standing by the bed, her coal skin glowing with satisfaction, while Tal drank her health potions down to the last drop.

Achilles also came to see how the new guest was and it very quickly came out that both Tal and Achilles are crazy about a musical style called deep house, and they sank into a secret-language conversation apparently understandable only to those crazy about deep house music, ignoring Yoel when he asked what is so deep about this particular house, and didn't stop sharing their exciting experiences on the topic—not to mention the fact that they both not only love the music but also play it: Tal on bass guitar and Achilles on drums. And while Yoel was astounded that he hadn't known any of these facts till now, his laptop seemed to be even more astounded when the two young men suddenly shook it out of the perpetual slumber it had been in until now and began to race it all over the virtual world to search out musical performances and play them at deafening volume. Yoel looked over their heads, and instead of his letters and words on the computer screen he saw masses of dancers bouncing to the rhythmic electronic music while drinking, smiling at the camera, and hugging each other in what appeared to be pure bliss.

I imagine, Yoel tells Tal, that when they did not arrive a week later, Sonia understood. But even when she realized that they would not be coming with Leo to Bergen-Belsen, she probably still hoped they would be waiting for her in the Netherlands. The last of the Jewish prisoners who managed to evade the transport lists and remain in Westerbork were liberated from the camp at the war's end. But Jozef de Lange and the Rosso couple were not among them, and it eventually became clear that they had been on the very last train that the Germans managed to send from Westerbork to Auschwitz.

Yoel and Tal stand by the window of Martin's shop, which is covered with photographs of apartments for sale or rent. Tal swallows. And the child, he asks. What happened to the child?

Nettie told me that Sonia's hopes that Leo might have nevertheless survived were shattered when eyewitnesses told her that Martin and Anouk Rosso boarded the train to Auschwitz with their little son. And years later, this was confirmed when she saw the list of names of Dutch Jews who perished, among them Martin Rosso, Anouk Rosso, and Sebastian Rosso. But she must have already mourned Leo even before she set out to sail to Eretz Yisrael. And she decided, already then, that the real Sebastian Rosso, the living son, would be her son.

Tal's beautiful face wrinkles with concern when he asks, So for her, you were a kind of substitute for the child she'd lost?

There was a moment, Yoel admits, that I thought so too. But there's no such thing, Tal. There is no substitute for a child.

They get to Jacob Obrechtplein, sit on the bench under the ancient oak, and raise four eyes to the sky peeking through its thick branches.

It would have been much more convenient for her if she would have gotten rid of me, Yoel tells Tal and also tells himself. She could, after all, have searched for Anouk's or Martin's relatives, handed me over to them, and carried on with her and Nettie's lives without me. She could have re-married, could have had more children. . . . I only hindered her recovery. Because of me, she even gave up her right to grieve for her son.

He has no one in the world, says Sonia to Nettie on the deck of the ship sailing to Eretz Yisrael. He has no one, but from now on he will have me and he will have you.

The girl nods with understanding and compliance. Sonia places one hand on Nettie's head and one hand on the head of the child who is im-planted in her lap as if in an external womb. We'll call him Yoel, she says. Those people gave him the name of a Christian saint but we will call him Yoel, after your righteous grandfather Yoel, and also . . . and also in mem-ory of our Leo, since this name was supposed to be his. From now on this is our Yoel. Yoel Blum.

Yoel Blum, Nettie repeats after her.

And never, Sonia whispers, never must he know his former name. Do you understand, Nettie? He must never know how he got to us, and he must never know that we had another child, because the main thing—you understand, my clever girl, don't you—the main thing is that he must never know that he came from those people.

The ship they are sailing in is a fleeting dot in the infinite space where the sun is sinking as red as blood. If there is a God, Sonia says, looking up at the horizon, perhaps he will forgive them. If there is atonement, perhaps their suffering will atone for what they have done.

55

picture: A grandfather and his grandson sitting at noon in an inner room of a small coffee shop on Keizersgracht. In the room facing the street, which, if not for the sweet smell, one might think is a room in a regular café, there are about ten customers sitting at the bar or around small tables, and in the inner room, which is veiled in a pleasant darkness, only the two of them are relaxing among the soft cushions of a corner sofa. Quiet rhythmic music plays in the background, spectacular predator animals are moving on a big plasma screen, and the world is a smoky cloud wafting in the distance, although they only ordered two cups of coffee and only came here so that Tal could introduce his grandfather briefly and superficially to the concept of Dutch coffee shops.

The thing is, sums up Tal, after explaining to him the details of the menu offered in the place, to be able to free yourself. To lose control, Grandpa. To relax, you understand? It's like releasing yourself from the limits of knowledge in order to be able to believe in God.

Yoel tries to remember how this happened, how recent events have brought him to this scene in which he is sitting in such proximity with his grandson from whom he had been so disconnected.

The truth, Yoel confesses, is that I am not so good at losing control and at relaxing.

Tal shrugs and smiles. I'm not really good at it either. The friends who I came to Amsterdam with got high and let go easily, but I needed more time and more effort until I finally began to feel something.

It doesn't matter, Yoel decides. It doesn't matter how it happened. Cats have more cats, fish spawn more fish, and intimacy gives rise to more intimacy. It was the condition of intimacy imposed on us that brought us closer together.

Was it because of that, he asks the boy in a low voice, that the cannabis wasn't enough for you that evening and you thought you had to consume the alcohol as well?

And Tal smiles and says, You found me out.

What a charming smile he has, and how much can a heart swell with love?

They walk up Spiegelgracht. To their right a tourist is examining a shop-window full of objets d'art, pointing at something with an excitement that makes Yoel jealous because he wishes he could get excited like that. To their left, a single duck is swimming in the center of the canal, all black, with a white stripe crossing its body from head to tail.

I do not know what I think about their cooperation with the Germans, Tal says.

And Yoel is silent, because what can he say?

It's clear to me that you're right, Grandpa, when you say we cannot judge them because what do we know, what do we know about them and what do we know about the situation they were in.

He is silent.

All they wanted to do was to just survive, Grandpa. It's the most basic instinct there is.

True, Yoel thinks. Thank you, my dear grandson, for understanding this complexity. Later I may explain to you that many collaborators also believed, believed truly and naively, that their cooperation was minimizing the hardships of the entire population and sparing the lives of many Jews.

They ascend the little bridge over Prinsengracht and stand facing opposite the direction of the flowing water. The truth is, Tal says, that it's really hard for me to avoid judging her. And Yoel asks, To avoid judging whom, even though it is perfectly clear to him about whom Tal is talking. And Tal replies: Grandma Sonia, the woman who raised you.

What is there to judge Grandma Sonia about?

I'm sorry, Grandpa, but I don't understand what right she had to judge your biological parents. Not only did she judge them, but she also sentenced them to the most terrible punishment: that you, their son, would not know of their existence.

They are leaning against the railing of a small bridge over the water. Yoel sees a woman hanging towels out to dry on the deck of a houseboat. He sees the water running slowly in the canal. Sees a child's face carried away in the current.

I am trying not to judge her, adds Tal, because what do we know and all that. But even if it's possible to understand what she had against de Lange and even what she had against Anouk, why did she obliterate Martin from you as well? What did she have against Martin, her and Eddy's best friend, who did whatever he could to save her and her two children?

At night, Tal sinks into a quiet, easy sleep on the folding cot that Achilles managed to squeeze into the small room for him. But the question he asked today is still wide awake.

What was Martin's sin?

In fact, Yoel now realizes that this question was already on his mind even before Tal expressed it in words. It seemed to be constantly and secretly smoldering within him, and perhaps it was this burning that translated itself, in his subconscious, into that imagined fear of a fire that could destroy the Mokum Hotel.

If a fire would break out, he would escape from the hotel exactly the same way he and Bat-Ami escaped from that hotel in Istanbul on the night of the violent earthquake that, to their chagrin, had to happen precisely that very night they had stopped for a short Turkish holiday on their way home from one of his lecture tours in the USA. When, that summer night, they were suddenly flung from sleep and found their room rocking wildly from side to side, they burst into hysterical laughter and Bat-Ami shouted: What is this? How can the Turks live like this? As if a seven-point-four earthquake was something that happened there every night. At the end of twenty long seconds, the rocking stopped and a deathly silence ensued, followed by the colossal flapping of tens of thousands of birds that emerged in unison from all the trees in Istanbul.

They tried to turn on a light in the room, but the electricity was out, so they simply threw on the first articles of clothing they could lay their hands on in the gloom and hurried out of the room to the dark stairs, feeling their way along with all the other hotel guests who were fleeing outside and gathering in the narrow street, comforting each other and smiling at each other with relief. There was an elderly lady who had come down wearing only a transparent nightgown and holding her passport. There was a man who came down without his eyeglasses, without which he could not see a thing. And there was a pair of sisters from Rishon LeZiyyon, for whom this was their first trip outside Israel, and while their husbands dozed off on the hotel's front steps, they did not stop castigating each other: You see what happens abroad? Didn't I tell you that it's better to stay in Israel? It was only two days later that the dimensions of the disaster began to unfold and they became aware of the multitudes—men, women, and children—who had been buried alive during those twenty seconds.

But what sin did Martin commit?

On Thursday, Tal announces that this is it, he is feeling strong enough, and that same night Achilles takes him to a deep house party in an authentic Dutch club, the kind of party not for tourists but only for local young people. (Achilles: It's a good thing that tonight I don't have classes. Yoel: Classes?! Achilles: I study four evenings a week. Law, second year, seven thirty to eleven thirty at night. You must have noticed, Mr. Writer, that because of my night classes I am almost always tired during the day.)

Too bad I'm flying back Saturday night, Tal says when he returns, giddy, from the party at the club. He enters the room just a few minutes after Our Lady of the Most Holy Rosary rang her bell three times, as fresh as if it were three o'clock in the afternoon and not three in the morning, throws his coat into the corner of the room, and says, on Shabbat, I'd like it if you and I could go to the Spanish-Portuguese synagogue for services. What do you think, Grandpa?

56

On Saturday morning they exit the Mokum Hotel and all the Sabbaths, all the Sabbaths that Amsterdam has ever known, accompany them through the streets and pass with them over the Golden Crown Bridge on the Amstel River and across Waterlooplein toward the Esnoga. On Sabbaths as cold as this one, services are not held in the main temple because heating such a huge space is impossible. Rather, they are held in one of the other buildings in the ancient compound, in a small hall where Rabbi Moshe Chaim Luzzatto, the Ramchal, taught between the time he fled persecution in Italy because of his involvement in kabbalah and his immigration to the Land of Israel, where he and his wife and young son tragically died in a plague. Now they are here, singing, Blessed be He who gave the Torah to his people of Israel, and reading the weekly Torah portion. At the end of the third section of the Torah reading, Kastiel the beadle clears his throat, raises his voice, and sings out: And Yoel Sebastian, son of Martin, will stand up, fourth.

Yoel looks to his right, to his left, and behind, as if he is checking if there might be another worshipper in the congregation named Yoel Sebastian, the son of Martin. Only when Tal pats him lightly on his shoulder and smiles at him with pent-up emotion does he realize that he is indeed the one being called up to the pulpit, and he hastens to fasten his prayer shawl onto his shoulders and rise. Under the soles of his shoes, the wooden floor trembles on its water-planted pillars, and he ascends to the pulpit on the very same steps that his forefathers ascended, touches the tip of his finger to the Torah scroll that has been touched by the fingertips of his forefathers, and chants, Who chose us, and gave us His Torah, exactly like his forefathers did. When Kastiel sings in the traditional Sephardic style, He who blessed our forefathers, Abraham, Isaac, and Jacob, shall bless Yoel Sebastian, son of Martin, Yoel feels alive more than ever before.

Later, from among the prayer shawls, cylinder hats, and handshakes, his grandson approaches him and they gather each other in an embrace of unconditional love.

That's that, he tells himself, late at night after escorting Tal to the airport, puffing up the four flights of stairs, and returning to his empty room. That's it, enough, soon you'll be free to leave this place and return home. On the balcony, in the cold that is already the cold of early winter and has ceased to be simply the cold of the end of autumn, he searches beyond the blackening trees for the golden harp on the Concertgebouw's roof and finds only clouds and darkness and expressionless windows. The house, too, seems to be deep asleep, though he thinks he notices two dim lights, one in a basement window and one in an upstairs window, and it seems to him that these two lights are winking to each other in the dark.

The memory of his aliya, his being called up to the Torah that morning in the Esnoga, still fills him with exhilaration. And no less than the aliya itself is the fact that the one who arranged it for him was Tal, and that the boy knew, even before he himself imagined it, how much he longed to be called by his real name.

How did you know that was what I wanted, he had asked him earlier, at the terminal.

And Tal shrugged his shoulders and smiled. I didn't know, but I hoped.

They were standing next to the El Al counter, which in Schiphol, just like in all the other airports in the world, is stuck in some remote ghetto at the end of the passenger hall, as befits the counter of a chosen people whom, because of their striped shirt of many colors, other peoples want to throw into the pit. Finally the two went together to the departures gate, and again they embraced each other in farewell.

Here, Yoel said to himself. Here is Anouk and Martin Rosso's son embracing Anouk and Martin Rosso's great-grandson. And all of a sudden the ten thousand pieces of the puzzle fell into place and he understood what he did not want to understand until now, and all his bones rattled and his knees trembled, and the boy, who felt this, tightened his embrace and held him in strong arms until he was steady again, and only then did he gently part from him and say, Thank you for everything, Grandpa, and he went toward his flight, and in a few days he will put on a uniform and become a soldier.

Is that true, Nettie? Is that what Mother told you Martin did?

I'm sorry, Yoel. I did not really want to tell you this part of the story.

What did she say about him, Nettie? What did she say about Martin?

She said what you said to me now, Yoel. What you, and probably your wise grandson, already understood by yourselves.

But what exactly? What did she say Martin did?

She said . . . she said that Martin deliberately switched the two children. That he exchanged them to save his son.

She said that to you exactly like that?

That's what she said, Yoel, I'm sorry. . . . In the beginning she talked about it quite a lot.

What did she talk about? What else did Mother tell you about this, Nettie?

She thought that Martin must have known from all those radio broadcasts and from his other sources that his family was in danger. And that he decided to increase the chances for his child to survive by finding someone who would get the child out of the camp as fast as possible.

. . .

Yoel?

Yes, Nettie. I'm listening. I'm listening.

That's it, that's all she said. And when you grew up, she stopped talking about it out loud, but . . .

But what? What did you start to say?

Nothing special. I think I've already said too much.

Don't hide anything from me, I beg of you.

The truth is that after many years, Yoel, Mother still told me that the more she thinks about it, the more certain she is that from the start Martin did not intend to bring her our Leo in time. That when he began to arrange for her to take one boy with her on the train, he did it solely so she would take his child, that is to say Sebastian, that is to say you.

. . .

Yoel, are you there?

I'm here, Nettie, I'm here, I just . . .

I'm sorry, Yoel, I'm really sorry you had to discover all this.

57

What does he want? What does he want and what is he doing on a Dutch bus on its way to the countryside south of Amsterdam? Who is he expecting to find there, as he does not, nor will he ever have, even the slightest idea of the name or whereabouts of the village where the boy Leo Blum was hidden. Nettie, with whom he has recently been speaking on the phone every day, sometimes even twice a day, says that Sonia also did not know the name of the village or the name of the family that hid Leo. There was a time, she reminded herself, after they had more or less become acclimatized in Israel, that Sonia tried to search for these details. But then it became clear to her that there were only two or three underground members who actually knew where her son had been hidden, only two or three young students, including that same little woman known as "Katya," and none of these young people survived the war.

Yes, Nettie said to Yoel. Yes.

And so Mother gave up on getting any information about the last days of Leo's life. And Yoel heard her words and thought of the Sonia of his childhood and youth, of Sonia walking upright along Herzl Street in Netanya and declaring to him from up on high: Whatever was, was. Those waters have already flowed onward.

Actually, how do we know that he did not survive, he asked his sister the next time they spoke. Maybe he is alive to this day?

Who is alive? Nettie did not understand. Who are you talking about?

Leo. I'm talking about Leo. Maybe Martin never sent anybody from the resistance to bring him, and he just remained in the village?

Nettie was shocked. Yoel, what's gotten into you? When she scolded him, her voice resembled Sonia's, not Sonia's loving voice with which she spoke to him, but the sharp, blunt voice that she used to distance herself from other people and to deter them from liking her and wanting to make friends with her. Nettie got angry. How could you ask such a question when you already understand (she was so excited that it came out "ven you understand") that poor Leo was murdered. Didn't people report seeing Martin and Anouk Rosso getting into the transport with a boy? Also, according to the official records they died together with a little boy. . . .

He heard her through the telephone receiver, saw her window overlooking Mount Gilboa and the date groves, and was speechless. But here he is, going from Amsterdam to the villages, traveling along the city's outskirts, past large industrial and factory buildings, across clusters of tall, balcony-filled apartment buildings, and then rows of trees towering alongside the road and beyond them fields and water canals and polders, where here and there stand an old-style windmill or a group of modern wind turbines.

My parents, Raphaels had told him, had to search a long time before they found me. It turns out that I had passed through several addresses, and they finally located me only by chance. My mother, he says, was sure from the very first moment that I was their son, but my father doubted it. Perhaps he continued thinking that I was some other people's child all his life. . . . Raphaels also told him about Jews who returned from the war broken in body and soul but immediately set out on bicycle or on foot to search for their hidden children all across Holland. Many families who hid children never registered them with any proper authority, and many became attached to the children they had hidden and tried to hide them from their own flesh and blood so that they would stay with them.

Remember, Yoel, and never forget, his mother would tell him as a child: You've got a mother and you've got a sister and you've got yourself. That's all; nothing else matters.

He gets off in the first village that the bus stops in and wanders here and there. The boy Leo lived in this place, or in a place like this place. His blue eyes saw these wide-open vistas, or wide-open vistas like these. He played on the banks of this canal, or on the banks of a canal like this one. And he returned through these picturesque alleys or ones like these to this shack, or to a shack like this one, where people like the people here raised him, through these picturesque alleys or ones just like them.

Is it not possible—unreasonable, perhaps, but still—is it not possible that one of these people is Leo himself? And he stares at every village man who seems to be at the age that Leo, if not dead, would be today. He searches the faces of each one for features similar to those of Sonia or Nettie. In the grocery store, where he goes to buy himself bread and yogurt, he recalls the words of the Talmud about the frequent similarity between a son and his mother's brother, and it seems to him that the grocery-store owner is of the appropriate age and that he resembles Yisrael, Nettie's deceased son. So he begins to interview the perplexed man in English, asking him about the number of residents in this beautiful village, and if he was born and raised here, and does not relent until his interviewee gets tired of him and turns to converse in Dutch with the next customer in line.

Stop hallucinating, he tells himself as he exits the grocery store's gloom into the glittering afternoon. There are dozens of villages in the immediate vicinity like this village, and many men of this age in them. Not to mention that there is no guarantee that Leo, if he lived, did not leave the village when he grew up and head to the city, where he may have walked, without even knowing it, in his biological father's footsteps to become a doctor in a big hospital. Or he might have joined a traveling circus, why not, or emigrated from the Netherlands to another country. Or perhaps he did indeed die in childhood, perished with Martin and Anouk Rosso or perished separately from them, perished like so many other Jewish children.

58

He shaved his face. He got a haircut. He wore his tailored jacket and put on his cap.

Soon he will board the plane.

Soon he will return home.

On his last day in Amsterdam, he went to Vondelpark to say goodbye to the fallen tree. Then he bid farewell to the museums and communed at length with Jan Toorop's sea, with Marc Chagall's seven-fingered hand, and with Vincent van Gogh. As he passed through the space under the arches for the last time, a Bach partita for violin was playing as if especially for him. And in Obrechtstraat he saw, as the sun was setting, the young mother pedaling her bicycle with her daughter sitting in front of her, and he saw the girl saying something and the mother sliding her large hand over the child's small head while riding slowly.

He decided he would buy a present (a little dress? a soft toy?) for Zohar's baby, to try to remember (or to ask Bat-Ami) what the baby's name is, and to show some interest in her well-being, as well as to ask after Zohar's health and to tell her that he is proud of her.

He saw darkness fall, saw the lights coming on in the windows. And inside the windows he saw living spaces framed by walls and padded with protective layers of pictures and lamps, dining tables and rugs, dishes and books and vases of flowers. On one window ledge he saw two jars, one in which paintbrushes were waiting and in the other tubes of paint. And in Martin's art shop, which is now a real estate agency, he saw people inspecting apartments for purchase or rent and maybe signing an agreement. The brown café on the corner was also filling up, and as he passed its entrance he heard Our Lady's bell and counted six rings, and saw Vij laughing behind the brown counter and near her the box of roasted walnuts and the basket of hard-boiled eggs.

His sunflower had long ago withered in its green bottle. He was sorry he couldn't at least take the orchid home, but he presented it to Josephine and she gave him an embarrassed, tearful embrace.

As he left the hotel, dragging his suitcase and his shoulder bag to the cab that was about to take him to the airport, he almost bumped into two slim young girls who were just coming off the street and walking down the steps to the lobby. As they passed him, he heard one turn to her friend and say in Hebrew, I can't believe it! That's Yoel Blum the writer. Did you see?

He wants to write this book like Vincent van Gogh painted: to pour the colors generously, knead them with his paintbrush as if he were molding clay, and form the contours of his soul layer upon layer upon layer. He wants, like Vincent, not to be afraid to take a sheet of paper on which he has drawn a city street or a bird's nest, to turn it over and paint another self-portrait on the other side. Like Vincent, he wants to also work outside, even in the wind and the rain, so that the day will come when within the layers of his portraits, grains of earth and stalks of grass will be found.

And he wants his new novel to resemble Vincent's painting in which, in a low, wide format shaped like a basement window, pear trees are wrapped in the light of dusk and gold sparkles through their branches onto a fading path.

———————

In the line at the Israeli airline counter, a group of elderly, stocky Dutch people are waiting, apparently happy to be traveling to the Holy Land and joking between them in their muddy, gravelly language. An Israeli standing behind him asks his wife why women must always be carrying things in a bag or in a womb. And another man, who looks like one of those high-tech successes that Israel prides itself on, sums up his conversation with the success standing next to him with: There's nothing we can do. We're an island, and the sea is the good side of this island.

On his way to the departure gate, Yoel ponders the identical methods that control all the airports in the world. About how all the terminals are so similar to one another that, on the way to the boarding gate, it is hard to remember in which country one is and to where one is going. And how the seriousness with which human beings adhere to the system and cling to the appearance of law and order is so touching although, like the figures in Escher's engraving of the infinite house that keep walking and walking to nowhere, each and every person is also going to his gate and to his plane seat to fly from point to point on a tiny planet that is rotating about itself, and the only route on which they are really progressing is the one leading to their deaths.

But as he approaches the gate that the square of paper that he has been given leads him to, he sees an aquarium sunk into the marble wall of the departure hall, and a little boy, almost just a baby, is standing below the aquarium, stretching out a toddler's hand toward the ornamental fish swimming in the transparent container and chirping: Fishies! I wanna see the fishies! And his young parents hear his voice amid all the chaos and go up to him, and his mother glows as his father picks him up in his strong arms so he can see the fish better.

AUTHOR'S NOTE

This book uses facts and data from a variety of sources, including the books *I Believed I Would Speak: Memories and Testimony* by Shlomo Samson (Mass Publications, Hebrew), *Damaged Lives: Conversations with Dutch Jews Who Gave Their Children to Strangers During the Holocaust* by Dr. Bloeme Evers-Emden (self-published, Dutch and Hebrew), and from the collection of video testimonies in the Yad Vashem Archives.

ACKNOWLEDGMENTS

My thanks to Renée Sanders, Amsterdam. To Dr. Bloeme Evers-Emden, Amsterdam. To Yael Stern, Amsterdam. Thanks also to Mr. Joop Sanders, former secretary general of the Amsterdam Jewish Community, and to the staff of the Library and Resource Center at the Jewish Historical Museum (JHM) in Amsterdam.

My thanks to my partners in the "Ta'azumot Hanefesh" journey to Poland (June 2013), to Rabbi Avraham Kriger, and the Shem Olam Institute.

I am grateful to Shlomo Samson, Tirza Levy, Rivka Kahana, Hadassah Nir, Hannah Goldberg, and Bakol Serlui.

I thank Professor Yigal Schwartz, Noa Menheim, Ruth Elon, Yael Maly, and Batsheva Peli Seri.

My gratitude also to Linda Yechiel, Nilli Cohen, and Daniella Wexler.

I am profoundly appreciative of the support given to me by my children and their families. The English edition of this novel is dedicated to the memory of my beloved husband, Rabbi Benny Elon, and of our own house on endless waters.

ABOUT THE AUTHOR

Emuna Elon is an internationally bestselling, critically acclaimed Israeli novelist, journalist, and women's activist. Born in Jerusalem to a family of prominent rabbis and scholars, she was raised in Jerusalem and New York. She teaches Judaism, Hasidism, and Hebrew literature. Her first novel translated into English, *If You Awaken Love*, was a National Jewish Book Award finalist.

HOUSE

ON

ENDLESS WATERS

Emuna Elon

This reading group guide for House on Endless Waters *includes an introduction, discussion questions, ideas for enhancing your book club, and a Q&A with author Emuna Elon. The suggested questions are intended to help your reading group find new and interesting angles and topics for your discussion. We hope that these ideas will enrich your conversation and increase your enjoyment of the book.*

INTRODUCTION

At the behest of his agent, renowned author Yoel Blum reluctantly agrees to visit his birthplace of Amsterdam to promote his books, despite promising his late mother that he would never return to that city. While touring the Jewish Historical Museum with his wife, Yoel stumbles upon a looping reel of photos offering a glimpse of prewar Dutch Jewry, and is astonished to see the youthful face of his beloved mother staring back at him, posing with his father, his older sister . . . and an infant he doesn't recognize.

This unsettling discovery launches him into a fervent search for the truth, shining a light on Amsterdam's dark wartime history and the underground networks that hid Jewish children away from danger—but at a cost. The deeper into the past Yoel digs, the better he understands his mother's silence, and the more urgent the question that has unconsciously haunted him for a lifetime—*Who am I?*—becomes. Evocative, insightful, and deeply resonant, *House on Endless Waters* is an unforgettable meditation on identity, belonging, and the inextricable nature of past and present.

TOPICS & QUESTIONS
FOR DISCUSSION

1. Do you think Yoel is right to visit Amsterdam despite his mother telling him not to? Why or why not?

2. After Yoel and his wife, Bat-Ami, see the images in the museum of Yoel's mother, he is plagued with questions. However, when he returns to his hotel room afterward, he doesn't call his sister, Nettie, to tell her what he just discovered. Why is he so reluctant to tell Nettie what he learned?

3. We learn that Yoel was the only one who didn't know about the other sibling. Why do you think his mother and sister kept this from him? Do you agree with their decision? Why or why not?

4. Yoel begins to contemplate all the relationships around him, including the one with his wife, daughters, and grandchildren. Why does the revelation about his mother instigate this? What does it say about the relationship we maintain with our mothers?

5. Why would Yoel's mother always remind him that "You've got a mother and you've got a sister and you've got yourself. That's all; nothing else matters"?

6. Do you agree with Yoel's mother's decision to isolate them from making friends and partaking in "the great human celebration"? Why or why not?

7. On page 60, it reads: "And he's sure that great danger is hovering over him: that they, all the people passing by in the street right now, can see he's a Jew and they're determined to murder him." Why does Yoel suddenly become paranoid about being Jewish in Amsterdam?

8. Yoel picks the smallest room in his hotel with a balcony. What purpose does this serve in his writing process?

9. When Sonia is first introduced, who do you think she is? How does your perspective change as you keep reading?

10. Does it make Sonia selfish when she says that "their life is complicated enough without being overburdened with what is going on in other places"? Why or why not?

11. As a child, Yoel didn't eat unless spoon-fed by his mother. What did you think about his character after learning this? What did you think about his mother's personality?

12. Do you think Raphaels's anger at his parents, biological and nonbiological alike, is justified or should he understand he was given away for his own safety? Why or why not?

13. What does the oak tree that Sonia notices growing horizontally in the park symbolize?

14. Sonia expresses resentment toward Sebastian, a toddler, one day when she encounters Anouk with him on the stairs at their house. What does it say about Sonia's character to feel such animosity toward an innocent child? How does this make you feel?

ENHANCE YOUR BOOK CLUB

1. Spend some time with Emuna Elon's 2007 novel, *If You Awaken Love*, and see if you can discover any similar themes between the two books.

2. *House on Endless Waters* takes place in Amsterdam and has many scenes in the Jewish Historical Museum. Take a moment to do some research on the history of Jewish heritage in Amsterdam. You can start here: www.amsterdam.info/jewish/.

3. The relationship between mother and child can sometimes be very complex. Explore this with your book club: What was your relationship like with your own mother? Did you learn anything about your mother that surprised you? If your mother has passed, were you left with any unanswered questions? How has your relationship with your mother affected you as an adult?

A CONVERSATION
WITH EMUNA ELON

Why did you decide to write *House on Endless Waters*?

Actually, it's not me who decides which story I am going to write. A new novel occurs to me when a specific character begins to gain control over my thoughts, followed by glimpses of images, phrases, and visions. Then I feel a powerful urge to start writing in order to find out what's going on.

House on Endless Waters began with two characters: lonely, caged-within-himself Yoel on one side, and young, vivacious Sonia on the other. At first I didn't know if there was any connection between the two of them, but I sensed that there was a personal secret that Yoel needed to reveal. When I spent a few days in Amsterdam, which was initially just another beautiful city I enjoyed visiting, I was stunned to see the past— Yoel and Sonia's past—come to life right before my eyes.

What sort of historical research informed the book?

My extensive research included reading books, articles, and other archival materials and watching filmed testimonies concerning Dutch history, Dutch Jewry, and Holland during World War Two. I also interviewed Dutch Holocaust survivors and children of survivors, trying to understand not only the historical facts but also their long-term implications. And I spent long periods of time in Amsterdam, taking in the sites and absorbing the atmosphere in which the story takes place.

As I worked on the story of Yoel's stay in Amsterdam, alone in a shabby hotel overlooking the neighborhood, I too stayed alone in the exact same setting, and many of his daily experiences were derived from my own.

Did any of the research surprise you?

Many of my findings surprised me, especially since beforehand I was under the (mythical) impression that Jews in Holland met a comparatively "good fate" during the Holocaust.

I was especially astonished to learn about Holland's hidden Jewish children, and to realize that many of their stories have remained murky and untold to this very day.

What inspired you to explore the mother-son relationship at the center of *House on Endless Waters*?

I think family ties are always fascinating, and mother-child relationships are one of the world's greatest mysteries. I find myself drawn to this mystery in every story I read or write, and can't say I have figured it out even now, when my own mother is no longer alive and I myself am the mother of six wonderful children who have already become six wonderful adults.

What motivated you to structure the novel as a story within a story?

Amsterdam has not changed for many years, so when I was there it was really natural for me to see the story of the city's past come to life within the story of the present.

Another reason for this structure was that Yoel Blum had to use his imagination in order to fill in the gaps of the story his sister told him. I knew that he had to be a storyteller, a writer, and that my novel would describe the writing process of *his* novel.

What was the most difficult aspect of writing this book?

I doubted my ability to tell a story from the perspective of a male protagonist, and I tried to switch to a female one but couldn't bring myself to reject

Yoel Blum's plea that I write him. I felt a little more confident when my [Israeli] publisher promised me that the book would have a male editor, and I was more than relieved when that editor, professor of Hebrew literature Yigal Schwartz, gave Yoel's thoughts and motions his unreserved approval.

Have you ever discovered anything shocking about your own family history?

When *House on Endless Waters* was published in Dutch (under the title *Sonia's Son*), I met with an audience in Amsterdam and someone asked me: "If Yoel Blum is a writer, why did he ask you to write his story rather than do it himself?"

That was when I decided it was time for me to write my own family history, which is what I am working on right now. I don't know if I will discover anything shocking, though I am already shocked by the mere realization of how little I know about the lives that yielded mine.

What are you hoping to leave your readers with?

I think my hopes are fulfilled when readers tell me that they feel as if this story is about them. We haven't all been through the exact same experiences that Yoel or Sonia have, but just like them, each and every one of us walks alone in this world. Each one of us reaches out to be loved and understood. Each one of us craves belonging and searches for meaning.

I felt rewarded when a woman told me that reading this book helped her comprehend her mother's behavior throughout the years; when a man said it gave him a new, more forgiving perspective of himself; and when a young mother confided that after she finished reading the book, with tears running down her cheeks, she went over to her child and gave him a big hug.